Hellish Book Five: Saving Grace

By Scott Dokey

This book is dedicated to artists and creators everywhere who pour their souls into everything they create.

PART ONE: PROMISES

CHAPTER 1

Hecate loathed her existence, a twisted wreck of what it once was. The cracked plaster walls and rotting floorboards of the derelict house she currently squatted in seemed to mock her, reminding her that this was all she deserved. The West side of town, a graveyard for the forgotten, held her captive in its bony grip. It hadn't always been this way. At one time, she had lived in a wonderful house, with wonderful parents, had a wonderful sister, and a wonderful dog. It had all been just wonderful.

But those days had been shredded, reduced to ashes in a single, blood-drenched night.

She reached for the whiskey bottle at her side and tilted it back, only to find it empty. An emptiness that resonated deep within her soul. With a growl of frustration, she flung the bottle across the room. It clattered loudly, startling Josh and Kerry, her temporary roommates in this current hell-hole. Josh's eyelids fluttered, and he rubbed his face, still disoriented, the alcohol fog clinging to his teenage brain. Kerry stirred briefly before collapsing back into unconsciousness, her chest rising and falling in shallow gasps. Despite being older, it was clear that she couldn't hold her liquor.

"What's going on?" Josh croaked groggily.

"Nothing," Hecate muttered, already rising to her feet. "We're out of booze. I'm going to get more." He nodded numbly, eyes slipping shut as she grabbed her torn jacket.

After lighting a candle in the bathroom, she looked at herself in the mirror and it greeted her with an unforgiving reflection. Dark, sunken eyes stared back from a gaunt face that barely resembled the girl she used to be. Her hair, greasy and matted, clung to her hollow cheeks, and her breath reeked of stale liquor and decay. Anger flared in her chest—anger at herself, at the world, at the memory of her mother's accusatory eyes the day she lost everything.

She recalled the night the monster came. The door had been left unlocked—a simple oversight—but it was a careless moment that ended in screams and blood. Her sister's innocent laughter, silenced. Her father's shouts, drowned in a guttural roar. The scent of iron and the gurgle of a final breath. It had been over a year, but each detail was branded forever into her memory. Her mother's voice cut through the memory like a dagger: "You did this."

Clenching her fists, Hecate forced down the bile rising in her throat. Dwelling on it would only push her closer to the edge—to more reckless, stupid choices. And stupid tended to lead to disaster.

She left the bathroom and stepped into the frigid night, crossing the yard to the splintered gap in the fence. The alley was dark, shadows slithering like vipers along the cracked pavement. The liquor store sat at the end of the block, a beacon of false salvation. Hecate approached, her skin prickling.

She knew the guy was a dick as soon as she saw him pull

up, but she didn't have any choice. Dressed in jeans and a black leather jacket, the guy climbed out of his beat-up Camaro and strode toward the door with his chest puffed out like he was God's gift.

Hecate rolled her eyes before she sauntered up to him, putting on her best pouty face. "Hey, mister," she said sadly as she batted her best puppy-dog eyes at him. "Do you think you could help me out?"

The man eyed Hecate up and down for a minute, grinning, "Okay, I'll bite. What'cha looking for?"

"Just a couple bottles of some hard stuff. My friends and I ran out a little while ago." She pulled some bills from her pocket and flashed them at the guy, "I got money."

The man's gaze swept over her, lingering too long. "Sure," he said, his grin widening. "How about we make a deal? Climb in, show me a good time, and I'll buy you whatever you want."

Disgust curled in her stomach. "How about you go fuck yourself?"

He shrugged his shoulders and laughed. "Your loss, sweetheart."

He sauntered inside, leaving her seething. "Asshole!"

Moments passed in tense silence until an elderly woman shuffled up to the store. Hecate followed, sliding into the corner past the clerk's inattentive eyes. Her fingers found the smooth glass neck of a bottle, and she tucked it beneath her tattered shirt. The alarm blared as she crossed the threshold, but chaos erupted when the clerk shouted, eyes darting between her and the old lady.

The street swallowed her whole as she bolted, only slowing when the dim shape of her hideaway emerged. But her relief flew away quickly when she saw the back door hanging limply from its hinges, shattered wood splintering into jagged points. Panic surged through her as she held the bottle upside down like a makeshift mallet.

"Josh? Kerry?" she whispered as she cautiously stepped inside. The silence was heavy and oppressive. The darkness seemed blacker than normal, as if all the energy had been sucked from the room, leaving a massive void that encompassed the world. Every hair on the back of her neck screamed for her to run. For a brief second, the moonlight broke through the window, casting a sliver of light into the room. That's when she saw it, and her whole world changed forever.

Bent over Josh's crumpled body, something monstrous turned to face her. Its blood-soaked jaws parted in a snarl, wings unfurling wide enough to blot out the room. Time stopped as it lunged forward. She tried to scream, but it was trapped in her throat. She hurled the bottle in a feeble attempt, but it barely thudded against the creature's chest.

When she turned to run, claws hooked into her arms, and she was yanked back, the beast's breath hot and fetid on her neck. She struggled for a moment under the creature's power, but it was useless. She would die tonight, in the same bloody way her sister and father had, Then, she heard a sickening thud beside her. The grip slackened, and the creature slumped to the floor, its head rolling away. Bewildered, Hecate turned to see the serene, almost cheerful face of an old man, his white beard stained with blood, and a bloody hatchet glistening in his hands.

"Hello," he said, as if meeting a friend. "I'm Solomon."

Her world tilted, and everything went black.

CHAPTER 2

The first rays of morning sunlight reached into the room through the fractured slats of the boarded-up windows, slicing the darkness with erratic beams. Hecate stood frozen, caught between disbelief and horror, as the dim light bled over the grisly scene. Josh's body lay sprawled and dismembered. One arm had been wrenched from its socket, cast aside as if it were no more significant than a broken doll. His chest gaped open, the space where his heart had once beat defiantly empty.

Kerry's death, though less brutal, carried its own stark finality. Her body lay motionless, eyes fixed in a glassy stare that told of a soul abruptly snatched away.

Hecate's stomach twisted in on itself, and without thinking, she turned and stumbled to the bathroom. The retching was sharp, tearing at her throat until there was nothing left but dry heaves and shudders. She splashed water on her face, the icy shock dragging her back from the edge of insanity. When she finally emerged from the bathroom, the house seemed more sinister, as if the walls themselves whispered of her impending death.

Unable to bear the suffocating presence of evil, even

though the creature lay dead on the rotting floor in a gruesome heap, she bolted for the front door, barely registering the splintered frame as she pushed it open and stumbled outside.

"Wait!" Solomon called as he appeared at her side, moving with a fluid grace that belied his age. His gaze was intense, full of something she couldn't name. "I want to help."

Hecate hesitated, her mind screaming at her to run and never look back. She'd been good at that—running from everything. But this was something different; something supernatural that her brain couldn't process at the moment. An instinct whispered for her to stop. She turned and looked at Solomon, her eyes wide and filled with questions she wasn't sure she wanted answered. "What the hell happened here?" she rasped.

His expression darkened. "You were attacked by a demon."

The word hit her like a physical blow. "A demon? You're serious?" The edge of hysteria in her voice didn't escape her.

Solomon nodded, his jaw set. "Very serious. Demons are real. They're the monsters behind the stories—the beings people fear but refuse to believe in. Vampires, werewolves, ghouls—at their very essence they're all demons transformed into abominations that prey on humanity. And this house was its den."

A shiver coursed down her spine, colder than any winter's chill. "How did you know it was here?"

His gaze drifted and she saw a moment of torment lingering there before he spoke again, his voice tinged with regret. "I've hunted this one for years. I lost its trail, and by the time I found it again..." His voice faltered, heavy with a remorse that settled into the space between them. "I was too late to save your friends."

Hecate's throat tightened as she glanced back at the house, at the bodies that would haunt her dreams. Josh and Kerry — kids she had barely known; who had been abused by their parents and had run away to escape the horror, only to find themselves in the middle of a worse nightmare. The kids who were now dead. "Are there more of them?" she asked.

Solomon exhaled slowly. "Not here, not now. But beyond this town? Yes. Always."

The weight of his words pressed down on her, and she sank onto the crumbling porch steps, the rough concrete scraping against her palms. "What do I do now?" she murmured, the question carried on a breath barely there.

"Do you have anywhere to go?" His voice was kind, the type of kindness she wasn't sure she could trust.

She shook her head. The motion felt final, like a door closing on the last remnants of what her life used to be. "No."

Solomon regarded her, eyes narrowing as if searching for something deeper within her. "Then come with me. I can offer you a place to stay, a way to understand this world you're caught in. But it's your choice."

"Teach me?" The word caught in her throat, edged with a spark of hope she hadn't felt in years. "Teach me to fight back?"

His lips twitched into the semblance of a smile. "If you're willing to learn, yes. But first, you'll need to tell me your name."

The pause stretched, as she weighed the unknown against the familiar pain she knew. Anything, she decided, would be better than where she was now. "Hecate," she said at last.

Solomon's eyes lit up. "Good. But know this: training comes with sacrifices. You've already seen what lurks in the dark. It only gets more dangerous."

She swallowed the knot of fear, thinking of the father and

sister she'd failed, the mother she'd left behind. She couldn't afford to be weak any longer. "I'm ready," she said, and for the first time, she believed it.

"Then follow me." Solomon led her down the street, the sky slowly shifting from gray to gold as dawn crept in. They stopped at a sleek, black sedan, its polished surface reflecting the new light. She hesitated, eyeing Solomon with one last measure of caution, but the pull of something greater compelled her to trust him.

"Where are we going?" she asked as she settled into the seat, the leather cold and unfamiliar beneath her.

Solomon glanced at her, a twinkle of mischief breaking through his seriousness. "Ever seen Touchdown Jesus?"

The question took her by surprise, pulling an unexpected laugh from her. "Only on TV."

He nodded, the engine purring to life. "Well, you're about to see it up close. And much more."

As the car pulled away, leaving behind the house and all its horror, Hecate looked ahead into the uncertain dawn, wondering if this path would lead her to salvation—or into a darkness she could never escape.

After a few tense minutes, Solomon turned off North Michigan Street and onto Angela Boulevard. The sun, in its slow, golden ascension, began to conquer the shadows that clung stubbornly to the edges of the road. They drove past the manicured golf course where early risers in bright polo shirts swung their clubs, oblivious to the dark truths that prowled beyond their perfect lawns. Hecate's gaze lingered on them, and a bitter thought clenched her mind, *They have no idea what's really out there.*

The car eased left onto Eddy Street, and for the first time, the university loomed before her. Notre Dame's campus had always been a silent, indifferent neighbor to her life, neither loved nor hated, just existing in a realm she never felt part of. But now, in this surreal turn of fate, she entered its grounds burdened with questions she never imagined asking.

Solomon's driving slowed as they approached the Hesburgh Library, its imposing façade anchored by the iconic mural known as 'Touchdown Jesus.' The figure's outstretched arms seemed almost like a benediction or, perhaps, a warning. "It's actually called 'The Word of Life' mural," Solomon said, breaking the silence. His voice held a tone caught between reverence and something bittersweet. "Ara Parseghian gave it that nickname back in nineteen sixty-four. The name stuck. He had a sharp wit, that one."

Hecate turned to him, curiosity sparking. "And you know that how?"

"Because I was there," he said simply, his eyes scanning the mural as if seeing layers no one else could.

Instead of guiding her to the grand entrance, Solomon led her around the east side of the building. A narrow set of stairs, chipped and worn, rose to a nondescript door. It opened into a dim hallway that stretched south, with two doors standing vigil on the west wall. Solomon paused at one, jangling a set of keys that seemed too ordinary for the strangeness of the moment.

A figure appeared at the corner, striding toward them with a briskness that spoke of authority. He was middle-aged, sharp-eyed, wearing a sport coat that suggested he belonged here. "Morning, Sam," the man greeted. His voice was friendly, but a watchful edge hinted at deeper knowledge. "How's it going?"

Solomon's reply was casual but weighted. "It's good, Aaron. How are you?"

"Busy already. Is this a new one?" His eyes flickered to Hecate, assessing her.

"Maybe. We'll see how it goes."

The man turned to Hecate and offered a practiced smile as he extended his hand. "I'm Aaron."

She stiffly took his hand. "Hecate."

"If there's anything you need while you're here, just ask," he said, eyes softening before he nodded at Solomon and disappeared through the door they'd entered from.

Hecate's brow furrowed as she watched him leave. "I thought you said your name was Solomon?"

"It is," Solomon replied. "I just prefer Sam. It's... more current."

Current. The word lingered, oddly unsettling. Before she could probe the answer, he pushed the door open and gestured for her to step inside.

The room was stark, almost disappointingly so—empty walls, cold linoleum floors, and not a piece of furniture in sight. Before she could question it, Solomon raised his right hand, the gold ring he wore catching a thin slice of light. He pressed a hidden mechanism at its center, and the floor shuddered beneath her feet.

A grinding noise echoed in the silence as the entire room began to descend. Hecate's breath caught, her eyes darting to Solomon, who stood calm, the faintest of smiles touching his lips. The descent was long, each second stretching out as if they were being swallowed by the earth itself. She felt like Jonah inside the whale, uncertain where the darkness would spit her out.

When the floor finally stopped, the west wall lifted with a mechanical groan, revealing a space that made her heart skip. The cavernous room was carved from stone, the ceiling disappearing into dim heights. Shelves stuffed with books loomed in shadowy corners, and a long altar stood like a sentinel on one side. Opposite it, tunnels yawned open, disappearing into the unknown.

What stunned her most, though, were the people. Dozens of them, moving with a purpose she could sense but not yet understand. Some were hunched over ancient tomes, their fingers tracing the spidery script of forgotten languages. while others were off in the corner practicing various forms of martial arts.

Solomon's voice, low and resolute, anchored her back to reality. "Welcome to our training facility."

CHAPTER 3

Hecate's head was spinning as Solomon guided her through a narrow, dimly lit tunnel. The walls seemed to close in around her, their shadows stretching long and heavy, as if trying to swallow her whole. The soft shuffle of their footsteps was the only sound, muffled and distant in the eerie silence. On either side of the tunnel were rows of doors—each hiding an unknown world behind it.

Solomon stopped in front of one, its wood old and worn. He swung the door open, revealing a room that felt like it came from another time. The space was small but comfortable—like a secret place tucked away from the chaos of the outside world. A modest kitchenette gleamed with the soft glow of a single hanging light, a plush armchair sat in one corner, while a bed was nestled against the far wall.

Hecate stood frozen in the doorway, her mouth dry, her mind a whirlwind of thoughts and emotions. She blinked, uncertain if she was still dreaming. "Is this for me?" she finally asked.

"If you want," Solomon replied.

Hecate glanced around the small room that seemed to promise comfort she wasn't sure she deserved. "But I'm not like any of those other people out there," she murmured.

Solomon's eyes softened as he studied her for a moment. "You're right. And none of those others are like you. You're special in your own way, Hecate."

Hecate chuckled bitterly. "I certainly don't feel special," she muttered, feeling more alone than ever before.

Solomon stepped closer and placed his hand gently on her shoulder. "Just relax. Get some rest for now. We can talk later when you're ready. No pressure here. Take your time. Let it all sink in."

His words were soft and kind as he walked past her, calming her down just a little, but they didn't completely chase the storm from her mind. She nodded as she slowly entered the room, the door clicking shut softly behind her, leaving her alone in the stillness.

Hecate sank onto the edge of the bed, her legs suddenly too weak to stand. She couldn't remember the last time she had felt this tired, this drained. Her body ached with exhaustion, but her mind refused to stop. She had so many questions, so many things she needed to understand, but there was no one to answer them, no one to guide her through the darkness. She closed her eyes, fighting the flood of thoughts, and as soon as her head hit the pillow, sleep claimed her.

It wasn't the peaceful rest she longed for—it was merely a momentary escape from the whirlwind inside her head. She let herself surrender to it, knowing full well that when she woke, the questions would still be there, waiting for her. But for now, she could only let the silence envelop her.

***

Hecate's mind was a twisted labyrinth, spinning with

shadows that reached for her even in the deepest corners of her dreams. She could feel *them*—hovering just beyond the veil of sleep, pressing in like the weight of a thousand unseen eyes. The sensation crawled under her skin, a chill that spread through her like cold fire. Her heart began to race as if it knew something she didn't.

Her eyelids fluttered, but she didn't want to open them. *No, not yet,* she thought, but the pressure only grew stronger, more suffocating. She half-expected to see Solomon's familiar form looming in that strange way he had, his presence oddly comforting despite the dark undertones of the world they found themselves in.

But when she finally forced her eyes open, she was terrified to see that it wasn't Solomon. It was *them*—her father and her sister. The same faces she had known her entire life, but now twisted by something far worse than death. Their throats were torn open, ragged and raw, gaping like torn paper. Blood streamed down their bodies in thick rivers, staining the air with the iron stench of death.

They reached toward her with outstretched arms, their eyes wide with a desperate plea, *Help us.* But when they opened their mouths to speak, only a torrent of blood poured out, gurgling, choking their words into a grotesque, unintelligible mess.

Her breath caught in her throat, and before she could react, she saw it—the monster. A hulking beast, its body like a shadow made flesh, looming behind her family. Its face was a twisted mass of flesh and sinew, eyes gleaming with madness, a grin so wide it seemed to stretch beyond its bulbous head. It let out a deep, rumbling laugh, a sound so terrifying that it reverberated through her very bones, paralyzing her with dread.

The creature's claws—long, curved, and drenched in

something dark—swept through the air with an inhuman speed. A sickening crunch filled the room as it decapitated both her father and sister in one brutal, simultaneous strike. The spray of blood was violent and explosive—covering Hecate in a torrential burst, drenching her body from head to toe in hot, sticky red.

Her heart stopped as the heads fell to the bed beside her, their eyes still wide, frozen in an expression of terror. But their mouths didn't stop moving. "How come you let us die?" her father hissed. His words were like a punch to her gut, slamming into her with the weight of everything she had failed to do that terrible night.

And then her sister spoke. Though her voice was softer, it felt like a dagger thrust deep into her heart. "You said you'd always protect me... but you lied."

The words pierced her, deeper than any blade or demon's claw ever could. They echoed in her ears, taunting her, gnawing at the fragile remnants of her sanity. *You lied.*

The demon lunged forward, its claws slicing through the air. A scream tore from Hecate's throat and her heart thundered in her chest as the darkness threatened to consume everything.

And then, just before the beast's claws could reach her, the world exploded in a blur of blood and terror, her scream lost in the chaos.

***

Hecate shot upright in bed, her body trembling violently. While she gasped for air, the words from her dead family echoed in her mind, a cruel reminder that she would never escape the suffocating grip of guilt that had all but consumed her. *How could I have let them die?* The images, grotesque and relentless, flashed behind her eyelids—her father and sister, their throats torn open, their lifeless eyes accusing her. She buried her face into her pillow, sobbing relentlessly, the first real release of emotion she'd allowed herself since their deaths. It wasn't just grief for their deaths that haunted her—it was also the unbearable weight of her self-proclaimed failure to stop them.

A soft knock on her door interrupted her moment of grief. She ignored it at first, but then a voice spoke up, "Hecate? My name is Landis. I'm just checking to make sure you're okay?"

She choked back her tears, but the effort was futile. Her voice, strained and fragile, betrayed her. "I'm okay," she lied.

"Well, if you need to talk, I'm here," Landis said softly. "We're all here for you."

His words—meant to comfort—only made the pain twist deeper inside her. *If these people knew the shit I've done,* she thought bitterly, *they wouldn't be so kind.* She had done things —said things—that would label her a monster in the eyes of anyone who knew. And yet, here they were: strangers who knew nothing about her past, offering her comfort, not understanding that she hadn't earned a single ounce of it. Hell, she couldn't even figure out how to accept it.

After a few quiet moments, Landis gave up, his footsteps retreating down the hall, leaving her alone in the suffocating silence. She knew he was only trying to help, but she wasn't ready—not yet. It had been hard enough to accept Solomon's help, and that was only because he had just killed a demon in front of her eyes.

She briefly considered trying to fall back asleep, but the fear of the demon returning in her dreams held her back. Instead, she got up, her legs unsteady beneath her as if her body couldn't decide whether it wanted to fight or collapse. The room was plain, simple even—a bed in one corner, a small refrigerator in the center, a desk pushed up against the wall next to the chair. But above the desk, a bookshelf caught her eye, filled with a collection of occult and esoteric tomes. The titles were cryptic, promising secrets about meditation, herbalism, demonology, and forbidden lore. It was a collection both unsettling and fascinating, like a dark promise that she wasn't sure she wanted to unravel.

Her fingers brushed over the leather-bound spines, hesitation creeping up her spine. She thought about pulling one out, scanning its pages for answers—anything to escape the madness of her thoughts—but quickly thought better of it. Her mind was fragile enough at the moment without delving deeper into things she wasn't prepared to understand.

Her gaze reluctantly drifted toward the door. "Might as well get this over with," she sighed as she pulled it open. The hallway stretched out ominously before her, its silence broken only by the soft thud of her own footsteps. She paused, cautiously peering both ways, before moving toward the main chamber.

What greeted her was a surprising sight. Small groups of people, standing together, talking quietly—too many for such an early hour. For a moment, she was back in high school, watching with mild interest as the groups splintered into cliques, divided by popularity and ethnicity. *The only clique I ever belonged to was me,* she thought bitterly. She considered turning around, retreating back into her solitude, but before she could make a move, one boy started walking toward her.

He was short, with a medium build and infectious smile. He extended his hand eagerly. "Hi, I'm Landis," he said.

Hecate took his hand hesitantly. "I'm Hecate," she murmured softly. "Thanks for trying to help earlier."

"No problem," Landis replied. "That's what we do here."

"To be honest, I haven't had much of that lately," she confessed, the words slipping out before she could stop them.

Landis saw the sadness in her eyes and changed the subject, "So, what's your specialty?"

Hecate blinked, confused. "Specialty?"

"When Solomon picks someone to join the group, they usually have some sort of ability. Telekinesis, divination, that sort of thing. Me? I'm an Empath."

"What's an Empath?"

"I feel things—residual energy from places or objects. And I can sense other people's emotions."

Hecate instinctively crossed her arms, a subconscious barrier against the vulnerability that seemed to be creeping into her soul. She didn't want him to see her—not now, not like this.

Landis smiled gently, noticing her discomfort. "Don't worry. I'm getting better at controlling it, and I only use it when it's necessary. I don't want to invade anyone's space. Sometimes, when I take in other people's emotions, it gets pretty messy."

Hecate's posture softened just a little, but she remained guarded. "To be honest, I'm not sure why I'm here. All I know is that last night a demon killed my friends, and Sam saved me. I don't have any abilities like that."

Landis's expression grew more serious, his gaze steady. "Well, you're here for a reason. Sam doesn't do anything by accident."

"Speaking of Sam," Hecate said. "Who is this guy?"

Landis's smile faltered for a brief second. "If you haven't guessed already, Sam's... pretty unique. Did he tell you what his real name was?"

"Yeah. The first time I met him, he said it was Solomon."

Landis's eyes gleamed with something darker, something

she couldn't quite place. "You know what that means, right?"

Hecate shrugged, "Not really."

Landis's eyes held hers for a moment before a grin tugged at his lips. "Think about it."

A sudden realization hit her, like a bolt of lightning. "How is that possible? He'd have to be three thousand years old!"

Landis shrugged nonchalantly. "I don't get it either. But I'm telling you, it's true. And the thing about him being the wisest man in the world? Totally accurate. The man knows everything about everything."

"So why is he here?" Hecate asked, incredulous. "With all that knowledge, he could be doing... anything. Making a fortune."

"Money doesn't mean much to him anymore. My guess is, he's already made his fortune a hundred times over. But he told us his focus now is solely on protecting the world."

"Sounds... noble," she said, though the word felt strange in her mouth.

"That's correct!" came a voice behind them, and Hecate turned to find Solomon standing in the doorway, his presence as commanding as ever.

Landis gave her a quick, understanding glance. "I'll leave you two alone," he said. "We'll talk more later."

As Landis stepped away, Solomon's gaze softened as he stepped into the room. "I hope you slept well."

Hecate glanced at him, her exhaustion still evident. "Not really."

Solomon frowned. "I'm sorry."

Hecate shrugged, trying to mask her inner turmoil. "It's okay. Everything's just happening so fast. It's a lot to take in."

He nodded, understanding. "Yeah, I know. But I wouldn't have brought you here if I didn't think you could handle it."

She hesitated before asking, "Landis asked me what my

special ability was. He said everyone here has one."

Solomon's lips quirked. "They do. In fact, everyone does. They just have to find it."

"Well, if I do have one, it hasn't helped me very much," Hecate muttered. "My life is pretty much shit right now."

"But don't you see?" Solomon said, his voice low but filled with conviction. "For all the shit you're going through—I prefer to call them tests—you'll come out of it stronger. Wiser. And that gives you the greatest gift of all: heart. The ability to push through, to survive. That's what I see in you. You're a fighter, Hecate. A fighter with a will to survive."

Hecate snickered, trying to deflect the praise Solomon was throwing at her. "Obviously you haven't seen me in some of my finest moments."

Solomon chuckled. "I think we've all been there a time or two. Myself included."

After walking for a few minutes, Solomon stopped and opened a door. He beckoned Hecate inside, "After you."

"What's inside?" Hecate asked nervously.

Solomon replied, "Your first lesson."

CHAPTER 4

It began as a faint buzzing in Father Gideon's ear, a subtle hum that barely registered. But it grew—slowly at first—until it became a murmur, an orchestra of whispered voices brushing against his mind. He sat upright in bed, his pulse quickening, closing his eyes as the whispers began to coalesce into one word. A name. *Azazel.*

His heart raced as he leaped from the bed, the name echoing in his mind like a command. He moved swiftly, walking out of his room, the voices trailing behind him, urging him forward. The dark energy that radiated from them felt familiar—inviting. The thought of serving Azazel, the Prince of Hell, thrilled him to his core. After his previous failure, this was his moment. His chance to prove his worth. The whispers grew louder, sharper, and Gideon's blood ran cold as he reveled in the moment. The time was near.

A sense of giddy anticipation swirled within him as he reached his study and pressed the hidden button under his desk. The staircase to the lower level groaned as it opened, and with a hurried glance around the room, he descended into the darkness. The door clicked shut behind him. The Church could never learn of his true allegiance. He had clawed his way to the top, and he would not risk losing it now—not for something as trivial as carelessness.

The bottom of the stairs greeted him with a low hum, and he flicked on a switch, illuminating the eerie space. The walls of the room were lined with ominous doors, but he moved toward the leftmost one. His breath caught as he entered the small chamber beyond, filled with ancient symbols etched into the walls and ceiling, glowing faintly in the dim light. In the center, a round tub sat, its contents dark and thick.

Gideon undressed without hesitation, stepping into the tub as he began to chant an incantation in a language older than time itself. He crossed his arms over his chest, lowering himself fully into the blood. His body submerged, and as his senses dimmed, his mind unraveled, slipping into the void.

He was drawn, pulled deeper into the abyss, a swirling vortex of darkness that tore at his astral form, dragging him through the countless layers of Hell. He landed in a field, the earth beneath him cracked and barren. In the distance, howls split the air, a warning to the realm's twisted inhabitants that an outsider had arrived. Another name whispered through his mind: *Jezebeth,* followed by, *Helena Thompson.*

Gideon wasted no time. Though in his astral form, he knew that any harm here would carry over into his physical body. He turned, his eyes scanning the horizon, and spotted a small tower, its weathered stone rising against the bleak sky. Quickly, he moved toward it, feeling the pull of the impending task upon him.

The door was heavy but opened easily under his touch, and he ascended the spiral staircase within. The air grew colder as he climbed, the silence pressing down on him. At the top, he came upon a small landing, and just beyond it, the sound of a demonic cackle echoed. He paused. Then, with a cautious hand, he opened the door.

The scene before him sent a chill through his spirit.

A woman was shackled to the stone wall, her wrists and neck bound by thick iron chains. Her skin was ashen, her hair a tangled mess, and her teeth—black, sharp, and decayed. Her eyes were wild, gleaming with a madness that only the damned could know.

Gideon swallowed hard. "Jezebeth?"

The woman's lips curled into a twisted grin. "Well, well... What have we here? At first, I thought you were just another snack. But now that I see you know my name, I suppose you're not here to feed me, are you?"

"I was sent by Azazel," Gideon answered, keeping his tone steady despite the cold sweat that now dotted his brow.

At the mention of the Prince of Hell, Jezebeth's laugh stopped, and her eyes gleamed. "Azazel, you say? Now that's a twist. What does the great Prince want with me?"

Gideon took a deep breath, bracing himself. "He told me to give you a name: Helena Thompson."

For a long moment, Jezebeth's expression shifted, her face contorting as she rummaged through her fractured memories. Then her eyes snapped wide, a smile stretching across her face like a predator's. "Helena Thompson... Yes... For that, I'm going to need a ride."

Gideon's stomach dropped. He had feared the request. The *ride* meant she would possess him—take control of his body, use him as her vessel—until they returned. And he would be powerless to stop her. He could only pray that the demon feared Azazel's wrath enough to comply with his instructions and not torment him for her own amusement.

But Gideon knew better than to trust in such fragile hopes.

Gideon's gaze flickered back to Jezebeth, her eyes wild and unwavering, locked on him with an unsettling intensity. He took a deliberate step forward. There was no turning back now. He had come too far, and failure was no longer an option.

"Okay, witch," he muttered, voice tight with control. "I want your word that you're not going to pull any tricks, and that you'll leave the moment we're back."

Jezebeth's lips curled into a mock pout, and she feigned an expression of hurt, her voice dripping with false sincerity. "I wouldn't dream of it! If Azazel himself sent you to free me, who am I to defy him? We've always had such a lovely little arrangement. I'd be a fool to jeopardize it now."

Gideon stared at her, his distrust evident in his eyes, but he pressed on. "How do I free you from these chains?"

Before she could answer, the growl of something massive echoed from outside the tower. Jezebeth's grin widened, her shining with excitement. "Ooh, that sounds like a Hellhound. And it sounds hungry. You better hurry, Gideon."

The sound of her using his name unsettled him. "How do you know my name, Witch?" he demanded.

She chuckled darkly, her tone casual, almost amused. "Don't be so surprised. Word of your past exploits has made its way through even the deepest levels of Hell. Though, I must say, your little mishap with Vizibir was... rather disappointing."

"That wasn't my fault!" Gideon snapped, frustration creeping into his voice. "If Solomon and his infernal cronies hadn't sabotaged everything, it would've gone according to plan!"

"But they did... and it didn't. And you were the one leading the charge." Jezebeth's voice was laced with mockery, the hint of a smile tugging at her lips.

"Enough with the damn history lesson, hag!" Gideon snapped. "Just tell me how to free you, so we can get this over with."

Another growl, closer now, reverberated through the stone walls, the sound shaking the very air. Gideon's heart pounded as he realized the beast was nearly upon them.

"These chains hold me to the wall," Jezebeth said, "but it's the cage carved into the ceiling that truly binds me. That's where my power is sealed."

Gideon's gaze snapped to the ceiling, following her pointed finger. The intricate pattern of symbols and runes wrapped around the room, forming a protective barrier.

Without hesitation, he jumped, his body twisting to grab the cold iron bars of the window. With a grunt, he hoisted himself up, wrapping his right arm around a bar for leverage. His left hand reached toward the ceiling, fingers scraping desperately at the intricate runes. Blood began to ooze from his fingertip as he scratched furiously, the pain intensifying with each pass, but he didn't stop.

The moment the outer ring of the cage cracked, releasing its grip, a surge of power shot through the room, and Jezebeth was free.

Gideon released the bar and fell to the floor just as the Hell-hound barreled into the room with a deafening roar. The creature was massive—its midnight-black fur gleamed like a shadow, its eyes burning with hunger. Its massive jaws dripped with saliva as it lunged toward them.

"Time to go," Jezebeth's voice whispered in his ear, just before she turned into a column of black smoke and shot into his mouth.

A wave of nausea washed over him as the demon's presence flooded his mind. For a moment, panic clawed at him—what if she didn't keep her promise? What if she took control and never left? But then, just as quickly as she had entered, the pressure lifted. Jezebeth expelled herself from his body, and Gideon was once again himself.

He flailed around in the tub, gasping for air, the feeling of her presence lingering like a cold, suffocating shadow. His heart hammered in his chest as he watched her ghostly form slip through the crack at the bottom of the door.

Never again, he vowed. Never again would he allow himself to be used as a vessel for something so vile. The sensation of another being clawing at his mind, scraping against his very soul, was enough to drive even the most hardened of men to madness. And yet, he had endured it. Barely.

Rising from the tub, he cleaned himself off, every movement mechanical, as though the effort to shake off the lingering effects of possession had drained him. He waited, straining for any sign, any command from Azazel, but the silence stretched on.

He had done his part. Now, all he could do was hope the demon hag would do hers.

CHAPTER 5

When Hecate stepped into the room, her eyes immediately fell on the boy huddled in the corner, his tiny body chained to the cold stone wall. His face was caked with dirt and smeared with blood, and his clothes were little more than tatters, barely clinging to his frail frame. The stench of urine and feces was overwhelming, thick in the air and almost suffocating, forcing a gag from her throat.

"What the fuck is going on here?" Hecate demanded, her voice sharp with disgust and disbelief.

Solomon closed the door behind them with a soft click, his eyes never leaving the boy. "The child's name is Joel. The demon inside him, however, goes by something far more... horrific."

A low, guttural laugh filled the room, the sound so unnatural, it seemed to come from somewhere far older and more sinister than the small body it emanated from. "Why don't you come closer, pretty little thing, and let me whisper it in your ear?" the boy said, his voice sending a shiver down Hecate's spine.

Instinctively, she stepped back, but the demon only laughed harder, twisting in a grotesque and unnatural back

28

bend. His head and neck contorted as he scurried up the wall, moving like a spider, his body bent at an impossible angle. He opened his mouth wide, and the shriek that tore from him pierced the air, high-pitched and searing, aimed straight for Hecate.

Terrified, she turned to Solomon, her voice filled with panic. "Why the hell did you bring me here?!"

Solomon's expression was calm, almost distant, as he responded. "I want you to help me with the exorcism."

"Say what?"

"That's right. We're here to cast out the demon and send it back to Hell where it belongs."

"But why me? I don't know anything about this kind of stuff."

Solomon's gaze softened slightly. "You've got to trust me, Hecate. I'm a pretty good judge of character, and something tells me you've got the gift. I wouldn't have brought you here if I didn't think you could handle it."

She let out a dry laugh. "You've certainly got a lot more faith in me than I do."

"Just believe, and everything will fall into place."

Joel's voice cut in with a mocking cackle. "You think so, huh? Unless you know my name, freak, I'll just keep coming back. Maybe next time, I'll fly down your throat, sweet little thing. I bet you feel just as good inside as you look on the outside."

Solomon's face hardened, his voice suddenly cold. "I guess your brothers in Hell didn't warn you about me, Valak," he snapped. "Or you'd think twice before mocking my abilities."

The demon's face twisted into fear at the sound of his name. It shrank back into the corner, trying to press itself into the cracks of the brick wall, its form suddenly much smaller, less menacing.

Hecate raised an eyebrow, impressed by the sudden shift. "What now?"

Solomon turned to her, a knowing smile tugging at the corners of his lips. "How's your Latin?"

Hecate blinked. "You mean, that's a real language?"

Solomon chuckled softly. "Don't worry. You'll get the hang of it."

He stepped toward a nearby bookshelf, pulling a dusty tome from its place. Flipping through the pages until he found the right one and handed it to her. "Just follow my lead. Recite the words with me as best as you can. But it's more than the words—feel the power behind them. Let them fill you. Believe in them. Without that, they're just empty sounds."

Hecate took the book, her hands trembling slightly as she opened it. She wasn't sure why she trusted this man so readily, but something in him made her willing to try. Taking a steady breath, she glanced up at him. "Are you ready?"

He nodded, his expression unchanging. "Whenever you are."

The first words she spoke were slow and unsure, as she sounded out the strange syllables, feeling the weight of them in her mouth. Then she heard Solomon's voice joining hers, steady and confident, reciting the ancient invocation from memory. "Exorcizamus te, omnis immunde spiritus, omni satanica potestas, omnis incursio infernalis adversarii."

A surge of energy coursed through her, electrifying her body in a way she had never felt before. It was as if she had tapped into something far greater than herself—something alive, crackling with power. Her eyes widened, and she looked at Solomon, who simply smiled at her, encouraging.

The words came more easily now, as if the language itself was flowing through her, not just her lips but deep inside.

"Omnis legio, omnis congregatio et secta diabolica, in nomini et virtute Domini nostri Jesu Christi, eradicare et effugare a Dei Ecclesia, ab animabus ad imaginem Dei conditis ac pretioso divini Agni sanguini redemptis."

As she spoke, she could feel the energy growing, swirling within her like a storm, each word infusing her with more power, more certainty. The demon inside Joel began to thrash and writhe, its body contorting violently as the exorcism took hold. It hissed and spit, thrashing against its prison as Valak's voice erupted, trying to disrupt their focus. "You'll have to do better than that, Old Man. Or have you lost some of your giddy-up along the way? You know, it's not uncommon for a man your age to have trouble getting it up."

Solomon ignored the taunts, his gaze never leaving Hecate. "Again. Stronger this time."

Taking a deep breath, Hecate did as he asked, pouring more strength into her words, more belief. The words seemed to take on a life of their own, building to a crescendo, the demon's resistance weakening. Joel's body twisted unnaturally, scurrying up the wall like a spider, screeching as black, viscous mucus streamed from his mouth.

As they reached the final words, Solomon darted forward, catching Joel's limp form before it hit the ground. For a moment, the boy lay still in his arms, and Solomon's heart skipped a beat. Had they been too late? Had the demon's grip been too strong? But then, slowly, Joel's eyes fluttered open, and he looked at Solomon with exhaustion.

"I'm thirsty," the boy rasped.

A sigh of relief escaped Solomon's lips as he pulled the boy close. He motioned for Hecate to take his place. As she sat down on the floor beside Joel, Solomon cradled his head gently in her lap. "He was terrified," Solomon said softly. "Especially when you came in."

Hecate frowned. "Me? Why was he afraid of me?"

Joel turned his head toward her, his voice quiet. "I'm not sure, but that's why he said those mean things to you. He was trying to make you weak."

Hecate smiled softly, brushing his hair from his forehead. "Well, it didn't work, did it?"

Joel shook his head, offering a small, tired smile. "Thank you."

Her heart swelled, and for the first time, she felt a surge of something new—a sense of purpose, of making a difference. It was a feeling she'd never known before, and she wasn't sure how to handle it. "I want to learn everything," she whispered.

Solomon's eyes gleamed. "I knew you would."

***

In the months that followed, Hecate threw herself into the study of the occult with an unrelenting hunger, consuming everything she could find. For the first time in her life, she had a sense of direction, and with each book she devoured, each new technique she mastered, she found herself more and more immersed in the world that had once seemed so distant to her.

She began with the basics—numerology, Tarot, meditation techniques that bridged her to the Kabbalah. The deeper she delved, the faster she learned, as if the very knowledge coursed through her veins. But it was the practice of exorcism that truly consumed her, igniting a passion she hadn't known she possessed. The rush of banishing evil, the sense of power when she watched an innocent freed from torment—it was exhilarating. Yet despite her desire, Solomon had yet to include her in another exorcism ritual.

"When do I get to help with the next one?" she asked, her voice tinged with impatience.

The answer was always the same. "You're not ready yet. There's still much for you to learn."

"But I've learned so much already! And you said I did well with Joel, didn't you?"

"Joel was a rare case," Solomon replied. "A controlled situation. If you're not fully prepared, it could go terribly wrong."

"Like what?" she pressed, frustration mounting.

"The host could die," he said simply. "Or the demon could transfer itself into you. And trust me, neither you nor I would want that."

Hecate knew he was right, but it didn't make it easier to wait. For the first time in her life, she had found something that pushed her to grow, something that made her feel alive in a way she never had before. Now that she felt truly useful in this world, she didn't want to stop.

Landis became a constant in her life, an anchor, a source of knowledge and comfort as she navigated this new, dangerous path. He helped her with Latin, constantly reminding her of its nuances—how verbs could have multiple meanings, how the word order differed from English, how every noun had a gender. His patience and presence grounded her, especially when the language seemed impossible.

One evening, the two of them sat together in a corner of Hesburgh Library, textbooks scattered around them. Hecate sighed in exasperation. "I'll never get the hang of this," she muttered, her head resting in her hand after an hour of struggling.

Landis smiled and squeezed her hand. "Don't be too hard on yourself. Latin's tough. But I know you... you'll get it."

Her gaze lingered on his hand in hers, and she met his eyes —eyes full of understanding, of something deeper. When he leaned in and kissed her, she didn't pull away. She welcomed it, savoring the tenderness of the moment.

"Let's get out of here," he said with a grin. "I think you've done enough studying for tonight."

Hand in hand, they left the library, strolling across the campus toward Saint Mary's Lake. The full moon cast a silver glow on the calm waters, and a pair of swans drifted lazily by. A family of ducks nestled together for the night nearby, and for a moment, everything felt perfect. The peaceful serenity was a welcome reprieve from the darkness that always lingered just beyond their world.

They sat on the grass, inhaling the sweet spring air that rose off the lake. The quietness enveloped them, and in that stillness, it was Hecate who leaned in and kissed him this time. For a fleeting moment, the rest of the world seemed to disappear as they embraced.

But the peace shattered when they noticed Solomon standing nearby, watching them.

Landis froze. "Sam, we were just—"

Hecate's voice faltered. "It's nothing—"

Solomon's smile was laced with amusement. "It's fine, guys. I actually believe that having a bond of love, especially in this line of work, strengthens both souls. It could mean the difference between life and death in a situation like ours."

Hecate blinked. "Who said anything about love?"

Solomon raised an eyebrow, glancing back and forth between them. Their blushes were so obvious even the night couldn't hide them.

Then, his demeanor changed, replaced with an urgency in his voice, "Unfortunately," he said quickly, "you'll have to put your courting on hold for now. We've got an appointment."

"Appointment?" Landis asked.

"Yes, all three of us," Solomon replied.

Hecate frowned. "Where are we going?"

"The Fourteenth Floor."

Landis's face went pale.

"What's the big deal about the Fourteenth Floor? And where is it?" Hecate asked curiously.

Landis's voice was barely above a whisper. "It doesn't exist. Not to the outside world, at least."

CHAPTER 6

Helena Thompson had once been the picture of happiness. She was a child who laughed easily, then grew into a woman who married the man of her dreams and started a beautiful family of her own. She had everything, or so she thought. But one night, in a single horrific minute, that happiness was ripped from her life, leaving behind a gaping, bleeding hole. And now, she was alone.

The memories of that night replayed endlessly in her mind. She tried, hopelessly, to convince herself that it wasn't her fault, but deep down, she knew. It was her carelessness that had cost her more than any one person should bear. Her husband and daughter were gone, dead. And her other daughter—she had abandoned her, leaving Helena in a hollow silence. She had died inside, too. The only thing that had stopped her from ending it all was the bitter truth that she was too much of a coward to pull the trigger herself. If only she'd locked that damn door!

Helena took another swig from the bottle in her hand and leaned back in the chair, the alcohol's warmth spreading through her limbs. *Hecate would be so proud,* she thought bitterly. She knew she had been wrong to blame her—wrong to push her away. Now, the chasm between them was too wide, too deep for either of them to cross.

With a final, heavy gulp, the bottle was empty. She let it slip from her hand, watching as it clattered against the floor. Maybe this time, she wouldn't wake up. *Please, just let me sleep...*

Unfortunately, her wish wasn't granted. Hours later, Helena woke up in an alcohol induced fog, dazed and confused. To her surprise, she wasn't in the chair where she had passed out. She was lying in her bed.

A voice broke the silence beside her, and a chill of terror shot through her.

"Thank God! You're finally awake!"

Slowly, Helena turned her head, and what she saw stopped her heart. There, beside her, lay Theodore—her husband—alive. "Teddy? Is it really you?" she whimpered.

He smiled warmly, brushing her hair from her forehead. "Yes, dear. Who else would it be?"

"But… I saw you die."

Teddy's fingers lingered in her hair as he gazed at her with soft, loving eyes. "You must've had a bad dream, sweetheart. Don't you remember? You were so sick. We were scared to death when your fever got so high."

Helena's eyes widened in disbelief. "We?"

Then, a small voice came from the other side of the bed. "I'm here, Mommy."

Helena's head whipped around, her heart leaping into her throat when she saw her daughter, Judith, lying next to her. Without thinking, she reached for her, pulling her into a desperate hug. "Oh, Judith! I thought I lost you forever. I missed you so much!"

Judith giggled, pushing gently at her mother. "You're silly, Mommy. I didn't go anywhere. I've been right here."

Helena's arms tightened around her. ""t doesn't matter. All that matters is that we're together again. Hecate's going to be so happy!"

Judith's brow furrowed. "Who's Hecate?"

"Why, she's your sister, silly."

Judith looked at her father in confusion. "Daddy, why is she saying that? She's freaking me out."

Teddy's smile faltered, though his tone remained gentle. "It's okay, sweetheart. Mommy's still not feeling well." He pressed his palm to Helena's forehead, his fingers cold. "Just as I thought, you still have a fever. Why don't you close your eyes and rest? Things will be clearer once you've had more sleep."

Helena started to protest, her heart racing. "But surely you remember her, don't you?"

Teddy's smile hardened, and his voice dropped into something far too calm. "You're being delusional, dear. Your mind's not right yet. You'll come around."

A jolt of fear shot through Helena's chest. *Something's wrong—something's terribly wrong!* Panic flooded her, and her breath came in shallow gasps. "This isn't right! I don't know what's going on, but something's wrong here!"

And then it happened.

Teddy's eyes went black, a void so deep it seemed to suck the light from the room. "The only thing that's wrong here, dear," he said, his voice low and cold, "is you. You refuse to accept the truth—that you're a monster, through and through."

Helena shrank back, tears spilling down her cheeks. "That's not true. How can you say such things?"

Judith's voice came again, but it was different now—dead, hollow. "It's true, Mommy. Look at what I am now. Look at what you made me."

Helena turned toward her daughter, and a scream tore from her throat.

Judith's face was half-eaten, maggots crawling in and out of her hollow eye sockets. Her hair was matted with dirt and dried blood. "What's the matter, Mommy?" the corpse of Judith asked, her voice a mockery of the innocence it once had. "Don't you love me anymore?"

Teddy's voice cut through the horror. "Well, answer her, bitch!"

Helena turned toward her husband, only to find that the man she had once loved was no longer there. Instead, what lay before her was a grotesque imitation—a thing that had crawled out from the earth to torment her.

A scream bubbled in her throat, but before it could escape, everything vanished. Teddy, Judith—they were gone. In their place stood Jezebeth, eyes wide with wild, gleaming madness.

Slowly, Jezebeth crawled onto the bed, straddling Helena. Terror seized Helena's chest, and though she tried to scream, only whimpers escaped her lips. "What do you want from me?" she begged, the words weak and trembling.

Jezebeth's lips curled into a cruel smile. "Sorry, darling. I like to play with my new hosts first... get to know them. And you, sweet Helena, have a lot of issues buried deep inside. This is going to be so much fun."

In a flash, Jezebeth transformed into a swirl of black smoke, coiling like a snake ready to strike. It hung in the air for a moment before shooting into Helena's mouth, plunging down her throat like a poison.

Helena's body convulsed briefly as the demon settled in. The room fell silent, and then Helena's eyes opened—black as night. And a twisted smile spread across her face.

CHAPTER 7

The elevator came to a halt and Hecate glanced nervously at Landis. He shot a questioning look at Solomon, who offered them a reassuring smile.

"Let me handle the talking," Solomon said, his voice calm, almost too calm. "If Uriel asks you anything, just be honest. He knows when you're lying. And if he seems to zone out, don't worry—he's having a vision. They don't last long."

He led them down a narrow corridor, pausing in front of a door with a security panel beside it. "And just so you know, Uriel tends to talk fast when he's agitated, which, given the circumstances, is likely tonight."

Solomon punched in a code on the panel, and a small compartment popped open, revealing a fingerprint scanner. After a brief scan, the door to the fourteenth floor slid open with a mechanical hiss.

The room that greeted them was nothing like what Hecate had expected. Gone was the notion of a lavish penthouse or a sacred sanctuary for the devout. Instead, they stood in a sprawling, high-tech control hub that seemed to swallow the space whole. The hum of a hundred computer terminals filled the air, each operator plugged into their own headset, voices overlapping like a chaotic stock market floor.

The far wall was completely covered with dozens of screens, each flashing with scenes that seemed to belong to another world—otherworldly creatures, visions, and landscapes beyond her wildest comprehension. Hecate felt a chill run down her spine as she took in the vastness of it all. She had seen a fraction of it, but this... this was something else entirely.

A man, tall and lean in khakis and a polo shirt, stood before the screens, flipping through them with unnerving speed. The moment she caught sight of him, Hecate was struck by an odd thought—a fleeting image of a State Farm commercial. She stifled a snicker, but it seemed out of place in such a tense environment.

As they approached, the man turned toward them, and Hecate's gaze was immediately drawn to his strange glasses —lenses that shifted in and out, adjusting like some kind of high-tech microscope. He looked at her and Landis with a detached curiosity, but there was something unnerving in the way his eyes lingered. It wasn't as if he was just looking at them—no, it felt like he was peering into them.

Solomon strode over and shook the man's hand with a firm grip. "Uriel, good to see you."

"You too, Sam," Uriel replied, his voice smooth but oddly distant.

Solomon turned toward Hecate and Landis. "This is Uriel, the wisest of all angels."

"Oh, Sam," Uriel chuckled, brushing off the praise with a humble wave.

Hecate's eyes widened in disbelief. "You mean, like... an actual angel?"

Solomon nodded. "Yes. Do you find that so hard to believe after everything you've witnessed?"

"I guess not... it's just... I always thought they'd look... you know, more radiant. More angelic."

Uriel's smile softened. "Like everything else, some things shine brighter than others. It doesn't make them any less important."

Hecate flushed in embarrassment. "I'm sorry, I didn't mean it like that."

Uriel's gaze shifted to Solomon. "Is she ready?"

Solomon nodded. "She's ready."

Uriel turned back to Hecate, his expression unreadable. "Are you ready?"

For a moment, Hecate froze, the weight of the question catching her off guard. "I... I guess so," she replied, her voice unsure.

Uriel focused on her once more, his hands adjusting the lenses on his glasses. The seconds stretched as he scrutinized her, and when he finally spoke, his tone was grave. "Very well. I trust your judgment, Sam. But... something has come up. Landis won't be able to accompany you after all."

Hecate glanced at Landis, confusion and concern spreading across her face.

Uriel raised a hand, signaling for them to wait. "Before we get to that, let's talk about why I called you here. We've been tracking an alarming increase in demonic possessions. It's starting to look like the beginning of something much bigger. I want you two to take the lead on a large-scale exorcism effort, and handle this before it spirals out of control."

Before Solomon could respond, Uriel suddenly froze. His body locked in place, as if suspended in time. Then, as quickly as it had happened, he snapped back to reality and bolted toward one of the cubicles, speaking in an agitated tone to a technician behind the desk. After a tense moment, Uriel returned, his face tight with worry.

"Apologies for that," Uriel said. "Now, as I was saying—your plane will be waiting for you. I'll send you the location of your first subject shortly. But before you go, let me talk to Landis for a moment."

Uriel beckoned Landis aside, his voice low and urgent as they spoke in hushed tones. Hecate couldn't make out the words, but she could see the expression on Landis's face—shock, sorrow, and a flicker of something else that made her heart tighten. When Landis walked away, his shoulders were slumped and tears were threatening to fall from his eyes.

"Are you okay?" Hecate asked softly. "What's wrong?"

Landis hesitated, his voice tight. "It's my parents. They... they were in an accident."

Hecate's stomach churned. "Oh, no! Are they going to be okay?"

"They're both in critical condition," he replied absently as he tried to make sense of the situation. "I'm flying to Arizona to see them. The doctors told Uriel... I don't know, Hecate. I haven't spoken to them in years. Not since—well, let's just say their... punishment methods were extreme. That's why I ran. To be honest, I don't even know how I feel right now. Part of me wants them to die, but they're still my parents. Is that wrong?"

Hecate's heart ached for him. She held him tight for a moment. "No, it's not wrong. You're human. I've felt the same way from time to time. A person's actions define them, though, not their thoughts."

Solomon's voice cut through the moment. "That's a wise perspective, Hecate. Now, let's head back. We've got work to do."

As they moved toward the door, Solomon called back to Uriel to say goodbye, but his words seemed to vanish into the noise of the control room. Uriel, lost in his work, was already adjusting his lenses again, scanning the screens with unwavering focus. It was as if they had never even been there.

***

Hecate and Landis stood by the terminal, clinging to each other as if the moment itself might slip away. Landis's voice wavered. "I wish I could go with you."

"I know," Hecate replied. "Me too. But your family needs you now."

"But you guys are my family too."

She squeezed his hand tighter. "We talked about this, Landis. If you don't go and see them, you'll regret it for the rest of your life."

He nodded reluctantly. "You're right. It's just... we're finally close, and I don't want anything to come between us."

Hecate smiled softly before pressing a kiss to his lips. "We'll have plenty of time to pick this up when I get back from wherever I'm headed."

Landis brushed a strand of hair from her face, eyes searching hers. "Promise me you'll be careful."

"I promise."

A boarding call echoed through the terminal, announcing his flight. With one last kiss, Landis turned and made his way to the counter, casting a final glance over his shoulder before disappearing down the tunnel, silently worrying that this might be their last goodbye.

As the space around them grew quieter, Solomon took a step forward, heading down the concourse. "Come on, Hecate. We have a plane to catch."

"Where are we going?" she asked, trying to mask the ache in her heart.

"To Menton, a town in the South of France."

"France?" She blinked in surprise. "When you said to get a passport, I thought you meant somewhere close, like Canada or Mexico—not Europe."

Solomon chuckled. "Evil knows no borders. It thrives everywhere, though it certainly has its pockets here—especially in the higher echelons of power. But that's another battle."

Hecate did a double-take at the last part of his statement, never really putting much thought into politics and how evil some politicians actually are. "So, how long is this flight?"

"It's an hour and a half to Atlanta, then a two-hour layover. From Atlanta to Paris is about eight and a half hours, followed by a quick hop to Nice. Plenty of time to practice your Latin."

She scowled at him playfully, the challenge sparking in her eyes despite her distaste for the language. Still, she knew better than to protest. Mastery could mean the difference between life and death.

Minutes later, they settled by their gate. Rain tapped lightly on the window beside them, casting a silvery sheen over the tarmac. The once-bright night felt heavy now, each drop amplifying the hollowness that threatened to swallow her. In a day, she had soared to elation and plunged to sorrow. It felt as if fate itself were mocking her, whispering, *Not so fast.*

Movement outside caught her eye. A shadow—a woman—stood in the rain, staring up at her through the glass. Pale, almost luminous, the figure was soon joined by others, their faces twisted with a silent, haunting recognition.

Hecate's heart slammed in her chest. She nudged Solomon, her gaze fixed ahead. "Do you see that?"

"What?" He glanced out the window.

"There," she insisted. "People. Watching us."

Solomon's brow furrowed as he reached into his bag, pulling out a pair of thin, wire-framed glasses. He slid them on, his face tensing as he looked again. "Ah," he muttered. "We have company. I'm surprised you see them so vividly. Have you encountered spirits before?"

Hecate's chest tightened at the memory. The night her grandfather died, she had seen him at the foot of her bed, his eyes wild with pain, mouth contorted in a silent scream, chest torn and bloody. For years, she'd carried the guilt, believing he'd blamed her for his death until she'd learned better.

"Once," she admitted, her voice low. "A long time ago."

Solomon nodded. "Then they're likely here with a message."

Her pulse quickened. "That's not creepy at all. What do they want with me?"

Before he could respond, the overhead lights flickered. The woman outside was suddenly at the window, skeletal face inches from the glass. Sunken eyes bore into Hecate's, and a ghostly wail split the air as the spirit opened her mouth. "Jezebeth!" she shrieked.

Hecate gasped as the apparition vanished. Trembling, she turned to Solomon. "Please tell me you saw that."

"I did," he said, his expression dark. "What did she say?"

"Jezebeth," she whispered, the unfamiliar name slicing through her like ice. "What does that mean?"

Solomon's eyes widened, then narrowed in thought. "If it's what I think... it's not good. Did she say anything else?"

"No, just that word. Is it... someone's name?"

"Not someone. A demon," Solomon said, voice taut. "One I believed I had locked away long ago. But if she's free, then we're facing a threat more formidable than you can imagine."

Hecate's heart thudded. "Perfect. No pressure, right?"

Despite the dire turn, a small smile tugged at Solomon's lips. "You've been preparing for this all along, Hecate. Trust your instincts. You were born for this."

The storm outside thickened, casting shadows deep and twisting across the tarmac as their flight drew closer. The voice over the intercom crackled, announcing the final boarding call, and it pulled Hecate from the strange, unsettling conversation. They stood and walked to the gate, Hecate casting one last glance out the window. Relief swept over her when she saw the runway empty of any spectral figures.

She hadn't flown since she was a young girl, and the memories were hazy—only the sharp pain of her ears popping and the queasy churn in her stomach remained. As they settled into their first-class seats, Solomon reached into his coat pocket and handed her a piece of spearmint gum. She raised an eyebrow.

"It helps with the pressure," he explained, a soft grin lifting the corners of his mouth. "The mint will ease the nausea too."

Hecate stared at him, taken aback. "Can you read my mind or something?"

"Not exactly. But I can sense your anxiety. Plus, the same thing happens to me when I fly."

She nodded slowly, accepting the gum and began chewing as if her life depended on it. The engines roared to life, and moments later, the plane shuddered forward, gaining speed. She clenched the armrest as the ground fell away and they climbed into the clouds, the hum of turbulence vibrating through her. Only when the plane leveled did she dare release her grip.

Solomon watched her, noting the pink flush that crept up her cheeks. He signaled for a flight attendant. "Can we have a bottle of water, please?"

The attendant handed one over with a smile, and Hecate unscrewed the cap, taking a long, grateful sip. "Thank you," Hecate said, her voice steadier.

"Feeling better?" Solomon asked.

"Yeah, I'm okay," she replied.

"It gets easier. Once you know what to expect, it's not so bad. I still remember my first flight—when there were only the pilot and one passenger. Now that was a hair-raising experience."

Hecate almost choked on her water. "What are you talking about?"

Solomon looked amused. "What do you mean?"

"It sounded like you were talking about flying back when the Wright brothers were around."

"I was."

Hecate's brow furrowed. Sure, she knew Solomon was older than he looked, maybe in his early forties at most. But if what he said was true…

"That would make you, what, a hundred years old?"

Solomon sighed, the smile fading as his expression turned thoughtful. "I thought Landis would've explained more. Seems I was wrong."

Hecate's confusion deepened. "He said something about you when I first got there, but I didn't really think about it after that. Then I got wrapped up in my training and forgot all about it. This whole time I thought you were just overly… eccentric?"

He took a breath, as if weighing how best to continue. "Do you remember the stories of King Solomon from the Bible?"

She shifted in her seat, shrugging. "Not much. Something about wanting to split a baby in half when two women argued over it."

Solomon winced. "Yes, not one of my finest hours. Effective, but dramatic. There were better moments, I assure you."

The realization hit her like a punch to the chest. Her mind raced, connecting the impossible dots. "There's no way…"

He nodded, a knowing glimmer in his eye. "Yes, I am that Solomon. And before you ask, I'm older than I look. A few thousand years older."

"But how?" The word came out as a whisper, thick with disbelief.

"My wisdom didn't just grant insight—it revealed ways to transcend the bounds of human limitations. It's cost me dearly but through it, God's grace allowed me to manipulate what others see as the immovable laws of time and space."

Her jaw dropped. "Are you saying you're immortal?"

"Not exactly. I can be killed. But I've been granted a state that's close."

Hecate's thoughts spun in dizzying circles. The man sitting beside her—thousands of years old, watching empires rise and fall, surviving through millennia. It was too much to grasp.

"Try not to dwell on it," Solomon said, his tone softening."I'm just a regular guy who knows some secrets, that's all. You'll be able to process it a lot better if you look at it that way. Now, why don't you relax and get some rest to take your mind off things?"

Easier said than done, she thought as she laid back in her seat and pressed her head against the window, looking out at the darkness. She wondered what other secrets she'd find out as they went along? The thought both intrigued and frightened her.

***

* * *

As the seatbelt chime sounded, signaling their descent, Hecate stirred from a surprisingly deep sleep. With her mind racing earlier, she hadn't expected rest to come so easily. Even the brief nap left her feeling clearer, more composed. Turning to her side, she glimpsed Solomon, slumped in his seat and lightly snoring. A hint of a smile played on her lips. *Maybe he really is just a regular guy after all,* she mused.

The plane jolted slightly as the wheels met the tarmac, and Solomon woke with a start, stretching out his arms and shifting upright. Hecate's smile widened. "What's so funny?" he asked.

She chuckled, "The way you snore. It's like a tiny puffing sound—it's kind of adorable."

"Is that so?" he smirked, teasing back. "Good to know my charm persists, even when I'm unconscious."

"Yeah, it does," she said, her tone softening.

"Glad to hear it," he replied. "The last thing I'd want is for you to feel uneasy around me."

"I don't. Not anymore. It just took some time to process everything."

Solomon reached over and gave her a gentle hug. "I'm glad."

Once the plane had rolled to a stop, Hecate stood to retrieve her carry-on. A book wedged behind Solomon's bag caught her eye. Only part of the title was visible—'beth'—and her heart skipped a beat. The name 'Jezebeth' echoed in her memory, vivid as the day she first heard it. But then Solomon shifted his bag, and she saw the full title: Macbeth. A wave of relief washed over her, followed by embarrassment.

Solomon frowned. "Something wrong?"

"No, just...jumping at shadows," she said, forcing a smile.

Their exit into the terminal was marked by a sleepy

quietness, the early hour reducing their dining options to a vending machine or a dimly lit IHOP Express. With little choice, they settled into the diner, both too tired to care much.

Hecate scrolled through her phone while they waited, her spirits lifting when she found a text from Landis. He'd made it to Chicago O'Hare and was preparing to board a flight to Denver. After that, he'd head to Palm Springs to reach his parents in the ICU at Eisenhower Medical Center. He promised more details as soon as he had them.

"Be safe," she murmured, fingers typing a quick reply.

Their food arrived shortly after. Solomon, predictably, opted for a spinach and egg-white omelet, while Hecate, famished, devoured a hearty plate of bacon, eggs, and strawberry pancakes. The first bite was bliss, bringing a rare, comforting moment amid the chaos.

They sipped coffee, lingering for a moment before Hecate spoke up. "What do you know about this girl we're going to see?"

Solomon set down his cup. "Not much. Just that she fell gravely ill overnight. Now she's lashing out and speaking in tongues."

"Tongues?" Hecate asked, eyes widening in confusion.

"It's common. Demons use ancient languages to curse and unsettle those around them."

"Curses that linger across generations?"

"Exactly. Part of an exorcism is not only banishing the demon but destroying its disease before it can spread."

"Got it."

Solomon pushed his chair back, stretching. "Let's walk a bit. We have a long flight ahead."

As she stood, reaching for her bag, Hecate felt a sudden, icy touch. Her breath caught in her throat. Glancing down, she caught sight of a pale hand beneath the table before it vanished. Solomon was already steps ahead, oblivious.

Heart pounding, she followed, eyes darting nervously. And then she saw him: a ghostly boy, dripping wet, standing to her left. Water trickled from his open mouth, pooling at his feet.

Suppressing a scream, she quickened her steps, grabbing Solomon's arm. "They're back."

Solomon adjusted his glasses, eyes scanning the room until they caught the shimmer of spirits, clustering like moths to a flame. "Now that your senses are open, they're more present. In time, you'll learn to filter them out."

"I'd rather start now," she said, her voice taut. "I don't want to see them anymore."

He nodded, placing a protective arm around her. "Most are harmless, seeking closure. But some... not so much."

Hecate shuddered. "One touched me, Solomon. It wasn't just a vision."

His eyes darkened. "It's rare, but it can happen. Stay close."

Suddenly, Hecate halted. Before them stretched a wall of spectral forms, a barrier of hollow-eyed figures daring her to move forward. It reminded her of a ghoulish version of the childhood game, Red-Rover, Red-Rover—but this was no game.

"Leave me alone!" she screamed, collapsing to her knees.

In an instant, they were gone.

Solomon kneeled beside her, pulling her to him as a gaping crowd gathered. "It's okay, Hecate. They're gone now."

Her breath came in ragged bursts. The crowd's murmurs stung her, shame coursing hot beneath her skin. She had fought too hard, grown too much, to be brought down by fear. Hecate was shaking, not just from fear, but also from anger—anger directed at herself. She had worked hard to grow out of the scared little girl she used to be, into someone with the power to push those fears aside and to go forward unafraid. Now these spirits were threatening to undo that hard work!

"What the fuck are you looking at?" Hecate hissed at the curious onlookers. A moment later, they shuffled away, each one shaking their head in disgust.

"Close your eyes," Solomon instructed softly. "Clear your mind."

She obeyed, though visions clawed at her consciousness. Solomon's hand rested firm on her shoulder. "Take a deep breath. They can't hurt you."

Hecate inhaled, seeking the calm within chaos.

Solomon continued, "Picture one spirit. Focus. Don't fear it."

The boy came to mind. Slowly, she opened her eyes. He was there, looking less spectral, more like a Sunday School student with eyes full of sorrow.

"What do you want?" she whispered.

The boy leaned in, his breath icy against her skin. "Go home," he rasped.

And then, he was gone.

Hecate sat back, her heart thundering in her chest. What did he mean? Was it a warning—or something worse?

Hecate stared into the void where the boy's ghost had stood. The whisper of his final words—"*Go home*"—echoed in her mind, twisting into a knot of anxiety. Was it a plea? A warning? Did the message mean danger awaited them on their mission, or was it more personal, a call to reconcile with her mother?

Solomon's voice broke her from her thoughts. "You did

well, Hecate. Most would have faltered. What did he tell you?"

"He told me to go home," she replied softly. "But I don't understand why?"

Solomon thought about it for a second. "Spirits often speak in riddles. It could be literal, or symbolic. Clarity comes with time."

"And if it doesn't?" Hecate asked.

"Keep watching for signs," Solomon advised. "When you know there's a message, the signs become easier to read."

He helped her up. "Come on. We've still got a trek before we find our gate."

Their footsteps fell into an uneasy rhythm as they navigated the expansive terminal. The lights above cast long shadows, and Hecate's senses remained on high alert. At last, they reached their gate. This time, Hecate sank into a seat with her back firmly against the window, unwilling to face what might lurk behind her.

Solomon settled in beside her. "You've come a long way, Hecate. I'm proud to call you my apprentice."

The word caught her off guard. "Apprentice? Me? But I've barely begun."

Solomon nod. "True, but your instincts, your resilience—they set you apart. You're progressing faster than most."

Hecate's eyes darted to the bustling terminal, then back to Solomon. "Are all the others under the library your apprentices too?"

"No," Solomon said, a chuckle escaping. "Most are students seeking knowledge, seeking purpose. Few carry the spark you and Landis have."

"How is Landis different?" she asked curiously.

Solomon's expression turned serious, his eyes narrowing as if weighing the depth of his response. "He's like you.

Sharp, compassionate, driven. But he carries burdens from his past that have shaped him. Has he shared much with you?"

Hecate shook her head slowly. "No, I didn't press. I figured, when he was ready, he'd tell me."

"That's wise." Solomon's voice softened. "His story isn't mine to tell, but know this—he's been through enough that we agreed he should step back from being my apprentice. I wanted him to have space to find his own way."

At the thought of Landis and whatever past torment he had endured, Hecate looked down sadly, wishing she could do more, be more, for him.

CHAPTER 8

Jezebeth slithered off the bed and glided toward the full-length mirror standing in the corner of the room. Slowly, she peeled off the clothes that clung to her, letting them fall in a careless heap at her feet. The room was silent, save for the whisper of her breath as she admired the form now under her command. Beneath the surface, she felt the frantic, futile scrabbling of Helena—the little mouse caught in her gilded cage. Jezebeth's lips curled into a smile.

"Not bad," she murmured, tilting her head as her eyes roamed over her new body. "I would've preferred someone with a touch more youth, but this will do nicely."

Her fingertips tapped lightly on the glass. "Little mouse? Are you in there, Little Mouse?" The mirror's surface shivered before stilling.

"It's safe now," Jezebeth cooed. "You can come out, Little Mouse."

The silvery surface rippled, then revealed the pale, stricken face of Helena. Her wide eyes met Jezebeth's, full of terror.

"There you are," Jezebeth purred. "What's the matter, my dear?"

Helena's quivering voice barely escaped her lips. "What do

you want with me?"

Jezebeth's smile deepened. "I think you already know the answer to that."

"But... why me?" Helena pleaded.

"Orders, darling," Jezebeth stated simply. "Trust me, Sweet Cheeks, you're just a means to an end. To me, you're nothing. But someone else," she leaned in, her eyes narrowing, "has grander plans for you."

She paused, her mouth twisting into a cruel smile. "But before I wear you out and toss you aside like yesterday's plaything, I'll do you one courtesy. We'll settle an old score— your husband, your daughter. You'll die knowing they're avenged. And I'll get a little bit of entertainment in the process. Sounds like a fair trade to me, wouldn't you say?"

Turning sharply, Jezebeth strode to the closet and flung it open. The hangers rattled as she tore through Helena's clothing, discarding dresses and blouses with a snort until her eyes caught a flash of crimson silk. The low-cut red dress hung like a trophy between her fingers.

"Ah, the color of blood," she said, pressing it against her body. "Perfect."

Jezebeth slipped into the dress, pulling down the neckline to reveal a glimpse of the prizes hidden beneath. Her eyes met Helena's in the reflection, holding a glint of satisfaction as she appraised the body she now wore like a second skin. "Not bad at all," she whispered, her voice dripping with menace. "For an older woman, you've got a few assets worth showing off. This will be fun."

Jezebeth felt Helena's presence shrinking away, recoiling in horror at the thought of her body being violated—the delicious feeling of helpless terror seeping through her like a fine wine. She added a smear of scarlet lipstick, exaggerated and bold, before slipping on a pair of stilettos sharp enough to draw blood.

Jezebeth swung the car door open and slid inside with ease. The engine roared as she flew down Bendix Avenue, before the tires screeched to a halt in front of Jeannie's Tavern. Instantly, the scent hit her like a wave—decay, violence, the raw edge of a man with nothing left to lose.

She found him inside. Damon. Alone at the end of the bar, hunched over a glass of whiskey, shadowed by guilt and rage. He was tall and rugged, with dark hair that fell over his brooding eyes. Jezebeth strode over, tugging the dress lower as she leaned into the bar.

"Is this seat taken?" she said in a silky voice.

He glanced up and scowled. "Beat it, Bitch. I'm not in the mood."

A flicker of fury surged through Jezebeth, hot and sharp. The urge to tear him apart nearly overcame her, but she forced it down, smirking instead. "Your loss, asshole."

Back in the car, Jezebeth's smile returned as she closed her eyes, the hum on her lips turning into a dark incantation. She reached into the bar, into Damon's mind, unraveling his secrets thread by thread. And there it was—a life steeped in cruelty, ripe for manipulation.

***

The bartender was an old, withered man, with sagging skin covered in dark blotches. His shirt was faded and frayed, and his baseball cap looked like it had seen better days. He dragged a towel across the bar, mopping up spilled liquor and pretzel crumbs. As he made his way back to Damon, who was still slouched in his seat, the old man shook his head.

"You're insane, you know that? How the hell could you pass up a piece of ass like that? You should've hit that like there's no tomorrow, man."

Damon didn't look up from his drink. "Shut up, Maury," he snapped. "I'm telling you the same thing I told her—I'm not in the mood."

Maury shrugged, "Whatever, man. It's your life. But you should know, it's last call. We're closing in twenty."

Damon grunted but didn't respond. He downed his shot and was about to stand up when the seat next to him creaked. He turned, prepared to give whoever it was a piece of his mind, but the words caught in his throat.

A little girl, no more than ten, sat there. His stomach churned. "Listen, kid," he growled. "What the hell do you want, you fucking little brat?"

The girl's eyes met his—unblinking, cold—and the corners of her lips twisted into something almost like a smile. "Don't you recognize me?"

Damon blinked. "No. Should I?"

The girl's body rippled with unnatural movement, her skin splitting open in small, violent tears. Blood leaked from her eyes, ears, nose, mouth—pools of red staining her clothes. "Is that better? I bet you recognize me now?" she asked, her voice a sharp rasp, like nails on a chalkboard.

Damon stumbled back in terror. "You're dead! No... no, I —I shot you!"

Her voice cut through the air in an unnatural growl. "Yeah, you did, you bastard. And now... you're gonna pay."

Before Damon could react, the girl was on him. Teeth bared, claws scraping at his flesh. He threw his arms up to shield his face, but she was like a feral animal, wild and relentless. He tried to shove her off, but her strength was like nothing he'd ever felt, inhuman even.

In his peripheral, another figure appeared—a man, tall and grizzled, his bloodied face twisted in a grotesque grimace.

Damon's heart froze.

"Is this guy giving you trouble, sweetie?" The man's voice was dark, dripping with venom.

Damon's breath hitched. "No… it can't be! I killed you too!"

The man didn't flinch. His eye socket was a gruesome hole, blood still oozing from the wound. He stepped forward, a booted foot pressing down on Damon's throat with a sickening crunch. Damon gasped, choking, desperate for air.

As the pressure mounted, he had no choice but to let go of the girl. The instant he did, she sank her claws into his chest, raking them down through flesh and bone. The blood flowed, soaking his shirt and pooling on the floor.

Everything went black.

When Damon's eyes opened again, he was back at the bar, hands trembling, heart still racing. Sweat slicked his skin. He blinked rapidly, the nightmare fading but the terror still clawing at him. He looked down at his shot glass, which was still full. *Am I finally losing my fucking mind?* The thought horrified him.

Maury was still there, wiping down the counter, unbothered. "Last call, Damon," he said, oblivious to the chaos. "Closing up soon. Time to get out."

Damon stared at him. "Didn't you see that?" His voice cracked.

"See what?"

"The girl! The… the dead girl and her father! They were just—" Damon shook his head. "You didn't see them?"

Maury didn't even look up. "Man, I think you've had enough. Whatever shit you're on, it's messed with your head. Now go home, sleep it off."

"Piss off, Maury," Damon said as he staggered out of his seat. He pushed through the door, the chill night air hitting his face.

As he made his way to the car, something felt wrong. His skin prickled. Every shadow seemed to move, every creak in the night louder than the last. He fumbled with his keys, his hands shaking. When he finally got the door unlocked, he saw it—the reflection in the window.

It was a ghostly shape, twisted and malformed, standing just behind him. He gasped as he whipped around, but the parking lot was empty.

He stumbled into the car, slammed the door, and locked it. For a moment, he just sat there, staring into the rear-view mirror, his face pale. "Jesus, get it together, man."

But when he went to start the engine, the shadow of Jezebeth appeared, blocking the way. "Not again. What the hell does she want now?"

She smiled at him, slow and deliberate, then started to sway—dancing, teasing him. Her skirt hitched up, revealing long, slender legs and a hint of something darker.

"Okay," Damon resigned as he rolled his window down. "You win. Get in."

She slid into the passenger seat. "I promise you, Damon, this is a night you'll never forget."

He shot her a skeptical look. "You're a crazy bitch, aren't you?"

She leaned closer, her breath hot on his neck. "You don't know the half of it."

He turned the key and put the car in drive. "So, what's the deal? You strung out on something, or are you just a walking sex dream?"

Her laugh was low, with a sinister edge to it. "Something like that."

Damon glanced over, a grin curling at the edge of his mouth. "Hope you can handle me, then."

"Oh, sweetie," Jezebeth whispered as her tongue slithered across the nape of his neck, "it's you who should be worried."

Damon smiled, "Okay, Bitch. Don't say I didn't warn you." He put the car back in gear and pulled away. "Where do you want to do this? Your place, or mine?"

Jezebeth replied, "Just drive. I'll tell you where to go."

Damon drove down Bendix Drive until he came to Cleveland Road. As he turned left, he felt Jezebeth's hand on his crotch. "Boy, you just can't control yourself, can you?" he said.

"Right now, I just want to eat you all up," Jezebeth said as she rubbed and massaged him vigorously through his jeans before she pulled down his zipper.

Moans of pleasure erupted from his mouth while he continued down Cleveland Road. As they approached Riverside Drive she lifted her head from his crotch and said, "Turn right here."

He obeyed, the road cutting past the Waste Water Treatment Plant, its smell of decay wafting through the air, until they reached the entrance to Pinhook Park.

"Turn in here," she commanded as she sat back in her seat, adjusting her lipstick and smoothing her dress.

Damon's tires skidded lightly on the gravel as he veered into the park, the road bending in front of him like a trap he was too eager to fall into. At the end of the drive, the lagoon came into view—its waters eerie and still, reflecting nothing but the deep blackness above. The moon had disappeared behind a blanket of clouds, as if even the heavens wanted to conceal the sins that were about to unfold.

He parked close to the water, the engine ticking in the sudden, suffocating silence. He turned to Jezebeth, a smirk playing on his lips. "Well, show me what you've got, bitch."

She leaned in, kissing him with a hunger that caught him off guard. It was fierce—raw—and for a moment, he let himself get lost in it. But she pulled back with a dangerous gleam in her eyes.

"Not here, though. Let's go down by the water."

She slid out of the car, walking towards the bank, her hips swaying in the dim light. After watching her for a moment, appreciating the view, Damon followed eagerly. She stopped a few yards down, where the earth dropped into a little sandy alcove.

"Down there," she whispered.

He watched her gracefully descend the embankment, standing just inches from the water's edge. Her presence felt like a storm waiting to break. Damon grinned, impressed. "You know, I gotta give you credit, Little Lady. You're certainly more interesting than I thought."

Jezebeth turned, her lips curling into a smile. "Just wait. The party's just begun."

Damon climbed down to join her. "Well, then. Let's start now."

With a rough hand, he seized her neck and brought her lips back to his. She responded with a ferocity that made his pulse race—her tongue dancing in his mouth before she bit down on his bottom lip, drawing a small drop of blood. The taste lingered, sweet and metallic, as she let out a soft moan.

With a sudden shift, she pushed him backward onto the ground. Her dress slipped from her body, and she climbed on top of him, straddling him while she ravaged him with her tongue. She held his arms down, but before Damon could react, the earth beneath them rumbled. Tendrils of vines and roots erupted from the ground, snaking around his wrists, ankles, and throat, binding him to the earth with an unrelenting force.

Damon gasped as he struggled, but the more he fought, the tighter the roots seemed to pull. His voice was stifled as the vines choked the air from his lungs.

Jezebeth smiled in twisted satisfaction. She jumped off him, leaving him to watch helplessly as the water before him began to churn. From the black depths of the lagoon, the girl and her father—both dead, covered in muck and decay—rose from the water, dragging their bodies forward like marionettes on invisible strings.

Weeds and algae clung to their forms, and leeches wriggled in and out of their rotting flesh, feeding off whatever remnants of life they could still find. Damon's eyes widened in horror as they approached, their movements slow but deliberate.

They stopped next to him, mouths gaping wide, and suddenly, a swarm of insects exploded from their open jaws, showering him with filth. He felt the sharp sting of pincers sinking into his skin as the creatures crawled over him, biting, burrowing into the flesh.

Then, from the corner of his eye, a viper slithered up to his face, its body coiling, its head reared back to strike. Damon squeezed his eyes shut, bracing for the impact.

But nothing came. He opened his eyes, confused.

Jezebeth remained atop him, still straddling him, but the grotesque apparitions were gone. He looked around in disbelief.

"What's going on here?" he croaked.

Jezebeth's smile twisted, darker now, as she pointed to her temple. "You see, Damon, I made a promise to a little mouse. I promised her I'd make you pay for killing her husband and daughter. And I always keep my promises."

Damon's face went pale as the weight of his past came crashing down. "I didn't mean to! I was fucked up, okay? I thought no one was home—I just wanted a score. And then he was there, and I panicked. The girl... I saw her... it was too late. I ran. Everything after that is just a blur."

Her gaze grew colder. "Let me make it clear for you, Damon. You're nothing but a worthless piece of shit. Your existence only serves to cause pain, to destroy, to ruin everything you touch. You're a stain on this world, and I'm here to rub you out."

Damon's anger flared, the words cutting deeper than the vines ever could. "How dare you judge me, you filthy whore!"

She slammed her face down to his, her teeth sinking into his neck with vicious precision. With a swift, brutal tug, she ripped his windpipe from his throat. He choked, his blood spilling, flooding his mouth, drowning him.

When the life left his body, Jezebeth stood, dragging the keys from his pocket with an almost bored indifference. She pulled him down into the cold, black water, watching with satisfaction as his body sank into the muck.

She dressed quickly, her fingers brushing through her hair as she stood up, smiling softly to herself. "See? Little Mouse, I told you I'd take care of him."

She felt the faint withdrawal of Helena's presence in her mind, a tug that no longer mattered. Whistling a cheerful tune, she walked back to the car, the night swallowing her whole.

"Goodbye, Little Mouse."

***

Tarek lingered in the shadows of the parking lot, his eyes locked on the woman as she slipped back into the car. His heart hammered in his chest, and a gnawing unease churned in his gut. Gideon had sent him on countless missions, each more dangerous than the last, but what he'd just witnessed? It was beyond anything he'd seen before. When that woman tore the man's throat out with her teeth and discarded his lifeless body into the murky water, Tarek knew—this wasn't just some deranged killer. This was something else. Something not human.

He shadowed her from a safe distance, his every move cautious and calculated. She drove through the quiet streets, winding her way through town with a fluid precision that made him uneasy. When she pulled into her driveway and parked, Tarek stopped a block away, the engine of his car humming low beneath his fingers. He watched as she got out of her car, and for a heartbeat, their eyes met—cold, black, and knowing.

A chill snaked down his spine, icy fingers pressing against his bones, but after a beat, she turned away, disappearing inside her house.

Tarek wasn't the type to get rattled. He had been raised under Gideon's strict tutelage, exposed to a world where the supernatural lurked behind every corner. Yet, seeing someone possessed—really possessed—that was something new. Something raw. Something visceral. The realization that what stood before him was no longer human sent a shudder through his body that he couldn't shake off.

His hand fumbled for his cell phone, and he dialed Gideon's number, his voice shaky despite his best efforts to remain composed.

"Gideon, I found her," he said nervously. "You're not gonna believe what she did."

Gideon's voice came through the line, cool and controlled. "Remember, you're not dealing with a normal person anymore."

"You're telling me," Tarek shot back. "She ripped a guy's throat out with her fucking teeth."

There was a pause on the other end, a moment where the silence seemed to grow thick between them before Gideon's voice returned, calm but insistent. "Stay clear of her. I just want you to keep an eye on her. Azazel sent her to that woman for a reason. We need to know why."

Tarek barely had time to respond before the car window shattered with a sudden explosion of glass, and before he could process it, Jezebeth's hand shot through the wreckage like a serpent, gripping his throat with terrifying strength, as she lifted him off the seat, her grip a vice that made it impossible for him to breathe.

"You have two seconds," she hissed, her voice a low growl, "to explain why you're spying on me, before I perform an encore."

Tarek's vision blurred as his airway constricted, gasping for air that wouldn't come. Panic flooded his veins. His mind raced, but there was only one thing he could get out before he suffocated.

"G-G-Gideon sent me," he managed, each word a struggle to force past the crushing pressure on his throat.

Her black eyes bore into him like twin pits of abyssal darkness, her grip loosening just enough for him to draw in a desperate breath. He coughed violently, his chest heaving as he fought for air.

Jezebeth stepped back, her lips curling into a cruel smile. "Tell Gideon to be ready," she said, her voice colder than the night air. "He'll know what to do when the time comes."

She eyed him for a moment, her gaze unreadable. "As for you... I'll let you watch. But I need you to help me with something first."

Fear rose in Tarek's chest like a tidal wave. What could a

demon like her want from him? He knew the stories—the fates of those foolish enough to make deals with demons. It wasn't a pretty picture. But the weight of her gaze, the raw power she exuded, told him one painful truth: he didn't have a choice.

Swallowing hard, he finally spoke, his voice small and hesitant. "What... what do you want me to do?"

The two-hour flight from Denver to Palm Springs felt like an eternity to Landis. The plane's hum did little to ease the rising anxiety in his chest. As soon as they touched down, he fumbled for his phone. He dialed Hecate's number, only to realize the connection would likely be lost as soon as he stepped outside the airport. The call went straight to voicemail. "Hey, it's me," he said tightly. "Just checking in. I landed in Palm Springs, heading to the hospital. Call me when you get this."

He slipped the phone back into his pocket and made his way to baggage claim, the weight of his parent's accident pressing down on him. As he grabbed his bag from the carousel, the lights above flickered, and a sharp jolt shot through his hand, as if the very air had turned electric. He shook it off, grabbed his bag, and moved quickly toward the taxi stand.

The taxi driver was an older man, whose face was long and wrinkled, weathered by years of hard labor. Landis guessed the man was in his sixties, his posture bent from a life spent hunched over the wheel. As he shuffled toward the car, his mind still racing with thoughts of his parents, something caught his eye—a flash of movement in the backseat. A woman was sitting there, her figure shadowed and ethereal. He blinked, and when he looked again, the seat was empty.

It's just jet lag, he told himself. Or maybe it was the overwhelming dread that had begun to settle in his bones and was now starting to play tricks on him?

He slid into the car, pulling the door shut with a slight squeak, and the driver adjusted the rear-view mirror with a grunt. "Where to?" the man asked in a thick voice.

"Eisenhower Medical," Landis replied softly.

The car pulled away slowly, merging into the streets, and Landis found himself staring at the San Jacinto Mountains in the distance, their jagged peaks cutting through the pre-dawn darkness. The scenery tugged at something deep inside him —memories of a time before his father had morphed into the monster he became. The change had been swift, a descent into something dark and unrecognizable. Landis couldn't pinpoint the exact moment it happened, but he had felt the shift, felt the rage that had consumed his father, and from the age of twelve until the day he ran away, he had borne the brunt of that fury.

He rested his head against the cool glass of the window, watching as the first slivers of dawn began to paint the sky in shades of pink and orange. The date palms lined the streets like sentinels, their fronds whispering in the soft breeze. He hadn't realized how beautiful Palm Springs was until now, and for a fleeting moment, he made a silent vow to bring Hecate here.

As the taxi turned off Ramon and onto Bob Hope, the car swerved suddenly, narrowly missing a coyote that darted into the road. Landis's heart skipped a beat as he watched the animal's dark eyes lock onto his. A chill ran down his spine. He couldn't shake the feeling that it wasn't just a random encounter—that something darker was at play.

The driver's reflexes were quick, and he regained control of the car immediately, but the unease in Landis only deepened. Something felt off. His anticipation of seeing his parents again now mingled with a strange, creeping dread—something more than just family history. Something otherworldly.

A few minutes later, the taxi pulled to a stop outside the hospital. Landis handed the driver a wad of cash, but the man lingered, his gaze sharp and concerned. "Everything okay, son?" he asked, his voice gentler than Landis had expected.

"Not really," Landis admitted, his throat tight. "My parents were in an accident. I haven't seen them in years, and I don't know if I'll get the chance to now."

The driver's expression softened. "I'm sorry to hear that, kid. Hopefully, they'll recover. Maybe you two can work things out."

Landis gave a tight nod, but inside, a part of him wondered whether he even wanted that. It wasn't their death he feared—it was actually their survival. He didn't want to wish them ill, but the thought of them living, still trapped in their old roles, was almost worse than imagining their passing.

He turned away without saying another word, walking toward the hospital entrance. As he neared the door, once again he saw something out of the corner of his eye—a figure standing just beyond the threshold. He spun, but when he looked again, there was no one there. The nagging feeling grew stronger. Something was following him.

Inside, the air smelled sterile and cold. Landis approached the receptionist, an older woman with graying hair and thin silver glasses. "I'm here to see my parents, Thomas and

Marsha Galloway. I was told they were in an accident and are in ICU."

The woman typed quickly on her computer, then looked up. "ICU's on the third floor. Go to the nurse's station there. They'll have more details."

She handed him a visitor's pass, which he clipped to his shirt before making his way down the hall. Overhead, signs directed him toward the elevators, and, to his surprise, the same ghostly girl from earlier appeared beside him, walking in step. He could feel her presence, a quiet sorrow in the air. He felt an odd guilt, as if he owed her something—perhaps the company she hadn't had during her dying moments, or the love she had never received growing up, something he could certainly relate to.

They reached the elevator, and the girl followed him inside, her gaze locked on him as they ascended to the third floor. As the elevator jolted to a stop, the lights flickering momentarily, the girl looked at him, her eyes filled with a stark warning, and mouthed the words, *Be careful*, before vanishing.

Landis took a steadying breath before he exited the elevator and walked down the hall, eyes fixed ahead, determined not to look at the shadows lurking at the edges of his vision—the spirits lining the hallway, their sadness hanging thick in the air. He could feel their presence as he moved, but he didn't dare acknowledge them. Not now, with everything else going on.

At the nurse's station, a middle-aged woman with a pencil stuck behind her ear glanced up from her typing. "Can I help you?"

"I'm here to see my parents, Marsha and Thomas Galloway."

The nurse typed their names into the system. "Are you

Landis?"

"Yeah," he replied tightly.

She pulled out an envelope from a drawer and handed it to him. "It's from your parents' lawyer. I was instructed to give it to you upon their passing."

His stomach dropped. "So, they're—?"

The nurse hesitated. "Not yet. But their injuries are severe. I'm afraid it's just a matter of time. I'm sorry."

"Do you know what happened?" Landis asked.

She shook her head. "Only that it was a car accident up on seventy-four. That road... scares me every time I drive it."

He nodded, swallowing the lump in his throat. "Can I see them?"

She led him down the hall to a room at the end. "Your mom's in here, and your dad's next door. We thought it would be better to keep them close."

"Thanks," Landis muttered, his heart pounding.

As the nurse left, Landis stood before the door, taking a deep breath before turning the handle.

What he found inside crushed him. His mother was hooked up to an array of machines, her frail and shrunken form looking nothing like the woman who had once held him close. He fought back the tears, guilt crashing over him for the years of resentment he'd harbored. The past felt like a lifetime ago, yet it still weighed on him.

"I'm here, Mom," he whispered, his voice cracking.

For a moment, the EKG machine beeped a little louder, giving Landis a brief sign of life. Then, seconds later, the machine flat-lined. An alarm screamed through the room, and the next few minutes passed in a blur as a mob of hospital staff rushed in, pushing him aside.

The nurse from earlier ushered him out of the room, but Landis barely registered her words as he sank into a chair in the hallway. His mind was a runaway freight train as he sat there, running back through all the memories he had of a better time, and then all the regrets that followed when things weren't so great. If he had to do it all again, he knew he could've done something different that wouldn't have hurt everyone so much. Then he felt a soft breeze on his cheek and a warm touch on his hand. He looked to his left and saw his mother sitting there with a bright smile on her face.

"I'm so sorry," he cried. "For everything."

Somehow her smile grew even brighter, as she shook her head and told him something he hadn't heard in a long time; "I love you."

Then she disappeared.

Time stretched into what felt like hours before the doctor finally emerged, his face grim. "I'm sorry, son. Her injuries were too severe. We did everything we could."

Landis didn't respond. He didn't know what to say. He just nodded, swallowing the lump in his throat.

Later, the head nurse approached. "How are you holding up?" she asked softly.

Landis shrugged, his eyes distant. "I don't know. I'm just numb."

She patted his hand gently. "You'll get through this. Are you going to see your dad?"

He had avoided looking at his father's room, the man who had hurt him more than anyone. He had made a promise to himself never to face him again. As far as he was concerned, the man got everything he deserved. He replied to the nurse, "No, I don't think I can."

Landis rose from his seat and started down the hall, but paused, turning back to the nurse. "Can you call me if there's any change?" he asked.

"Sure, kid."

He handed her his number and walked to the elevator, passing the faded shapes of lost souls, drifting aimlessly through the hospital halls. The sight stirred something in him—he found himself feeling more sympathy for them than he ever had for his own father, who had lived a life of darkness. How strange, that his heart ached more for the dead than the living.

Slipping into the elevator, Landis shoved his hands into his jacket pocket and felt the cool paper of the envelope he had nearly forgotten. His fingers trembled as he tore it open, uncertain of what it held. The contents surprised him: a living will, and a key to a house he hadn't even considered. The will stated that in the event of an accident requiring life support, all ownership of the house, along with everything in it, would transfer to him. He couldn't believe it. The house, everything tied to his parents—it was his now. Maybe because he was the only child, or maybe because he had always been distant from them, but the thought of owning their things felt wrong. It felt like a debt he'd never agreed to.

Stuffing the will and key back into his pocket, he turned and headed toward the entrance, ignoring the silent pleas of the spirits that surrounded him. He had nothing left to give.

At the fountain outside, he pulled out his phone once again, trying to reach Hecate. Her voice-mail picked up. With a sigh, he left a brief message before using a ride-share application to request a ride.

As he waited, a wave of loneliness washed over him. In all his years of running, he had never felt as lost as he did now. If only he could hear her voice, if only she could calm the chaos swirling inside him.

A black Honda pulled up, breaking his reverie. The driver was a kid, no older than Landis himself. "Where to, man?" he asked.

Landis hesitated, the weight of the paper, the key, and his father's death pressing down on him. "The Marriott on Country Club," he finally muttered.

"Gotcha."

As they drove away from the hospital, Landis glanced back, almost certain he saw his mother standing there for a fleeting moment. He blinked, and she was gone.

At the Marriott, he normally would have admired the sleek lobby, but tonight, the glitzy surroundings held no appeal. He just needed to rest, to sort through the tangled mess of emotions that had overtaken him.

The hotel attendant handed him his key card, and he made his way to the elevator. A short ride up to the fourth floor, and he found himself standing outside a small lounge where two older men chatted idly over coffee about the previous night's Dodgers game. *If only life were still that simple,* he thought. Landis envied them for a moment.

As he reached the door to his room, his hand froze, a memory piercing through his haze. This was the same room his family had stayed in when they first moved to the desert. The same room that had seen the beginnings of all their turmoil. Landis felt a hollow ache in his chest. *I guess things really have come full circle.*

He tossed his bag to the floor and collapsed onto the bed. The moment his head hit the pillow, his phone rang, slicing through the silence. He fumbled for it, his heart leaping with the hope that it was Hecate. But when he answered, it was the head nurse's voice that greeted him.

"Landis?"

"Yes," he responded flatly.

"I'm so sorry," the nurse said. "I know it's so soon after your mother's passing, but your father just passed as well. If it's any consolation, he died peacefully."

Landis couldn't speak. He didn't have the words, so he hung up instead. Peaceful? The thought of his father dying peacefully felt like a cruel joke. He imagined his father's curses trailing him into the afterlife.

The phone dropped from his hand, and within moments, sleep claimed him, dragging him into a world of fragmented dreams and nightmare visions.

****

Landis stood frozen at the threshold of the last place he ever wanted to be. The front door of the large two-story house on Shadow Vis hung open, its darkened interior beckoning him like the mouth of some twisted fun-house. The shadows inside seemed to stretch, pulling at him with invisible fingers, and he felt a coldness seep into his bones, like icy tendrils wrapping around his very soul. Every instinct screamed at him to turn and run, to flee from the darkness that hung over him.

But then, a voice cut through the silence—his mother's voice, soft and insistent, whispering in his ear, "You need to go home."

He spun around, hoping to see her; hoping she would be there to provide the strength he needed to persevere through this ordeal. But she wasn't there. No figure, no comforting touch. Just the same hollow, empty space.

Her voice came again, clearer now, though still as faint as a breeze. "It's the only way to stop him. Go home, Landis. Go home!"

The words reverberated in his ears, echoing the same warning the ghost girl had whispered to him in the elevator: *Be careful.*

Landis stood there, torn between the urge to retreat and

the pull of something deeper, something darker within those walls. He didn't know what awaited him inside, but he felt the desperation of his mother's plea, and a part of him knew he had no choice but to move forward.

CHAPTER 10

Hecate was halfway through her overseas flight when she jolted awake, the soft hum of the plane around her barely registering as her mind fought against the remnants of a restless sleep. She had been trying to focus on her Latin, her eyes glued to the screen of her phone as she navigated the Rosetta Stone application. But the constant interruptions of an unreliable Wi-Fi signal, each crash of the program more frustrating than the last, had sapped her patience. In the end, her eyelids had grown too heavy, the world blurring into the chaos of dreams.

But these weren't the kinds of dreams that comforted. They were disjointed, a jagged mix of nightmares that clung to her even as she woke. Images of the dead, faces twisted in silent screams, flashed before her mind's eye, their hollow eyes reflecting the terror she'd seen at the airport. But the last image, the one that made her stomach churn with unease, was of Landis.

In the dream, she stood before a grand two-story house, nestled at the edge of a serene golf course. A Great Heron soared overhead, landing gracefully on the lake at the center of the course. The sun was bright, casting a warm glow over everything, a peaceful, idyllic scene. Yet, the moment Hecate heard Landis's scream from within the house, all of that serenity shattered.

She rushed to the door, but it was locked. She threw herself against it, desperate, as his cries grew louder, more urgent. Panic clawed at her, and she kicked at the door with everything she had. Finally, it gave way, splintering as she rushed into the house.

"Landis!" Her voice cracked as she called for him, but only muffled sounds of pain answered her. The cries came from upstairs, but as she searched for a way up, she was met with dead ends at every turn. Frantic, she spun around, her heart hammering in her chest, until—out of the corner of her eye she saw a narrow spiral staircase, leading up.

She bolted for it, the stairs stretching on forever. She climbed, each step echoing in the silence, until she neared the door at the top. But, in an instant, she was back at the bottom again, staring up in disbelief. She didn't have time to question it; she ran up again, her feet flying, and this time when she reached the door, she flung it open.

The hallway before her was lined with doors, and behind each one came the sound of suffering—cries of anguish that echoed in her bones. She flung open door after door, but each room was empty. Her heart sank lower with every failure, every room she found devoid of Landis.

Finally, when she was at her most desperate, she found him. He was on his knees, his back to her, his arms stretched wide and chained to the walls. Blood flowed from deep gashes across his back, and Hecate watched in horror as an unseen force lashed out at him, striking him again and again, as if he were being whipped by some invisible torturer.

She ran to him, frantic to free him, but the chains were too tight. Landis lifted his head weakly, his bloodied face contorted in pain. Through ragged breaths, he managed to rasp, "Run."

Before she could move, she saw him. A tall figure, a man like no man she'd ever seen, emerged from the shadows. His body was thin, his eyes beady and black, his smile twisted into something cruel and wicked. He raised a barbed whip high, his gaze fixed on her with sinister intent.

And then, with a jolt, Hecate was awake, the dream slipping away, but its chilling remnants still clinging to her.

Solomon turned to her, sensing her distress. "Is everything all right?" he asked, his voice steady but concerned.

Hecate fumbled for her phone, trying to reach Landis, but the signal was dead. It took a moment before she could answer him. "I hope so. I just had the worst nightmare... about Landis."

Solomon's brow furrowed as he closed his eyes, his mind reaching out. A moment later, he opened them again, his expression darkening.

"What's wrong?" Hecate asked, her voice tight.

"Nothing," he replied, though there was an edge to his tone. "I was trying to locate him, but something's blocking me."

Hecate opened her mouth to ask what that meant but stopped herself. She didn't want to hear another one of Solomon's explanations about metaphysics. It was always more than she could follow.

"We could check on him, though," Solomon offered.

"Are you sure it's safe? I haven't exactly mastered astral projection yet."

"It'll be fine," Solomon assured her, taking her hand gently. "I'll be with you every step of the way."

Hecate hesitated, the darkness from her dream still lingering. The thought of spying on Landis felt wrong, like an invasion of privacy, but the fear gnawing at her made her nod. "Okay," she said hesitantly.

With a deep breath, Solomon closed his eyes, and within seconds, Hecate felt herself lift from her body, her physical self stilling in the seat beside him. The experience was unsettling, the familiar sensation of her body now distant, like being tethered to the air itself. She knew Solomon would protect her, but the unknown dangers of astral projection still gnawed at her.

As they soared through the dark expanse, the physical world below them blurred into a monochrome streak, while vibrant neon colors swirled around them, the presence of other astral travelers marking their path. Solomon guided them carefully, avoiding those wandering the plane as they searched for Landis.

Solomon tried once more to locate him, but again, came up empty. Luckily, Landis had crossed the astral plane with him before, and Solomon could pick up his unique signature. They followed it, from the airport to the hospital, and then to the hotel.

When they found him, asleep on his bed, Hecate breathed a sigh of relief. But as her eyes fell on his slumped form, the dark circles beneath his eyes and the redness in his cheeks told a different story. This was not the happy, carefree Landis she remembered. This was a man weighed down by something heavy, something she couldn't yet understand.

"Do you feel better now?" Solomon asked, his voice gentle.

"A little," Hecate replied, her voice barely a whisper. "He looks so sad. I just want to be there with him."

Solomon's expression softened. "He'll be okay. It'll just take time."

Hecate nodded, but her heart ached for him, for the man he had become. Before she could speak again, Solomon stiffened, his gaze shifting toward something unseen.

"What's wrong?" she asked nervously.

Solomon's face grew serious. "Astral parasites," he muttered. "They're closing in."

Before Hecate could react, she saw the dark swarm approaching. They moved like a pack, fast and determined. Solomon made a swift gesture, and in an instant, they were pulled backward, streaking across the astral plane toward their own world.

A jolt of energy snapped through Hecate as she was yanked back into her body, gasping as she sat upright. Her senses were disoriented, her heart still racing.

"What were those things?" she asked, voice trembling.

"Astral parasites," Solomon explained calmly, though his eyes remained alert. "Individually, they're nothing to worry about. But in groups, they can cause serious harm. They're like psychic piranhas. Not something I wanted to risk, especially with you here."

Hecate shuddered at the thought. Her stomach churned, a wave of nausea rushing through her before it passed. "Can you ask the flight attendant for a bottle of water?" she asked.

Solomon waved the attendant over, but before she could return, something caught Hecate's eye. A hand, black and shriveled, reached from the back of the attendant's head, a grotesque appendage that vanished before she could react. Her breath skipped, but she said nothing, not wanting to alarm Solomon.

After a few moments, the water arrived, and Hecate felt the familiar sense of calm return as she sipped. She closed her eyes, hoping the nightmares wouldn't follow her. But even as the plane descended toward the Cote d'Azur, a chill ran through her, and the unease settled deeper into her bones.

As the plane hit turbulence, Hecate gripped her seat

tighter, bracing against the disorienting motion. But when they finally landed safely, the dizziness returned, overwhelming her. She swayed, nearly blacking out, her lungs constricting painfully. Solomon kneeled beside her.

"Are you okay?" he asked, concern evident in his voice.

"I'm fine," she replied weakly. "I think I just stood up too fast."

"Just sit here for a minute and relax. We'll let all the other passengers go first."

Hecate nodded and took the last swig of water from her bottle. By the time the last one had gone, she was feeling better.

And then, out of the corner of her eye, in the back of the cabin, she saw her. Her mirror image, with a smile that was wrong, twisted and maniacal, a smile that sent a shiver of fear through her. Hecate's heart skipped a beat. Something was very, very wrong.

Jezebeth's foot slammed onto the accelerator, her car roaring to life as it tore down Riverside Drive. There was a wild gleam in her eye and a savage hunger in her veins. The night whispered its sweet promise of freedom, and she reveled in it, not caring about the hows or whys—just the now. Azazel's plans were distant at the moment, almost irrelevant. Tonight, she was hers alone, free to embrace the madness and to chase the chaos with reckless abandon.

The wind howled in her ears as she swerved down the winding path beside the Saint Joseph River, taking each curve with a manic grin that split her face. She felt like a beast, something untamed and wild, laughing wildly as the world blurred by.

As the headlights flashed across the city's streets, her mind suddenly clicked—something was brewing, and it was going to be fun. Her fingers gripped the wheel as she veered onto North Michigan, then jerked a sharp right onto Navarre Street. Her destination? Memorial Hospital. Time for a show.

She brought the car to a screeching stop, nearly slamming into an idle ambulance. With staggering, unsteady steps, she lurched toward the hospital entrance, her movements erratic and unnerving, like a creature from some fresh grave that had just clawed its way to the surface.

Dan, a tall, muscular man with an easygoing demeanor, noticed her first. He was guiding a clean gurney into the ambulance when Jezebeth's figure caught his eye. Jack, the other man, shorter but sturdy, followed close behind, his arms laden with a heavy case of supplies. Both of them stopped in their tracks, watching as Jezebeth lurched toward the emergency entrance.

When she arrived at the wall and began slamming her head into it, splattering blood on the once-pristine surface, the two men exchanged a look of utter disbelief. "Shit!" they both cried in unison and rushed to her.

Dan grabbed her around the shoulders to keep her from hurting herself anymore. "Calm down, Miss. We're here to help."

Jack pulled out a small pen light and shone it in Jezebeth's eyes. He saw craziness looking back at him. "Can you tell me what's going on here?" he asked. "Are you on something?"

Jezebeth tapped her temple, eyes wild. "There's a little mouse in my head. I'm trying to get it out, but it won't come out."

The two men looked at each other and rolled their eyes. Neither was in the mood for this kind of shit at this hour. "Does this mouse have a name?" Dan asked.

Jezebeth's grin spread wide. "Yes! Her name's Helena. But I call her Little Mouse. She likes it. I think."

Jack hesitated, but played along. "And you talk to this Helena?"

"All the time! She doesn't always answer, though. I think she's scared of me. But I just want to have some fun!"

Jack took her hand, leading her to the waiting gurney. "How about we go inside, get you settled, and maybe warm up a little? It'll be better in there."

"That might be it!" Jezebeth exclaimed. "I think she's cold in there! Maybe she'll come out and play when she warms up?"

"She might. Just lay down here and we'll give you a ride inside."

Her head tilted as if considering. "That sounds fun! Little Mouse will like that!"

Dan chuckled uneasily. "We'll take care of that cut on your forehead first. Is that alright?"

Jezebeth squinted at him, eyeing him as though making a judgment. "I suppose he'll do."

The comment made both men pause, but neither thought too much of it. With Jezebeth settled onto the gurney, Jack began to push her inside, and Dan carefully applied antiseptic to her forehead. The instant the cool liquid touched her skin, Jezebeth screamed, a sharp, piercing cry that echoed through the entrance doors. Before anyone could react, her hand shot up, grabbing Dan by the throat with a force that made him choke.

"You didn't tell me it was going to hurt, you fucker!" she snarled.

Her teeth sank into Dan's ear, tearing it off in one savage motion. Blood sprayed from the wound as Dan howled in agony. Jack stood frozen for a moment, watching in shock, before he sprang into action, trying to stop the bleeding and yelling for help.

The chaos exploded. Nurses rushed in, trying to tend to Dan's wound as a security officer wrestled Jezebeth into submission. Jack secured straps to hold her down, the wildness in her laughter growing in intensity.

"Get her out of here!" Jack shouted.

Two orderlies, Adam and Josh, appeared, big men with

grim faces, and took hold of the gurney, guiding Jezebeth down the hall.

Seconds later, Dr. Chapman, a lean, older man in his fifties, arrived. "What've we got here?" he asked.

Jack said quickly, "She attacked Dan. Not sure why."

"Attacked him how?"

"His ear's on the floor of the lobby."

Dr. Chapman's eyes widened in shock. "Is he okay?"

Jack shrugged, "Not sure. But Dr. Steinbrook's with him."

Jezebeth's laughter echoed through the room like a low growl, sending chills through everyone. She suddenly stopped, her face contorting as she began chanting in a guttural, foreign tongue.

Dr. Chapman acted fast, pulling a syringe from a nearby cabinet and injecting her. Within seconds, Jezebeth's wild eyes fluttered shut, and she slumped into unconsciousness.

"What do you want us to do with her? Take her up to the sixth floor?" Adam asked, eyeing the unconscious woman warily.

Dr. Chapman hesitated, something gnawing at the back of his mind. A feeling he couldn't shake. "Take her to the basement," he said, his voice low and unsettling.

Josh and Adam exchanged nervous looks, but neither questioned the order. They were employees, and following orders meant keeping their jobs.

The elevator doors slid open with a soft ding, and the two orderlies carefully wheeled Jezebeth inside, pressing the button for the lower level. As they descended into the bowels of the hospital, Josh muttered under his breath, "I don't like this one bit."

"Tell me about it," Adam replied, his voice shaky. "This chick's a freak."

Suddenly, the lights flickered, then went out completely.

Both men cried out in terror as an unnatural chill swept through the elevator. When the lights snapped back on, Adam screamed, staring down at his leg. Blood poured from a deep gash in his calf, yet his pants were untouched.

Josh's eyes went wide. "What the hell just happened?"

Adam clutched his leg. "I don't know, man... but it burns like hell."

Their gaze fell on Jezebeth, still strapped to the gurney, her face pale and peaceful in sleep—though the faintest hint of a smile tugged at the corners of her lips. And somehow, it made both men shiver all the more.

CHAPTER 12

A cold, unsettling shiver crept through Hecate as she pulled her phone from her pocket. The eerie image of the ghostly figure at the back of the plane still haunted her, lingering at the edges of her thoughts. Her fingers trembled as she dialed Landis's number, desperate to hear his voice and ensure that he was safe.

With each unanswered ring, her heart sank a little deeper. She didn't know how long she could stand the silence. Finally, on the fourth ring, his voice came through the line, and she let out a breath she hadn't realized she was holding.

"Hey, Hecate. Is everything okay?" he said, his voice thick with exhaustion, and she felt both guilty and relieved in the same breath.

"I should be asking you the same thing," she said, trying to keep the tremor out of her voice.

A small chuckle broke the tension. "Great minds think alike."

"That they do."

For a moment, neither of them spoke, the weight of the situation hanging in the air like a heavy fog. Then his words cut through the silence. "They're both dead, Hecate."

Her stomach twisted. "I'm so sorry, Landis. Did you... did you get to see them before they passed?"

"I saw my mom. I think she was holding on, waiting for me. I hope she's at peace now, though. Finally."

"And your dad?"

Landis hesitated, the words coming slower now. "I... I was going to go see him, but I couldn't bring myself to. And then, I got the call. He passed a few hours ago."

"Are you going to be okay?" she asked softly.

"Yeah. I think eventually. Their lawyer left me a living will they'd prepared. And the key to their house."

Hecate winced, her thoughts spinning. "That's a lot to deal with. What are you going to do?"

"I don't really want to go back there," he admitted.

"Then don't."

"I think I have to. My mom... she came to me in a dream. Told me I needed to go home."

Hecate's heart fluttered with the sudden sensation that something was being left unsaid, but she didn't push it. And for a brief second, a jagged memory of her nightmare rushed back before disappearing once again into the ether.

The subject shifted abruptly as Landis asked, "So, has your flight landed? Where are you headed?"

"A little town in France, Menton," she replied, trying to sound calm, but her nerves were beginning to fray at the edges.

"Lucky you," he sighed wistfully. "I'd give anything to be there right now."

"You and me both." She forced a laugh, though it felt strained. "I'm scared to death."

"You'll do great. I know you will. Solomon wouldn't have brought you if he didn't believe in you."

"I know," she said quietly. "I just wish I was as confident

as he is."

"It's like anything else. The more you do it, the easier it gets."

Hecate grunted half-heartedly in agreement as they kept walking down the main thoroughfare toward the baggage claim area. Then, just as she thought she could breathe again, she saw her—the girl. The one who looked just like her. Hecate froze.

"I'll call you back," she said quickly, ending the call before Landis could respond.

It was just a fleeting glimpse, but enough to send a shiver down her spine. As they passed a tourist gift shop, she caught her own reflection in the window—except it wasn't quite right. Her reflection moved slightly out of sync with her, a subtle shift of hands, a sly wink, her smile too wide, with a deranged feel. It was as if the reflection was alive, an entity unto itself. Hecate quickly looked away. She focused her attention straight ahead, forcing herself to dismiss what she'd just seen as a product of jet lag.

When they reached the baggage claim, she tried to shake the feeling of dread that clung to her. "So, what's the plan?" she asked, hoping to distract herself.

Solomon gave a small, reassuring smile. "We've got a room at a place near the subject, Menton chambre d'hôte. It's a quiet, rustic spot. Not one of the big, crowded hotels where we'd draw attention."

"Attention?" Hecate raised an eyebrow, confused.

Solomon nodded. "As outsiders dealing with what we deal with, it's better to keep a low profile. And, God forbid, if something goes wrong, it helps to be somewhere less conspicuous. Plus, I know the owner."

Hecate rolled her eyes. "Of course you do."

When their luggage finally appeared, they made their way

outside, where taxis lined the curb. The driver, a disheveled young man in his twenties, barely looked up as they approached. Solomon spoke to him in fluent French, the words smooth and practiced.

"Emmenez-moi à la chambre d'hôtes de Menton, s'il vous plaît?" Solomon said.

The driver nodded, "Oui, je connais l'endroit," and popped open the trunk, tossing their bags inside before climbing into the driver's seat.

Hecate stayed silent during the ride, lost in her thoughts. The quiet hum of the car was a welcome respite, though her mind kept racing. They pulled up to the small hotel, which looked more like a quaint Bed and Breakfast, nestled on the edge of the street. Solomon gave the driver a handful of bills, and they climbed out.

"Is everything okay?" Solomon asked, his eyes narrowing with concern.

Hecate forced a smile. "Yeah, just... a lot on my mind right now. Trying to keep it together."

He nodded. "If you need to talk, I'm here. As a friend... and as your mentor."

"Thanks, Solomon." But she wasn't sure talking would really help. Something was shifting within her, something she didn't fully understand. It was like she was losing her grip on reality, and there was nothing she could do to stop it.

Inside the building, Solomon was immediately greeted by Jacques, a tall, round man in his sixties who engulfed him in a hug. Hecate was surprised when the man spoke to him in English, albeit with a thick accent, "Solomon! It's good to see you, my friend!"

"It's good to see you too, Jacques," Solomon said. "How are things going?"

"You know...how do you say in English?..Same ol', same

ol'."

Solomon chuckled. "Jacques, I'd like to introduce you to Hecate."

Jacques gave warm smile, "Bonjour, Hecate."

He turned to Hecate, "Hecate, this is Jacques. He's been a friend of mine for a long time."

"Bonjour, Jacques," she said to the man, trying her best not to sound like a foreigner. Then she asked Solomon, "Is he like Uriel?"

Jacques answered the question for him, "No, little lady. I'm all flesh and blood, through and through."

Before Hecate could answer, Solomon said, "Jacques was one of my students a long time ago. He was with me for nearly thirty years. Then he went and got married so he could live a normal life."

"Best choice of my life. Now I am retired and living in the best place on earth."

Hecate asked, "Where's your wife, if you don't mind me asking."

Jacques' face grew long for a moment before he answered, "She is no longer with us. She died from pneumonia six years ago."

"I'm so sorry. I didn't mean to pry."

"It's okay, Little Lady. Here we do not mourn the passing of a loved one. Instead, we celebrate their life and keep those good memories close to our heart."

Hecate grew quiet as the man's words rang true, and for a moment, memories of her father and sister came flooding back.

Jacques immediately sensed her pain and quickly changed the subject. "Forgive me, my manners," he said. "I know you two are exhausted from such a long flight. Solomon, your normal room is prepared, just the way you like it. Daniel will escort you."

A young boy, barely sixteen, appeared at the door, waddling over to grab their bags. He grunted as he motioned for them to follow him.

They were led down a narrow hallway, finally stopping in front of a small room with a single bed in the corner. The walls were bare, the only other furniture a small desk and chair. Hecate blinked in surprise.

"Where's the rest of the furniture?" she asked.

"This is it," Solomon replied casually. "I prefer it like this."

"But... how are we supposed to sleep?"

"I don't sleep like you do," Solomon answered simply. "I meditate. That's all I need."

Hecate shook her head, though it was a little harder to find humor in his strange ways tonight.

"So, what's next?" she asked, her exhaustion starting to weigh on her.

"First thing tomorrow, we meet with the local priest at the Basilica St. Michel. After that, we go to the house where the girl is."

Hecate's chest tightened as the reality of their mission sunk in. A young girl's life hung in the balance, and as much as Solomon believed in her, she wasn't sure she was strong enough to face what was ahead. But she knew she'd have to try.

***

Landis tossed the phone onto the bed beside him and stretched out, his body still buzzing from the conversation with Hecate. Her voice had offered him a small reprieve from his grief, but the last few words, the fear in her voice as she hung up, gnawed at him. It was the kind of fear he couldn't shake, the kind that clung to the air long after a call had ended.

He tried to close his eyes again, hoping for sleep, but his thoughts wouldn't settle. They swirled faster, more insistently, growing larger and louder with every passing moment. Landis knew what he had to do. But the truth was, he was terrified.

With a deep breath, he dragged himself off the bed and walked into the bathroom. The hot water from a shower probably wouldn't ease the weight on his shoulders, but it felt like the only thing he could do. He shed his clothes, stepping under the spray, and for a moment, the warmth was soothing, the rush of water washing over him like a temporary escape.

To his surprise, it worked. The tension loosened, his mind clearing, if only for a moment. When he finally stepped out, he felt almost human again, his mind calm enough to think. But as he looked up, his eyes froze.

There, on the fogged-up mirror above the sink, were the words: 'Go Home!'

A chill ran down his spine. He knew instantly who had written it. His mother's nagging voice echoed in his head, reminding him that he couldn't delay any longer.

He sighed deeply. He couldn't keep running. It was time to face the house, to face everything he had been avoiding for far too long.

With slow, reluctant movements, he changed into fresh clothes and left the bathroom. A few minutes later, he was stepping out of the hotel and into the cool night air, heading toward a taxi waiting by the curb.

"1101 Shadow Vis," he said with a hollow, resigned note in his voice, sliding into the backseat.

The drive was short—just ten minutes—before they

reached the entrance of the Bighorn gated community. It took nearly as long to convince the gate guard to let them through. Landis fought the urge to ask the driver to turn around. He didn't want to go. But his mother's voice, now a constant presence in his mind, reminded him he couldn't avoid it forever.

The guard had been a close friend of his father's and couldn't accept that the man had passed away. It wasn't until Landis showed him the will and hinted at calling management that the guard relented, finally waving them through with a grumble.

The car wound its way through the community, taking a few turns before they reached Shadow Vis. And then, a few houses later, his… property. The realization hit him harder than he expected. This was it now. This was his responsibility.

He handed the driver a tip and walked slowly toward the front door, clutching the key in his pocket. For a split second, he wished it wouldn't work. He wished it would refuse to turn, just to delay the inevitable. But when he slid the key in, it clicked easily. No resistance. No miracle.

The warning from his mother whispered in his mind: *Be careful.*

With a heavy sigh, he pushed the door open and stepped inside. The house was bigger than he remembered, or maybe it just felt emptier now. There was an absence here, a void that stretched out before him. The silence was deafening, oppressive. It wasn't just the house—it was him, too. He could feel it in his bones, the hollowness that had settled there after his father changed into something monstrous. And his mother… she had suffered too, but had never left. That fact, that betrayal of her own soul, twisted something inside him. He had always promised he would save her. But now?

Now that day would never come.

Landis moved through the foyer into the living room, flipping the light switch. The room looked nearly the same as he remembered: the gray walls, the leather couch where he had spent so many nights, the old lamp in the corner. But a few things had changed—there was a large painting of a seascape on the wall, and a massive ceiling fan spun slowly overhead. The most unexpected change, however, was in the corner of the room, where a black cat slept soundly on a small bed.

His heart skipped. Thomas had always hated animals. His father had forbidden any pets in the house, and yet here was a cat, curled up and content. Landis watched as it stirred at his entrance, stretching and waking, a small bell tinkling around its collar. It stood, then padded toward him, a soft meow escaping its throat.

"Hey, little guy," Landis muttered, crouching down to pick the cat up.

He glanced at the collar. The name 'Abaddon' dangled from a small tag. "I guess it's little lady, then," he murmured, though he didn't much care for the name.

The cat gave another meow, nuzzling his hand, and Landis scratched behind her ears, feeling a small, fleeting warmth in his chest. But then, without warning, the cat's demeanor shifted. The meow turned to a sharp hiss as her head whipped around, eyes wide with fear.

Landis froze, his breath catching in his throat. He turned, his gaze locking on the figure standing behind him.

His father.

Dead. Standing in the living room. Staring at him with hollow, lifeless eyes.

CHAPTER 13

Hecate was relieved when the first light of morning broke through the window. The night had dragged on endlessly, filled with disturbing visions of demons and spirits, each one more haunting than the last. She knew her restless mind was the result of her anxiety about the upcoming exorcism. That, and the sight of Solomon floating a foot off the ground in the lotus position, his still form suspended in the dark room, had kept her on edge. She'd seen strange things in her life, but that had been unsettling in ways she couldn't explain, no matter how much she learned about him.

At some point, though, Solomon had disappeared, leaving her to her restless thoughts. And that was probably for the best. She wasn't in the mood to deal with him before she'd had a chance to caffeinate, especially when she hadn't gotten a wink of sleep.

With a deep sigh, she pushed herself out of bed, dragging her feet toward the bathroom. Even though the shower was warm and soothing, it didn't melt away the knots of tension gnawing at her. She turned the water off with a groan, reaching for a towel, when an icy hand clasped hers. She jerked her hand away, pulling the shower curtain back in a panic, but the room was empty. An icy chill lingered, creeping up her arm, and she had to flex her fingers, opening and closing them until the sensation faded.

Wrapping the towel around herself, she caught her reflection in the mirror. Her eyes were heavy from lack of sleep, but it wasn't just exhaustion that made her face look worn. She'd learned to accept the spirits around her, to co-exist with the odd, but the touch of one was a completely different story.

Hecate shook her head and refocused. Today, for the girl's sake, she needed to be sharp. There was no time for fear. She took a deep breath, and moments later, she was dressed and heading for the kitchen.

The smell of bacon and pancakes hit her before she even stepped inside. Jacques was at the stove and greeted her with a warm smile, "Bonjour, belle Hecate," he said.

"Bonjour, Jacques," she replied with a tired half-smile.

"Il y a un pot de café frais sur le comptoir si vous le souhaitez," he added in French, as he flipped a pancake.

Hecate chuckled softly, "Sorry, my French begins and ends with 'Bonjour'."

Jacques laughed. "There's a fresh pot of coffee on the counter."

"Thanks," she said, grabbing a mug and pouring herself a cup. She sat down at the small table, pulling out her phone to check for any messages from Landis. Nothing. Her stomach tightened as she remembered she'd promised to call him back but hadn't. *Damn it, Hecate,* she thought.

"Where's Solomon?" she asked.

"He went out to run an errand. Should be back soon. In the meantime, breakfast is ready. I assume you like pancakes?"

Hecate nodded before she eagerly dove into a hearty plate of food.

A few minutes later, Solomon walked in. "Couldn't wait for me, I see," he said sternly before his face with a soft grin.

"Nope," she replied with her mouth full. "You didn't say you were leaving this morning, so I didn't feel like waiting."

"Fair enough," Solomon said. "Did you sleep at all?"

"No," she snapped, barely looking at him.

He sighed. "I'm sorry."

Hecate grunted in response as she dug into her food, shoveling another bite into her mouth before fixing her gaze on Solomon. "Where'd you go, anyway?"

"I went to get us a car," he replied simply. "Thought it'd be better than walking."

"Oh," she replied curtly.

But something was off. Solomon could feel it. Her energy, her aura—it wasn't right. He focused, concentrating on her, trying to gauge how she was really feeling.

Hecate caught the shift in his attention. Her eyes flashed with irritation. "Are you fucking trying to read my mind?" she shot at him.

"No," Solomon said, holding up a hand. "I was just reading your aura."

"Well, whatever the hell you're doing, stop!" She pushed her chair back from the table. "Thanks, Jacques. Everything was delicious."

Jacques smiled and nodded. "*Vous êtes les bienvenus, belle.*"

Hecate blinked at him, confused.

"It means, 'You're welcome, beautiful one'," Jacques explained.

Hecate turned to leave, but stopped when Solomon called after her.

"Are you feeling okay, Hecate?" he asked.

She whirled around, a storm raging in her eyes. "Why do

you keep asking me if I'm fucking okay? No, I'm not fucking okay! This shit's just too much!"

Without waiting for a response, she stormed out.

Solomon was about to follow, but Jacques held him back. "Let her go. It's just her nerves. It happens to everyone, even to you, remember?"

Solomon paused. "Yeah. I guess you're right. I'm starting to wonder if I've pushed her too hard too soon."

Jacques grinned. "She'll be fine. She just needs to work through this. And remember what I was like when I started."

Solomon chuckled. "Yes, I do. You were vomiting for an hour after your first case."

"Don't remind me," Jacques muttered with a wince. "But the point is, I was terrified, and you helped me through it. She'll come around. She's strong."

Solomon hugged his friend tightly. "Thank you. For everything."

Jacques patted his back. "Anytime. And may God be with you today."

Solomon nodded before heading out the door.

He found Hecate sitting on the porch steps, her face buried in her hands. When she looked up, her eyes were red from crying.

"Sorry about that," she murmured.

Solomon sat down beside her. "It's okay," he said gently. "You're under a lot of stress. I just want you to know, I'm here for you."

She wiped away the last tear, taking a breath. "I just hope I don't mess this up. For you. For the girl."

Solomon pulled her into an unexpected hug. "You won't mess it up. I know you won't."

"You're more optimistic than I am," she said softly as she sniffled. "I guess that's something I need to work on."

Solomon stood up, offering her a hand. "Come on. It's time. We have an appointment with the priest."

The drive to the church wasn't far, and in minutes, they were stepping onto the grounds of a grand building, its towering spires and Gothic architecture casting a shadow over them. Hecate couldn't help but marvel at its beauty.

The Basilica was under renovations, so access was restricted for most people. Solomon, however, wasn't most people. After climbing the long stone stairway to the top, he simply walked up to the front door, inserted a key, and walked right in.

Hecate's breath was taken away the second she stepped through the door. Inside, the air was thick with history. Marble pillars reached up to a dome painted with Baroque artwork, and the massive statue of Saint Michael slaying a demon loomed over the high altar. She could almost picture herself in another time, gazing through the eyes of a partisan during worship service.

Father Benjamin, an imposing figure in priestly robes, met them halfway down the aisle. He greeted Solomon with a warm handshake and a bow.

"Father Benjamin," Solomon said with reverence. "Thank you for meeting us on such short notice."

"Mon ami, the pleasure is mine," the priest replied. "It's been far too long since you've been here, though I wish it were under better circumstances."

Turning to Hecate, Solomon introduced her. "This is my apprentice, Hecate."

The priest smiled warmly. "It's an honor to meet you, mon cher Hecate."

Father Benjamin led them down the hall to his office, where they took their seats.

"What can you tell me about the girl?" Solomon asked.

Father Benjamin explained. "Her name is Sophie, sixteen years old. Her father passed away from a heart attack, and she lives with her mother, Laina. I've sent one of my acolytes to help keep her subdued until you arrived."

"And her behavior?" Solomon pressed.

"Speaking in tongues, rashes, boils... others report the smell of sulfur, and she's levitated above her bed."

Hecate frowned. "I didn't notice anything like sulfur around the boy. Is that normal?"

"It's not always there, but it's common," Father Benjamin explained.

Solomon asked, "Do we know the demon's name?"

"We think it's Angrboda," Father Benjamin said. "Her mother heard her whisper the name."

"That's helpful," Solomon said.

"How does it help?" Hecate asked.

"Knowing the demon's name strengthens the ritual," he explained. "It gives you more power over it, and a better chance of protecting the host."

Father Benjamin nodded. "The demon might injure or even kill its host if it knows it's about to be defeated. That's why the ritual must be done quickly and precisely."

"That's horrible!" Hecate said.

"All the more reason to end this as quickly as possible," Solomon said. "The longer the demon is present in the girl, the stronger the foothold it has on her soul."

Hecate stared down at her hands. "What if I fail? What if I'm not good enough to do this?"

Solomon squeezed her shoulder. "We won't let that happen. You're not alone."

"That is correct," Father Benjamin said. He turned toward Solomon, "It's time for you to do what you do best, my friend."

The priest gave each one a powerful hug and blessed them. "May God be with you," he said.

"Thank you," Solomon said before he turned and led Hecate from the room.

With every passing moment, Hecate's stomach twisted tighter, a coil of dread that tightened with each mile. But as they approached the house, she realized the drive had been far too brief to calm her nerves.

The house was small, worn down by neglect—its foundation cracked, its paint chipped—a home once filled with warmth, now a victim of tragedy. Tragedy that had left the woman who lived there unable to maintain it. And now, tragedy had struck again. Hecate could only hope they could restore a sliver of love to that broken place.

As they drew closer, Hecate caught a fleeting glimpse through a window—a figure standing in the far corner, watching them. When she looked more closely, a middle-aged man appeared at the window, his eyes hollow with sorrow. A heartbeat later, he vanished. It was Sophie's father, gone but still tethered to this world by grief. Seeing the pain etched into his features filled Hecate with a new sense of resolve. They had to save Sophie, no matter the cost.

Solomon broke the silence. "Are you ready?"

Hecate nodded, the words barely escaping her lips. "Yeah, I'm ready."

With a light knock, Solomon rapped on the door, and within seconds, it creaked open to reveal a frail woman standing in the doorway. "Laina, c'est ça? Je suis Salomon. Et voici mon partenaire, Hecate. Nous sommes ici pour sauver votre fille."

Laina's voice was frantic as she grasped his hands. "Oh, merci! Dépêchez-vous! Tu dois sauver ma petite fille!"

Solomon gave a reassuring nod as he entered, and Hecate

glanced at him, asking quietly, "What did she say?"

"She said to hurry and save her little girl."

"I agree," Hecate whispered, though her heart thundered in her chest.

Laina led them through a cramped, dimly lit living room, and toward a door at the far end of the house. Outside, Betran, an acolyte, stood guard, his expression tense.

"What's the status?" Solomon asked, his voice low.

"It comes and goes," Betran responded. "She's sleeping for now, but the demon could return at any moment. Stay ready."

Solomon nodded and turned the handle, pushing the door open with a quiet creak.

The bedroom smelled of decay, the stench of urine and feces heavy in the air. Hecate fought the bile rising in her throat, her body repelling the rancid odor. In the corner, Sophie lay bound to the bed, her limbs strapped down with rough ropes. Her white nightgown was stained, her pale skin pocked with boils and blisters. A trail of dried mucus lined the girl's chin, and her breath was ragged.

Hecate's breath caught in her throat when Sophie's eyes flickered open as they entered. The girl's pupils were pitch black, a void of darkness, and her lips stretched into a grotesque grin that seemed to split her face.

"My, my, what have we here?" Sophie's voice, no longer her own, rang out in a deep, malevolent tone. "New toys to play with!"

Solomon's voice cracked through the silence, sharp and commanding. "Shut your mouth, demon! Today is the day you release your hold on this girl and return to the pit you crawled from!"

A stream of saliva shot from Sophie's mouth, splattering across Solomon's face.

The demon inside Sophie cackled wickedly. "I knew you'd show up eventually, Solomon."

Sophie's eyes turned toward Hecate, and her smile widened. She switched to French, the words dripping with venom as she looked Hecate up and down. "Qui est la jolie petite garce ? Elle est assez bonne pour manger?"

Solomon's anger flared. "Enough!"

With a sharp motion, he gestured for Hecate to take her position. She stepped toward the bed slowly, Sophie's teeth snapping together like a wild animal eager to tear flesh.

The air in the room thickened with tension. Solomon's eyes locked on Hecate's, and with a shared understanding, they began the ritual. The chant rolled from Solomon's lips in a steady cadence, and the air seemed to hum with energy. Beneath them, Sophie's body twisted violently, the ropes straining as she fought to break free.

A low growl erupted from deep within her chest, and Sophie's body jerked against the restraints. The demon's voice grew guttural as it clawed its way to the surface.

"Hold her legs," Solomon barked, and Betran rushed in, grabbing the girl's legs with firm hands.

Hecate took her place at Sophie's side, her palms pressing down onto the girl's arms to keep them pinned.

The demon cackled again, a chilling sound that reverberated in Hecate's bones. Sophie's neck twisted unnaturally, her eyes never leaving Hecate. With a sickening lurch, the demon lunged, snapping its teeth toward her exposed arm.

Hecate pulled back just in time, but the ropes around Sophie's right arm gave way, snapping free. In an instant, the demon's hand shot upward and closed around Hecate's throat, its grip tightening with monstrous strength.

Solomon moved swiftly, slamming a crucifix against

Sophie's forehead. The demon recoiled with a shriek, releasing Hecate's throat as it flailed.

But in the chaos, Sophie's nails raked across Hecate's arm, the sharp sting burning through her skin.

Hecate winced, but held her ground. Solomon glanced at her, his face drawn with concern. She gave him a nod, though her expression betrayed her worry.

Together, they continued the ritual, their voices growing louder, stronger.

Sophie's body began to shake violently, foam spilling from her mouth, her skin pale and clammy. Then she stopped suddenly.

The room fell silent as they all waited and watched nervously.

After a few tense moments, the demon's eyes snapped open again. "Nice try, fucker!" it hissed. "You'll have to do better than that. And you better check on your bitch there, Solomon. Her blood smells sour."

Solomon's voice rose, "Enough, Angrboda! Time for you to go back to Hell!"

At the mention of its name, the demon froze. Solomon lifted his voice, louder and more forceful than ever, and with a final, commanding chant, he spoke the last of the ritual.

"Exorcizamus te, omnis immunde spiritus, omni satanica potestas, omnis incursio infernalis adversarii, omnis legio, omnis congregatio et secta diabolica, in nomini et virtute Domini nostri Jesu Christi, eradicare et effugare a Dei Ecclesia, ab animabus ad imaginem Dei conditis ac pretioso divini Agni sanguini redemptis."

Sophie's body arched violently, her back straining as her limbs fought against the last of the ropes holding her. A shrill, ear-splitting scream echoed as a black whirlwind of smoke poured from her mouth and spiraled upward, dissipating into the air.

Then, silence.

They stood frozen, waiting for any sign of life. A minute passed, then two. Doubt began to settle like a heavy weight in their chests.

Hecate couldn't take it any longer. "What do we do now?"

Solomon's voice was steady, though the edge of concern was evident. "Just a little longer."

"But we have to do something! We promised her mother we'd save her."

Then, finally, a shallow breath escaped Sophie's lips.

"And so we have," Solomon said, relief washing over his face.

Slowly, Sophie's eyelids fluttered open. The black voids were gone, replaced by eyes that were now a bright, vivid blue.

"C'est fini?" Sophie asked, her voice weak and raspy.

"Yes, it's over," Solomon replied, his voice softening.

Together, they untied the ropes binding Sophie's limbs, revealing the raw, burned marks on her wrists and ankles—scars of the torment she had endured.

They helped her to her feet, guiding her carefully out of the room and back into her mother's arms.

"Momma," Sophie whispered.

Laina rushed forward, her arms enveloping her daughter, tears streaming down both of their faces. "Oh, Sophie, ma douce petite fille, j'avais peur de te perdre pour toujours."

Laina turned to Solomon, gratitude flooding her eyes as she whispered, "Je vous remercie."

Solomon smiled warmly, nodding. "It was our honor."

As they stepped outside, Hecate leaned against the car, exhausted. "Holy fuck! That was intense."

Solomon gave a tired chuckle. "Indeed, it was. You did

well in there."

"Really? I almost got myself killed," Hecate replied, the words slipping out before she could stop them.

"But you didn't," Solomon said firmly. "You held strong."

Hecate glanced down at her arm and froze. The cut the demon had left behind was swelling, now glowing bright red with infection. Green pus oozed from the wound in sickening streaks.

"I don't feel so good," Hecate murmured, her vision blurring.

Before Solomon could react, her knees buckled, and she collapsed to the ground, unconscious.

CHAPTER 14

The fury on his father's face was now a grotesque reflection of what it had once been in life—magnified and distorted by death. The rage that burned in those hollow eyes was the kind that could scorch the very soul, and Landis knew that his life was in imminent peril.

Abaddon leaped from his arms just as he grabbed the fire poker from the hearth, swinging it at the apparition. The poker passed through the spectral form with an eerie howl, but the figure only dissolved into the air, vanishing without a trace.

Landis didn't have much time. He could feel the malevolent force rebuilding its strength, preparing for a second strike, and now the warning from his mother echoed in his mind with terrifying clarity. He had to stop his father's rage—if he didn't, he'd be dead before he could understand why.

In a frantic rush, Landis ran to the kitchen, the poker still gripped tightly in his hand, and began pulling open cupboards until he found a box of salt. Abaddon trailed behind him, her watchful eyes glinting from the counter, her feline curiosity never wavering.

Next, Landis stormed into the library, praying it would still be the sanctuary it had once been, the place where he had often found solace. But deep down, he feared that it had become something else—something darker.

The second his fingers touched the doorknob, the entire house trembled beneath his feet. At first, it felt like an earthquake—common enough in Southern California—but Landis instantly recognized that this was not nature at work.

He grabbed the door frame, his pulse hammering in his throat, as the ground beneath him buckled and groaned. Abaddon darted past him, her lithe form seeking refuge beneath a nearby table, her eyes wide with an eerie calm. When the tremor subsided, only a few objects—a vase, a knick-knack or two—had fallen from their shelves.

Landis slammed the door behind him and threw a line of salt across the threshold, praying it would buy him precious moments. He needed time to find the source of the madness —and fast.

His gaze swept the room, heart racing, his eyes scanning every corner. He almost didn't see it at first—the small, silver-framed mirror resting against a shelf. If this was the same as he remembered, it would be his salvation. If not, then death was a certainty.

His chest tightened as he moved closer, only to be stopped in his tracks by the sudden rise of his father's form through the floor. The once-familiar face was now a grotesque mockery, contorted in an unnatural snarl. Landis swung the poker at him, but before it could land, he was violently hurled across the room, slamming into the bookshelf. He hit the ground with a sickening thud, pain radiating through his body.

He tried to push himself up but his arm gave out and he fell back to the floor. As he lay there in pain, a barrage of books flew off the shelves, aimed at Landis like hard-bound torpedoes. He curled himself into a tight ball to protect himself, crying out in pain of pain as he was pelted over and over.

A hiss rang out in his ear. Landis flinched, his body curling tighter to shield himself. And then, the storm of books stopped. He looked up, confused, and saw Abaddon standing before him, her back arched and teeth bared in a protective stance. Her eyes, wild and glowing, locked onto his father's apparition.

With a bone-chilling growl that seemed to vibrate the very air, Abaddon let out a scream—a high-pitched wail that could never come from a normal cat. Landis watched, stunned, as the spirit of his father recoiled in terror, disappearing into nothingness.

Breathing heavily, Landis pushed himself to his knees, clutching his shoulder. It was dislocated, and he knew he couldn't afford to wait for help. The pain was unbearable, but he had no choice.

Using the back of the door as support, he braced himself. With one final, agonizing effort, he slammed his shoulder forward. The sickening pop echoed in his ears, and he collapsed back to the floor, gasping in relief.

Abaddon padded over to him, her tail flicking with satisfaction as she rubbed herself against his legs. Landis managed a weak smile, scratching behind her ears.

"It looks like there's more to you than meets the eye," Landis said as he reached out with his right hand and scratched her behind the ears. "Thank you."

She meowed softly in response, then padded over to the corner of the room, as if beckoning him to follow.

Landis dragged himself to his feet, his head still spinning from the fall, and shuffled over to where Abaddon had stopped. The bookshelf had been pushed away from the wall, revealing a narrow, black void behind it.

The air grew icy, and Landis's heart sank when he saw the iron poker lying on the far side of the room, abandoned and useless.

Abaddon's fur bristled, and she stepped cautiously toward the dark opening. Landis had no choice but to follow. With a grunt, he shoved the bookshelf aside, and to his surprise, it moved easily. With one final push, he managed to squeeze into the narrow space behind the wall.

The air inside was freezing, and behind him, Landis heard Abaddon's feral hiss followed by a low, guttural cry from his father.

The narrow tunnel led to an even smaller space—barely five feet wide, with a low ceiling. As Landis moved through the cramped room, his head collided with something hard. Reaching up, his fingers brushed against the cool surface of a wooden door handle. Without thinking, he yanked it open, revealing a steep set of stairs leading upward.

Quickly, he scrambled up the stairs, heart pounding, unsure of what he'd find. A moment later, he was in the attic —a small, eerie space that felt separate from the rest of the house, as though it existed outside of time itself.

The light flickered on, and Landis froze in horror.

The walls were covered with strange symbols and runes, the shelves crowded with jars containing the remains of various creatures—some unidentifiable, others horrifyingly familiar. His stomach churned as he scanned the room, his gaze falling on the table at the far end. There, amidst a circle inscribed with blood and bordered by cryptic sigils, lay the book he feared—the Heptameron.

It had once been a tool for contacting angels, but in the wrong hands, it became a vessel for hellish power. And now, it was the source of his father's torment. Beside the book, a silver dagger lay, its blade stained with blood.

Suddenly, the house shook again, more violently this time, throwing Landis to the floor. His hand caught the edge of the table as he fell, sending the table—and its dark contents—crashing to the ground.

Abaddon ran over to him, sitting in front of him with a serious, focused gaze. And then, the voice entered his mind, *Destroy the book.* A spell raced into his mind. Whether it was one that he had learned before, or Abaddon had communicated to him, he didn't know.

Landis grabbed the dagger, slashing it across his palm, his blood spilling onto the floor. He quickly drew the sigil he had seen, a complex pentagram bordered by ancient runes. Once it was finished, he placed the book in the center of the circle.

He began to recite the words that burned in his mind, words he didn't understand but knew to be powerful. The circle began to glow, and then, in a blinding flash, it exploded into light.

A scream ripped through the room as his father's apparition flew toward him like a missile. Landis brought the dagger down, plunging it into the book, and as he spoke the final words of the spell, the world seemed to stop.

His father froze in mid-air, an agonized wail echoing through the room. The sound rattled Landis to the bone, a soul-less cry for help, desperate and weak, from someone that didn't deserve it, before he and the cursed book were gone in an instant.

CHAPTER 15

Solomon tore through the streets of Menton, the engine of the car roaring like a wild animal in pursuit of its prey. His mind was singularly focused: Hecate was dying, and he was the only one who could save her. Jacques' place wasn't far, but every second felt like an eternity.

He slammed on the brakes in front of the motel, the tires screeching in protest. Without wasting a moment, he rushed around to the passenger side and pulled Hecate's limp form from the car. He cradled her close, her body a dead weight in his arms, and bolted into the building, his voice cracking as he called out. "Jacques! I need help!"

Jacques appeared in the foyer, his eyes wide with confusion, quickly replaced by horror as he took in the sight of Hecate in Solomon's arms. "What happened?" he asked, his voice tight with fear.

"The demon poisoned her during the exorcism. But there's something else," Solomon said, his voice strained as he carried her into the kitchen and laid her on the table.

Jacques looked down at Hecate, brow furrowed. "What else?"

Solomon's eyes darkened. "Something the demon said

before we drove it out—'Her blood smells sour.'"

Jacques blinked, uncertain. "What does that mean?"

"I'm not sure... but I think she picked up an astral parasite when we were checking on Landis during our flight."

"Landis? What does he have to do with her?"

A wry smile tugged at Solomon's lips, and Jacques' face shifted as realization hit. "Oh, I see." He did a double-take, his voice tinged with disbelief. "Wait—what were you doing astral traveling with her on an airplane?"

Solomon sighed, pacing. "It's complicated. Hecate felt something was wrong. I should've known she wasn't ready."

"Don't beat yourself up, my friend," Jacques said. "What do you need me to do?"

"I need my bag from my room and some cold towels. We've got to get her fever down."

Jacques nodded quickly, darting toward the room. Within moments, he returned with the black satchel, followed by a stack of towels. He tossed the bag onto the table, swiftly draping an ice-filled rag over Hecate's forehead.

Solomon's hands trembled as he opened a vial of red liquid from his bag, pouring a generous amount down Hecate's throat. They waited in silence, each second feeling like an hour. Then her body went rigid, shaking uncontrollably. Jacques gripped her shoulders to steady her, while Solomon held her legs. The violent tremors seemed endless, but after what felt like a lifetime, they ceased.

A thick, black ooze began to leak from the cut on her arm, dripping onto the table, where it hissed and smoked before it disintegrated completely.

"Is she okay?" Jacques asked softly.

"I hope so," Solomon replied, his eyes never leaving her form. The demon blood had been expelled, but a deeper threat still lingered. The astral parasite needed to be eradicated before it could latch onto her soul.

Solomon took a deep breath, closing his eyes. His spirit rose from his body, drawn to the ether, leaving his physical form behind. Below him, Hecate's fragile body lay, and a surge of guilt hit him hard. In his eagerness to train her, he'd pushed her too far, too fast. If something happened to her… he would never forgive himself.

From his vantage point, he saw the parasite—a writhing black tentacle pushing its way up her leg, another quickly following, until her entire body was entangled. The darkness was spreading, inching from the astral to the physical. If he didn't act fast, the damage would be irreversible.

Solomon grabbed one of the tentacles, squeezing tight. The black form writhed fiercely, resisting his pull. Then, finally, it began to give way. Slowly and steadily, he disengaged it, pulling it free from her chest. The creature was twisted, malformed—a half-formed human from the waist up, its lower half a mass of wriggling, serpentine tentacles.

Solomon gritted his teeth, pulling harder, careful not to tear anything vital. For a moment, the parasite refused to budge, but then it finally gave in. Slowly, the parasite detached, releasing its hold on Hecate. Solomon pulled himself away from her body, as the black mass floated through the astral plane like a dead jellyfish drifting through dark waters.

When the parasite was gone, he hovered over Hecate, assessing her condition. Satisfied that she was free from the creature's hold, he descended back into his physical body, his consciousness snapping back into place.

"Did you remove the threat?" Jacques asked, as Solomon sat up.

Solomon nodded. "I think so. She should wake up soon."

Hecate's eyelids fluttered open. "What happened?" she

asked weakly as she looked around the room in confusion.

"You collapsed," Solomon answered. "You should be fine now. Do you remember anything?"

Hecate rubbed her arm, wincing as she touched the cut. "Yeah… I remember. The demon… it cut me during the exorcism. Why?"

"And how do you feel right now?"

She pushed herself up on the table, wincing slightly, and sat with her feet dangling over the edge. "I'm okay. A little hungry and thirsty, though."

"When the demon cut you, it injected poison into your bloodstream. That's why you passed out. I gave you an antidote to expel it. Your appetite is a good sign."

The sound of a bell ringing from the other room caught their attention. "I'll go see who it is," Jacques said, helping her down from the table.

Moments later, Jacques returned with a tall woman following him. She wore a long black dress, heels that seemed as sharp as weapons, and a red scarf that wrapped around her neck like a streak of blood. Her piercing blue eyes locked onto Hecate.

"Solomon?" Jacques said. "This woman wants to speak with you."

Solomon stepped forward cautiously and Victoria extended her hand. "Je m'appelle Victoria, et je suis en charge de la division occulte Français de la recherche surnaturelle."

"What can I do for you, Victoria?" He asked as he took her hand.

"My English is not so good," she replied with a thick accent. "But I will try my best. I want to ask you about the exorcism you performed on the girl, Sophie, today."

Solomon raised an eyebrow. "What would you like to know?"

Victoria didn't answer right away. Instead, she stood there studying him like a predator sizing up its prey. Solomon felt the weight of her silence and knew immediately that this wasn't a simple inquiry; it was something more.

When she finally spoke, her voice was icy and measured. "Can you tell me how you found out about the girl?"

A sharp warning flaring in Solomon's mind. "I have my sources," he replied guardedly.

"I see. And under whose authority did you perform this ritual?"

"My own, with guidance from the Church," Solomon answered.

"Father Benjamin?" she asked with a thin smile.

"Yes."

"Are you aware that he is being investigated—and has been threatened with ex-communication?"

Solomon's eyes narrowed. "No. What's he being investigated for?"

Victoria's smile widened, her gaze darkening. "The unauthorized practice of demonology... and giving classified information to untrained, unlicensed subjects."

Solomon's anger flared. "That's ridiculous! How could he be accused of such things?"

Victoria turned to Hecate. "Who is this young lady?"

Solomon answered through clenched teeth. "This is Hecate."

"And is she a licensed agent?" Victoria asked pointedly.

"She is under my direct supervision, and is currently undergoing extensive training in the field."

"But she's not licensed?"

Instead of answering, Solomon just stood there regarding the woman coldly.

Victoria chuckled, turning on her heel. "Merci, Solomon. Je

crois que j'en ai assez entendu. Et, je serai sûr de garder un oeil sur vous, cher Hecate."

She left without another word, and Solomon stood staring at the door for a long moment. "Something's wrong here. Jacques, find out everything you can about Victoria. I don't trust her."

***

As soon as she was clear of the building, Victoria pulled out her phone and made a quick call. After a couple of rings, the person on the other end answered. She said in an excited tone, "I have some information that I think you'll find quite interesting..."

CHAPTER 16

The elevator shuddered to a halt on the basement floor, and as the doors slid open, Adam and Josh scrambled to push the gurney into the hallway. The metal frame scraped against the wall, a jarring sound that echoed through the quiet, sending both men into a tense silence. They held their breath, hoping the noise hadn't stirred the woman strapped to the top.

Josh gritted his teeth as he shoved the gurney forward, the wheels squealing against the floor, while Adam slowly limped behind. They made a sharp turn, and then another, as they pushed toward the set of double doors that marked the entrance to the part of the basement no one liked to talk about—the place where the dark things were kept. At least, that's what the whispers said.

As they approached a door on the right, the lights above them flickered. Josh swiped his key-card at the panel beside the door, the soft click confirming it was unlocked. Adam hobbled ahead and swung the door open, revealing the cold, dimly lit room beyond. Josh followed behind, pushing the gurney in and locking the wheels in place against the back wall.

"Let's get the fuck out of here," Josh muttered nervously.

"This place is giving me the creeps."

"You and me both," Adam said while his eyes darted around the room as if he expected something to jump out from the shadows.

Josh swiped his key-card again, the familiar beep and green light signaling that the door was unlocked. But when he tried the handle, the door didn't budge. "What the hell?"

Adam limped over and grabbed the handle, giving it a hard tug, but the door wouldn't budge. "This doesn't make any sense," he grumbled.

Then a voice hissed from behind them, "It makes perfect sense to me."

The two men froze, their blood running cold as they turned to face the source of the voice. Jezebeth stood by the bed, her figure twisted in a grotesque parody of humanity. Her eyes were pitch-black, voids of darkness that swallowed the light. Teeth—razor-sharp and unnaturally long—jutted from her mouth, and her fingers, now grotesque claws, twitched with anticipation.

Before they could react, a chilling cackle erupted from her throat, and the lights above them flickered one last time—then went out, plunging them into darkness.

***

Dr. Chapman retreated to his office, shutting the door behind him with a quiet click, and drew the shades, cutting off the world outside. His sixteen-hour shift had caught up to him and he could feel his cognitive functions beginning to dull. He told the head nurse he needed a break and instructed her to call Dr. Phillips if anything urgent came up. An hour—that was all he needed.

Tossing his glasses onto the desk, he slumped onto the

small couch in the corner, a makeshift bed that had become all too familiar. The moment his head hit the pillow, sleep claimed him.

He woke up some time later to the sound of a fly buzzing near his ear. Swatting at the pest with a groan, he checked his watch and was alarmed to see that three hours had passed. He sighed, *Oh, well.* He'd needed it, and hopefully, the Director wouldn't find out.

Then the skin on the side of his face began to itch and burn. He scratched at it, but when he pulled his fingers away, they were smeared with blood. His heart raced as he stumbled out of his office, rushing to the bathroom across the hall.

A scream tore from his throat when he saw his reflection. The skin on his face was peeling away in chunks, exposing the raw, white bone beneath. For a moment, the horror of it was unbearable. But then, the illusion shattered—his reflection was back to normal, his face untouched. He stood frozen, trying to steady his breath, his mind scrambling to make sense of what had just happened.

After a long minute, he forced himself out of the bathroom and made his way back down the hall toward the E.R. Lucinda, the head nurse, was at her desk, sorting through papers. She barely glanced up as he approached.

"Hey, Luci," he said, trying to keep his voice steady. "Have you seen Josh and Adam?"

"Not for a while, Dr. Chapman," she replied, barely sparing him a second glance. "Want me to have them page you when I see them?"

"No, it's fine. They were running an errand for me. Just wanted to check in."

She grunted in acknowledgment, going back to her paperwork. He didn't have the energy to explain, and frankly, he wasn't in the mood to deal with her disapproval, especially when it came to the basement. As far as Lucinda was concerned, the entire area should be sealed off.

He knew he should've checked on the patient before now, but his exhaustion had taken over. Hopefully, she'd still be sedated when he got there.

Taking the elevator down to the basement, Dr. Chapman almost choked as he stepped into the hallway. The air was thick with the stench of decay, like someone had forgotten to close the morgue door, leaving the foul odor to fester. He pulled his lab coat over his nose, a futile attempt to shield himself from the oppressive air, as he made his way toward the restricted area.

When he passed through the double doors, the smell intensified, a foul, sickening stench that seemed to claw at his lungs. It felt like something evil, something ancient, had been trapped here in the dark.

His eyes burned, the acrid smell stinging his nostrils as he approached the door to the room where the woman had been placed. His stomach twisted as he saw a swarm of flies covering the door, writhing and buzzing in a grotesque frenzy, desperately trying to get inside.

In a panic, Dr. Chapman grabbed the fire extinguisher mounted on the wall and sprayed it wildly at the insects, the white cloud billowing in the air. As the mist cleared, he saw the hallway was once again free of the pests and the stench had vanished, but a deep feeling of dread lingered in his chest.

Shaking, he pulled his key-card from his pocket and swiped it in front of the door panel. The familiar beep sounded, and he pushed the door open, but it wouldn't budge. With a grunt of effort, he shoved harder, the door creaking open just enough for something heavy to tumble out onto the floor.

Adam's body.

His eyes were missing, black empty sockets where his pupils should have been. His nose was gone, and his throat had been torn out. Blood and bits of flesh painted the walls and floor in a grotesque display.

Josh sat in the corner, slumped against the wall, his skin a mottled shade of blue, streaked with black veins. His eyes were still there, but they were lifeless and hollow. The blood drained from Dr. Chapman's face as he looked around, scanning the carnage, until his gaze landed on Jezebeth.

She was still strapped to the gurney, unmoving—but her eyes were open. The wicked gleam in them made his blood run cold.

"Hello, Doctor," she purred, her voice a sinister whisper in the silent room. "I was wondering when you'd show up."

CHAPTER 17

Landis sat on the couch, staring blankly at the cold, lifeless fireplace, his thoughts swirling like a storm. Abaddon was nestled in his lap, purring softly, her eyes closed in contentment as he absentmindedly stroked her fur.

His mind raced with questions he couldn't answer, each one feeding the gnawing uncertainty that plagued him. What was she? Abaddon wasn't just any animal—he knew that with every fiber of his being. The mystery of her existence, her origins, was a riddle that tugged at the edges of his sanity. He doubted he'd ever uncover the truth, but the questions lingered, relentless and insistent.

The presence of his father's spirit wasn't unexpected, not entirely. The man had been consumed by rage in life, so it only made sense that his fury would bleed into the afterlife. But the book—the damned book—was a different story. It wasn't just the source of that rage; it was a gateway to a darker side of himself, one that Landis hadn't even known existed. The power inside the tome had twisted him in ways he couldn't begin to understand. What kind of person would he be if the book had never entered his life? And what had his mother's role been in all of this? Had she unknowingly

127

fueled the darkness, or was she just a helpless bystander, trapped in the middle of some cosmic war she had no chance of escaping?

He closed his eyes, trying to silence the chaos in his mind, but it didn't help—not really. The questions still bounced around inside his skull, relentless. What he needed was someone who could offer clarity, someone who could help him make sense of it all. He needed Hecate. Her presence grounded him, even when everything else felt like it was falling apart. She didn't need to have all the answers—just her support, her understanding. That's what he craved, even more than the answers themselves.

He sighed, pulling his phone from his pocket, the soft weight of Abaddon's body shifting on his lap as he moved. For a brief moment, her eyes fluttered open, a lazy glance at him before she sank back into sleep. He hesitated, finger hovering over Hecate's number. The exorcism… he couldn't risk interrupting them now, not when things were so volatile. Reluctantly, he set the phone back down beside him.

Landis closed his eyes again, trying once more to calm his thoughts. But the questions remained, unanswered, like shadows in the corners of his mind, just out of reach.

***

Hecate lay back on the couch, her gaze fixed on the ceiling, replaying every moment of the last few hours in her mind. Her first field assignment—and she could barely shake the feeling that she had failed. Always her own harshest critic, she couldn't help but feel that her carelessness had put everything at risk. The injury she'd sustained, the jeopardy it had brought to the exorcism—it all haunted her. But at least they'd saved the girl. That was something, right?

She pulled her phone from her pocket. She needed to hear Landis' voice. His words had a way of calming her soul, and she was counting on that again, hoping he'd lift her out of this depression. She wasn't sure why she was in such a mood. Maybe it was the letdown after the rush of the ritual, like the comedown from some drug-induced high. Regardless, the sound of his voice was always the one thing that could steady her.

The call connected immediately. Landis sounded almost like he'd been waiting for her. "Hecate! Hey! I was hoping you'd call soon. How did everything go?"

"It went fine," she replied, trying to sound more confident than she felt. "We saved the girl."

"That's great! I'm so proud of you!" he said.

"Thanks," she murmured, though the praise didn't ease the knot in her stomach. "It could've gone better, though."

"What happened?"

"I was careless. She scratched me—infected me with something. Solomon had to save me."

"Don't be too hard on yourself. It was your first time. I'm sure you did awesome."

"Yeah, but you have a biased opinion."

"So what if I do? I'm not denying it."

Hecate smirked softly. "And I won't ask you to. I have my own bias for a certain male that I know."

Landis chuckled. "And who might that be?"

Hecate hesitated, then, with a slight edge of uncertainty, said, "The man I think I'm falling in love with."

The silence that followed felt like an eternity, and for a moment, her heart sank. She had said too much, too soon. She scrambled, fumbling for words. "I mean... what I was trying to say—"

"I love you too," Landis cut in, his voice steady and sure.

Her breath caught in her throat. "You do?"

"I was trying to work up the nerve to say it myself, but I thought it might be too soon. Looks like you beat me to it."

"Is that okay?" she asked, her voice barely a whisper.

"It's perfect," he replied.

She smiled, feeling lighter than she had in days. "How are you doing after everything with your parents? Did you go to your mom's house like she wanted?"

Landis hesitated for a beat, and Hecate sensed that something was off. He didn't want to spoil the moment, so he changed the subject. "Yeah, I went. It felt... different. Oh, and I got you a surprise, by the way."

Her eyes lit up. "Oh, yeah? Like what?"

"I can't tell you. Wouldn't be a surprise then, would it? But I'll give you a hint. You'll need to feed it regularly."

Her eyes widened even further. "Now you really have to tell me."

"Nope. Not until you get back."

"Brat," she teased, laughing. "It's not fair to leave me hanging like this."

"All's fair in love and war, right?"

Before Hecate could respond, Solomon's voice interrupted from the doorway. "Hecate, I need you in the kitchen."

She held her hand over the phone, turning toward him. "I'll be there in a minute."

"Tell Landis I said hi," Solomon added with a grin before heading out.

"I have to go," Hecate told Landis, a reluctant smile tugging at her lips. "Solomon needs me. And he says hi."

"Okay. Just keep me posted. I know the time difference is crazy, but I want to hear from you whenever you can."

"I will. Talk soon."

She made her way to the kitchen, her thoughts still with

Landis as her steps quickened. What did Solomon want to talk to her about? A small part of her wondered if he was going to scold her for getting injured during the ritual. She wasn't sure she could handle being reprimanded by him.

But when she entered the kitchen, the sight before her threw her off completely. Jacques and Solomon were standing behind a table, both grinning like fools. On the table in front of them sat a large chocolate cake, its layers gleaming in the light. "What's this?" Hecate asked, stunned.

"It's just a little something to celebrate your first case," Solomon said with a wide smile.

Jacques chimed in, "It's a tradition we started years ago, a little ritual to ease the tension afterward."

Hecate blinked. She had been so focused on her own failures that she hadn't expected anything like this. How was she supposed to accept this celebration without feeling like a fraud? "Thank you, guys," she said softly. "But I don't think I earned this."

"Nonsense," Solomon countered with a wave of his hand. "You performed admirably. In fact, better than Jacques did his first time, I'd wager."

Hecate raised an eyebrow. "Really?"

"Well, I wasn't there to judge your performance," Jacques teased.

"But I got hurt... I put everything at risk—"

"No," Solomon interjected firmly. "You fought through a demon attack and saved that girl. You showed strength. That's what matters."

Hecate paused, reflecting on his words. "Is this one of those 'glass half-full' kind of deals?"

Solomon gave a soft smile. "Isn't life always a matter of perspective?"

Before she could reply, Solomon's phone rang. He glanced

at the screen and excused himself. "Sorry, I have to take this. You guys cut the cake. I'll be back in a minute."

"You don't have to tell me twice," Jacques said, already cutting the cake. Hecate's mouth watered as he served her a slice of the decadent triple-layer cake, filled with rich chocolate and caramel icing. She took a bite, closing her eyes in bliss—but the euphoria was short-lived when Solomon returned, his expression dark.

"What's wrong?" she asked, a knot forming in her stomach.

Solomon's brow furrowed. "Our celebration will have to be shorter than I hoped."

"Why?"

"I was hoping we'd have more time between cases—allow you to rest and prepare—but unfortunately, we have to leave in the morning."

"What happened?" Jacques asked.

Solomon turned to him, trying to hide his expression from Hecate, "There's a young man in London that needs our immediate attention. The team that was assigned to the case can't make it."

Brandon and James are feared to be dead, Solomon said silently to him. *Their plane went down mysteriously somewhere over the English Channel. Uriel has already assigned someone to investigate.*

Jacques tried his best to hide his reaction, but Hecate knew something was going on. "Okay, spill it," she said.

When Solomon didn't answer right away, she said, "Listen, if I'm going to be part of this team, you need to tell me everything. No secrets between us. Okay? And none of this 'trying to protect me' shit. We all know that only makes things worse."

Solomon sighed, "You're right. You deserve to know

what's going on. We don't really know what happened to the other team. Their plane went down and we fear they may be dead."

Hecate's heart skipped a beat. "What's going on? What happened to the team?"

Solomon hesitated for a moment, then lowered his voice. "Their plane went down somewhere over the English Channel. We fear they're dead. Uriel's already assigned someone to investigate."

Hecate's stomach sank. "Wow," was all she could say.

Solomon sighed. "I just want to make sure you're ready for the next case."

The thought of another case so soon filled her with anxiety. She wasn't fond of flying, and hearing about a plane crash only made it worse. But then she thought of Sophie, free now, with a chance at a normal life. *That's why we do this,* she reminded herself.

"I'm ready," she said firmly.

Gideon scanned the room one last time, ensuring he was alone, before pulling out his phone. His impatience grew with each unanswered ring, the call stretching to the third ring before he figured it was heading straight to voice-mail. But then, finally, Victoria answered.

"It's about time you picked up," he said, his voice laced with frustration.

"Don't get snippy with me, mon ami," Victoria's replied. "You, of all people, should understand how difficult it is to play both sides and not get burned."

Gideon couldn't argue with that. "True. My apologies, mon cher. So, what's the word?"

"Everything's in place. Solomon and the girl are headed to London first thing tomorrow."

"And the other team?"

"Gone. No trace. By the time they pull that wreckage from the water, Brandon and James will be forgotten. Like they never existed."

"Good. Just keep the truth buried. No slip-ups."

"Relax," she replied. "Everything's taken care of. Though, if you're still bent on getting rid of Solomon, we could always make his plane go down too. The English Channel has a nasty reputation for that sort of thing."

Gideon's thoughts darkened at the idea, but he knew the timing wasn't right, not yet anyway. "No. Let them land. As much as I'd love to see Solomon gone, the girl is the priority. She's the key. Whatever happens to her, we can't let her fall into the wrong hands."

Victoria fell silent for a moment. "And what exactly does she have to do with all of this?"

"I'm not sure yet," he admitted, rubbing the back of his neck as he thought. "But I'll figure it out soon enough. I'm heading to Indiana. There's something I need to see there."

"Indiana?" Her tone was skeptical. "What's in Indiana?"

"The girl's mother," he said. "Or what's left of her, anyway."

***

Gideon pulled up in front of the hospital, exhausted and irritated. His flight had been delayed—four hours late, to be exact—and on top of that, he'd been forced to endure a whiny, obnoxious brat kicking the back of his seat the entire time. He made a mental note to spring for first class next time, even if the church frowned upon it.

He parked the car, adjusted his stiff white collar, and walked toward the entrance. *I'll be glad when I never have to wear this cursed thing again,* he thought, as he pushed open the door to the lobby.

Inside, Tarek was already waiting. He met Gideon as the door swung open and handed him a cup of coffee. "I didn't know how you take it, so I left it black," Tarek said.

Gideon took the cup with a grunt. He took a sip and grimaced. "This tastes like shit," he muttered, then handed it back to Tarek. "Have you spoken to the doctor?"

"No. I was waiting for you."

Gideon nodded and made his way to the reception desk. Behind the counter sat a young woman in her twenties, typing rapidly on her keyboard. She paused when she noticed Gideon standing there, her eyes briefly lingering on his disfigured left hand—a cruel reminder of his previous failure that still lingered.

"Can I help you?" she asked after a moment.

"I'm here to see Dr. Chapman," Gideon replied.

"And who can I tell him is asking?"

"My name is Father Gideon. He's expecting me."

The woman looked him over before hanging up her phone. "Dr. Chapman will be out shortly. You can have a seat in the waiting room."

"Thank you," Gideon replied, settling into a chair.

Tarek leaned in close and lowered his voice. "I'm telling you, Gideon, that bitch is completely insane. Whatever's going on here, we need to be careful around her."

Gideon's gaze never left the door. "The woman is no concern. She was lost the moment Jezebeth took hold of her. It's her daughter that's the key."

"I don't understand."

"Neither do I at the moment, But we will, soon enough. We just need to be ready to act when the time comes."

A few minutes later, Dr. Chapman entered the room. He looked like he hadn't slept in days, his face drawn and haggard. Gideon didn't know the man personally, but judging by his appearance, it was clear what kind of torment he'd been under. He almost felt sorry for him—if he were the type to care.

"Father Gideon?" Dr. Chapman's voice cracked with desperation.

Gideon stood and shook the man's hand. "Yes," he said coolly. "This is my assistant, Tarek."

Tarek extended his hand, which the doctor took quickly. "Nice to meet you both. I'm so glad you're here. I need your help immediately."

"From our conversation on the phone and your current condition, I take it things have gotten worse?" Gideon asked flatly.

Dr. Chapman nodded, the panic in his eyes barely contained. "Yes, but we should talk somewhere more private. You need to understand the full scope of this situation."

He led them down a long hallway, constantly looking over his shoulder as if something might leap from the shadows at any moment. After a series of turns, they reached his office. He glanced nervously toward the bathroom door across the hall before opening the door to his office and ushering them inside.

"Please, have a seat," he said, his voice trembling slightly.

Gideon and Tarek sat across from the doctor, watching as he fidgeted in his chair, unable to settle. After a few long moments, Gideon leaned forward, cutting through the man's discomfort. "From what you told me on the phone, you believe you have a patient possessed by a demon?"

Dr. Chapman didn't hesitate. "I don't just believe it—I know it. She's pure evil."

"Tell me everything that happened," Gideon pressed, though he already knew what the answer would be.

The doctor took a deep breath before beginning. "She arrived two nights ago, outside the emergency room, acting either high or in the middle of a psychotic break. Two EMTs found her in the parking lot, and they immediately knew something was wrong. As they tried to get her inside, she bit one of them in the ear and ripped it clean off."

He paused, clearly unsettled by the memory. "We got her into one of the back rooms. When I checked on her, I knew something was terribly wrong. I didn't know just how wrong." He shuddered before continuing. "She started speaking in a language I didn't recognize—low, chilling, almost... ancient. It terrified me. I gave her a sedative and had the orderlies move her to a special wing in the basement. I didn't know then that would be the last time I'd see them alive."

Gideon raised an eyebrow. "You have a special wing in the basement?"

The doctor seemed uncomfortable, clearly unsure of how much to reveal. "It's just an extension of our psychiatric department. A temporary holding area for dangerous patients until we determine the next course of action."

"I see. And how many patients are in the basement?" Gideon asked, though he had a pretty good idea.

"She's the only one. Helena Thompson. But I'm telling you—this isn't just a psychotic episode. This woman is the devil incarnate."

"We'll decide who or what she is after we hear the rest of the story," Gideon said, though he was already certain of what she was.

Dr. Chapman nodded. "I took a break and went to my office for a nap. When I woke up, I found out from the head nurse that no one had heard from the two orderlies for a while. I went downstairs to check on her myself. That's when I saw the horror and realized what she was."

"What did you see?" Gideon asked somewhat eagerly.

The doctor inhaled sharply. "It wasn't just what I saw—it was the smell. The unmistakable stench of death and decay. It was like it was alive, choking me as it filled the air. Then I saw the insects—flies, covering everything. It was like a scene from Amityville. They were everywhere. Then, just as quickly, they were gone."

He shuddered again. "Looking back, I wish I'd walked away. I wish I'd never opened that door. Now, the image of what I saw haunts me every second."

Before Gideon could respond, Dr. Chapman broke into a violent coughing fit. He bent down, grabbing a trash can, and as he coughed, blood and mucus splattered into the can. The fit lasted for several long moments, and when he looked up again, his eyes were blank—his face a mask of horror. Blood poured from his eyes, nose, and ears. He slumped forward in his chair, dead.

Tarek jumped back, eyes wide. "Holy shit! What the fuck just happened?"

Gideon glanced at the doctor's lifeless body. "I assume Jezebeth happened. He must've gotten too close to her at some point, and she poisoned him."

Tarek swallowed hard. "So what's to stop her from doing the same thing to us?"

"Don't worry. That's not Azazel's plan. She'll behave around us."

"I hope you're right," Tarek muttered.

Gideon stood, shoving the dead doctor back into his chair to snatch the key card from around his neck. They left the office and headed down the hall toward the elevator.

It took a few minutes of wandering the basement before they found the right room. As they approached, Gideon could feel the demon's presence—heavy, oppressive, like a weight pressing against his chest.

"Just stay on guard," he warned, his voice low.

Tarek frowned. "But you said she'd behave herself around us."

"She will. But she's still a demon. And demons are always

unpredictable."

"That makes me feel so much better," Tarek muttered.

Gideon slid the key card through the reader, and the door buzzed open. He stepped inside, surprised to see Jezebeth sitting calmly on the bed, her feet dangling like she was relaxing on a porch swing. In her arms, she cradled the severed head of one of the orderlies.

She grinned as soon as she saw him. "I knew you'd come back for me! Oh, and you brought your little boy toy. I've been dying for a three-way!"

Gideon's expression hardened. "Shut up, wench. I'm not in the mood for your games. We're getting you out of here."

"Oh? Where are we going?" she purred, her smile widening.

"We're taking you home."

Jezebeth's grin never faltered. "And then a three-way?"

After a long, lingering farewell, Solomon and Hecate headed back to the Aéroport Nice Côte d'Azur. She felt a pang of regret at leaving Jacques behind—he was one of those rare, genuinely good people who would do anything to help. She hoped she'd have the chance to see him again someday.

Her mind drifted back to Landis. She tried calling him a few times, but each attempt went straight to voice-mail. Frustrated, she sent a quick text asking if everything was okay, then tucked her phone away. Despite what he'd told her, a small, nagging doubt gnawed at her. Had she been too forward? Too aggressive? Had she scared him off?

Relief washed over her when, a few minutes later, Landis replied with an apologetic text. His phone had died. The weight in her chest lightened, but only slightly. She knew her insecurities had deep roots from past relationships, but she hoped that Landis would be the one to help her overcome them.

Once they'd returned the rental car, they made their way through the bustling airport concourse toward their gate. In her mind, Hecate replayed the details of Sophie's exorcism over and over. She was determined not to make the same mistakes again. As her fingers brushed her neck, she could still feel the phantom pressure of the grip that had once strangled her, that unearthly force stronger than any girl her size should have been able to wield.

Boarding was quick, and they had barely settled in when a shiver ran down her spine. As they went to hand over their tickets, she felt a distinct pressure on her arm. Turning, she found nothing but air. Dismissing it as one of those odd sensations she'd grown accustomed to—another lost soul reaching out—she continued without a second thought.

But then, as they walked down the ramp and entered the plane, the whisper came. Soft, barely audible, but unmistakable: *"Hecate."*

She froze. Her heart skipped a beat, and she scanned the crowd, her pulse quickening. But just as suddenly as it came, the sound was swallowed by the noise around her, replaced by a child laughing and darting through the line. Hecate's eyes followed the girl as she disappeared into the crowd, still uneasy but unwilling to acknowledge the dread gnawing at her.

They reached their seats, and Hecate stowed her carry-on overhead before sinking back into her seat. She sighed. "I'm going to try to sleep for a bit, if that's okay with you?" she asked, her voice thick with fatigue. "I didn't get much rest last night."

Solomon nodded, offering a sympathetic smile. "Go ahead. Yesterday was rough on all of us."

"Yeah, sorry about that," she murmured, guilt creeping back.

"What do you have to be sorry for?" he replied. "You've got nothing to apologize for."

Hecate gave a wry smile and shrugged. "I guess it's just a habit."

Solomon chuckled. "Well, you can break that one any time."

She reached for his hand, giving it a gentle squeeze. "Thanks for everything. You've been a great teacher... and an even better friend."

Solomon raised an eyebrow, his grin widening. "Are you trying to make me blush?"

She opened one eye to shoot him a teasing look. "Alright, enough chit-chat. I'm going to sleep now."

Then darkness hit Hecate fast, and within seconds, she was fast asleep.

****

The darkness ebbed, slowly giving way to the soft glow of dawn. Hecate found herself standing on a vast, sandy beach, the air cool and crisp against her skin as she gazed out over the restless sea. The sky was painted in shades of pink and orange, the sun rising behind thick clouds and casting its radiant hues onto the black, rolling waves. The rhythm of the ocean's gentle lapping against the shore felt soothing, almost hypnotic.

Her eyes narrowed as a figure began to emerge from the water, moving with deliberate grace toward her. The man's long, golden hair swirled in the breeze, his body strong and confident as he approached. But it was his eyes—green like the deepest forest—that held her, locking her in place as though they were a force in themselves.

She tried to move, but her body betrayed her, rooted to the spot. A strange sense of peace settled over her, as though this was meant to happen. His presence enveloped her, and before she could process what was happening, he lifted her effortlessly into his arms. She responded instinctively, wrapping her legs around his waist, her hands finding the warmth of his skin.

He lowered her onto the sand, the world around them melting away until only they existed. As the sun rose higher, they became lost in each other, the warmth of their bodies and the sensation of being together like nothing she had ever known. Moans of pleasure escaped her lips, mingling with the soft crash of waves and the rising wind. It was a sensation unlike any she could describe, a union of body and spirit beneath the glowing sky.

The tide swelled, creeping higher as the water slowly overtook them. For a brief second, Hecate felt the panic of drowning enter her brain, until she realized that she was dreaming, and in dreams reality could be altered. She quickly quieted her mind and immersed herself in the dream.

But then, as quickly as it had come, the water began to recede, dragging her lover with it. She gasped, calling out before he disappeared into the retreating waves. "Wait, I don't know your name!"

The man turned and whispered one word as he vanished into the water's depths, "Azazel."

***

Hecate stirred from her dream, her eyes flicking open as she absently wiped the drool that hung from the corner of her mouth, her hand moving instinctively to brush it away. The motion brought her gaze to Solomon, who was watching her with wide, almost startled eyes.

"Well, that must've been some dream," he said with a teasing smirk.

Hecate shrank back into her seat, her cheeks flush with embarrassment.

"Don't worry," Solomon reassured her. "I put a shield around us, so no one else noticed."

She offered him a sheepish grin, and was just about to speak when the plane suddenly jolted, followed by the seatbelt signs flickering on. The plane then buckled violently in the air. Hecate's hands gripped the armrests hard, her knuckles turning white as the aircraft was tossed about like a toy in a storm. The pilot's voice crackled over the loudspeaker with the obligatory "turbulence" warning, but it did little to calm the terror building inside Hecate's chest.

The turbulence dragged on relentlessly, and even Solomon grew concerned. The memory of the last team's tragic crash lingered in the back of his mind, like an uninvited shadow, and he began to wonder if there was more to the storm than mere chance.

Minutes felt like hours before the plane finally steadied, finally allowing Hecate to breathe again, though she refused to release her grip on the armrests. Solomon kept his relief hidden from her. He knew all too well how far the fingers of darkness could reach, and for a moment, thought they'd fallen victim to that darkness.

The rest of the flight was ridden in relative silence, as all the passengers were shaken from the experience. When they landed an hour later, people shuffled somberly through the exit and into the concourse, each one measuring their near-death experience intimately.

When they reached a quieter section of the airport, Hecate found an empty seat and sank into it with a long sigh. "I just need a minute to calm down," she muttered.

Solomon nodded. "Take all the time you need," he said gently. "But I need to warn you—we're not waiting until morning for this one."

Hecate's head snapped up. "What do you mean?"

"As soon as you're ready, we're going in," he said, his tone grave. "We need to perform the exorcism now."

Her eyes widened in disbelief. "You're joking, right?"

He shook his head solemnly. "Afraid not. This one's more dire than Sophie's case. Especially after what happened to the last team. Time is of the essence here."

"Why?" she asked, the chill of worry creeping up her spine.

"The victim is a young man with a violent history. Under the demon's influence, there's no telling what he's capable of."

"Great," Hecate muttered, her stomach sinking.

Solomon chuckled softly, trying to lighten the mood. "Don't worry. We've got plenty of help."

She didn't share his confidence, but had learned that trusting Solomon was often the safest choice. She stood up, steeling herself for what came next. "Let's do this, then."

They made their way to Terminal 1, where a young man in a black jacket waited for them. He was tall, with a wiry frame and a youthful, boyish smile that softened his sharp features.

"Solomon!" he said, shaking his hand with enthusiasm.

"Good to see you, Dante," Solomon replied. "How's your father?"

"Good, good," Dante replied. "Some days are better than others. The arthritis is rough on him when it's cold, and his sight's not what it used to be, but he still cracks a joke now and then."

Solomon nodded warmly. "That's good to hear. I'll be sure to tell him you asked after him."

Dante turned to Hecate. "And you must be the famous Hecate we've been hearing about?"

Hecate blinked in surprise. "What do you mean?"

"Well, it's not every day Solomon takes on an apprentice,"

Dante explained with a grin. "When he does, it becomes big news. And big news travels fast."

Hecate blushed. "I—I don't know what to say."

Solomon chuckled, slinging an arm around her shoulders and mock-scolding Dante. "Now, Dante, leave the poor girl alone. It's been a long few days."

Dante raised his hands in surrender, a sheepish smile on his face. "My bad. I didn't mean to be forward."

"No big deal," Hecate replied, her voice quiet but amused.

Dante led them across the parking lot to a sleek black sedan, opening the door for Hecate before sliding into the driver's seat himself. As he started the engine, Hecate was taken aback to see another man already seated in the front passenger seat. He was shorter than Dante, but stockier, with a heavy, somber expression that contrasted sharply with Dante's upbeat demeanor.

"Hello, Brett," Solomon greeted the man.

Brett gave a nod of acknowledgment before returning his focus to the road, his silence thick in the air.

Solomon leaned toward Hecate, whispering, "He's a good man—strong as an ox, but not much for talking."

Hecate gave a small nod, her curiosity piqued.

A few minutes later, Dante turned the car onto Faggs Road, and Hecate asked nervously, "How far is it?"

"Not far," Dante answered. "We've got the subject cornered in a warehouse on Central Way. About five minutes from here."

Hecate's eyes widened. "Five minutes? That doesn't leave us much time to prepare."

"Don't worry, Hecate," Solomon said calmly. "If I know Dante, he's got everything under control. Right, Dante?"

Dante glanced in the rear-view mirror and gave her a wink. "Yeah, we're good. Besides me and Brett, we've got two more guys and a couple local cops inside, plus some extra hands guarding the entrances."

Hecate had expected a broken, run-down building and was a little surprised when they parked in front of a relatively new structure. As they got out of the car, one of the officers guarding the entrance walked toward them. He was an older man in his forties, tall and wiry. "It's about time you got here, Sam," he said. "I'm getting too old for this shit.

Solomon smiled. "Good to see you too, Leo."

Hecate raised an eyebrow as she followed them toward the building. "Is there anyone you don't know?"

Solomon just shrugged, his gaze focused ahead. "Where's the subject?" he asked Leo.

"East side of the building," Leo said, his voice low. "He broke in through a window in the back. We've been hunting him for days."

"What happened?" Solomon asked, already preparing for the worst.

"One of our guys got hurt. The bastard bit his finger off during an altercation."

A chill ran down Hecate's spine at the grisly thought.

Leo led them carefully through the building with Rueben, the other officer who had been stationed at the entrance, following closely behind. They had only gone a short distance when a loud crash echoed through the hallway, followed by the sight of a black cat darting past them, something clutched tightly in its mouth.

Leo stopped at the overturned trash can and saw the body of fellow officer O'Conner, lying cold and lifeless with a hole in his chest. Beside him lay another officer, Patrick, his throat slashed and eyes missing.

A tortured scream sounded from behind the door at the end of the hall. Brett took the lead and skirted over the dead men toward the door, with the rest of the group right behind. Hecate averted her eyes the best she could, but couldn't block out all the carnage. Her stomach buckled in protest to the images.

Brett pulled a gun from his waist and nodded at Leo, who yanked the door open as Brett stood to the side for a second before springing to the doorway.

He stood there motionless as he looked around the room. Blood splattered the walls and ceiling in all directions. One of the men who had been sent to guard the possessed man was Thomas, who was lying in one corner of the room with his arms and legs bent and broken in unnatural angles. Blood poured from numerous wounds across his body like he had been thrown around and beaten by an angry gorilla. On the other side of the room was the body of Amos, the brother of Thomas. Next to his body was his dismembered head, the mouth still open in its dying scream.

In the middle of the room, tied to a chair behind the desk, was a broken young man, his body clearly suffering from numerous unidentifiable wounds, but his eyes held firm by a force of evil. He smiled a devious smile and suddenly, the gun in Brett's hand started to turn. He could no longer control his muscles as he brought the weapon around to aim at his own head. Sweat and tears streamed down his face as he desperately struggled to regain control.

Solomon sprang into the room and pointed his ring at the man. A beam of energy shot out, hitting him in the chest. Brett's hold on his gun returned to normal, and he quickly dropped it from his hands.

Solomon shouted, "Hecate! I need you in here!"

Hecate rushed in and stopped immediately when she saw the scene before her. Her knees started to buckle.

The demon inside the possessed man chuckled, "How

sweet, fresh meat!"

"Shut up, demon!" Solomon said as he held the man pinned down in the chair.

The demon ignored Solomon and addressed Hecate instead, "How about you come here, Sweet Cheeks, and I'll show you what a real man is like?"

Something inside of Hecate snapped. Instantly, the images of all the men that had tried to subjugate her in the past came flooding forward. From the class jocks in High School, to the man outside the liquor store, their faces stirred a fire inside her.

Something inside of Hecate snapped, a boiling fury rising to the surface. She faced the demon, her voice trembling with rage. "Listen, you fucking bastard, you're going back to Hell whether you like it or not!"

A sudden, intense inspiration struck her, and she closed her eyes for a moment, tuning herself to something far beyond the tangible. When she opened them again, the room transformed. She saw the demon for what he truly was: a tortured, twisted black soul—its essence writhing in agony. And around him, spectral figures gathered, the victims of his cruelty, bound by their torment. She didn't need to speak; they already knew what she wanted them to do.

With fierce clarity, Hecate began the exorcism. The words, steady and commanding, flowed from her lips. As she spoke, the spirits converged on the man's body, one after another, merging into him. The temperature in the room grew colder, the air heavier, as they took their place inside him. When the final spirit dissolved into the man, she spoke again, her voice now an unshakable force.

When she was done, a violent spasm tore through the man, and a dark vapor expelled itself from his mouth. His head drooped forward, and for a moment, Solomon feared they had failed—that the battle had cost the man his life. He rushed forward and felt for signs of life. Then he pressed his hand on the man's chest and closed his eyes. For a moment, nothing happened. Then, with a slow, shaky breath, the man's chest rose.

As soon as Leo saw that the situation was under control, he radioed for assistance. Within a few minutes, a crew of forensic scientists, paramedics, and emergency crew had converged on the scene.

"I'm sorry about your men, Leo," Solomon said somberly.

Leo bowed his head, grief settling in the lines of his face. "Yeah, me too."

He looked at Hecate, who was sitting on the curb to the side as paramedics attended to her. "That's some woman you've got there."

Solomon looked over at her, a hint of pride mixed with worry in his eyes.

"I'd keep a close eye on her if I were you," Leo said. "Wouldn't want her getting tangled up with the wrong people... if you catch my drift."

Solomon grew quiet. For the first time, he felt a flicker of fear—not of Hecate, but of what her power could attract. The dangers it might bring.

Hecate had a distant look in her eyes as a paramedic finished tending to her.

Solomon nodded at Leo and walked over toward Hecate. "How are you holding up?" he asked softly.

She shrugged, her voice quiet, "Okay, I guess."

"We couldn't have done it without you," Solomon said as he sat down on the curb beside her.

Her eyes lowered. "People still died."

"That wasn't your fault," he reassured her.

For a brief second, brief images of the carnage assaulted

her, before she quietly cast them away. "I know... I just keep thinking about it. How horrible it all was."

"It was," he agreed sadly.

She tilted her head and looked at his hand, changing the subject. "I didn't know your ring could do that."

"And I didn't know you could call spirits like that."

A faint smile curved her lips. "It just kind of... came to me."

Solomon placed an arm around her shoulders, squeezing gently. "I guess we both learned something about each other today."

Hecate smiled. "Something tells me you've got more secrets than me."

Solomon chuckled softly. "Come on. Let's go home."

Hecate's face brightened. "Really?"

"Yeah. You've earned it."

Hecate threw her phone onto the chair beside her, the frustration radiating off her in waves. She'd tried reaching Landis again—countless times—but each call went straight to voice-mail.

"Everything okay?" Solomon asked.

"Yeah, no... I don't know?" she muttered, running a nervous hand through her hair. "I can't get ahold of Landis. I'm starting to worry."

"I'm sure he's fine," Solomon replied softly. "He's dealing with a lot right now, probably just busy getting things sorted. He'll get back to you when he can."

"I hope you're right," she replied.

The loudspeaker crackled to life, announcing that boarding for their flight would begin soon. It was a sound she'd grown all too familiar with over the past few days. After everything, she vowed to herself that once they got home, she'd take a long break from flying—if Solomon would let her.

"Thank god," she muttered, half to herself. "I can't wait to get home."

Solomon's voice held a hint of excitement. "Me neither. In fact... I was thinking maybe we both need a little vacation after all this."

Hecate's eyes widened. "Really? Wait... were you just reading my mind?"

He chuckled. "Not at all. But it's been a hell of a week for you, and you've definitely earned some rest."

Her arms wrapped around him tightly. "I can't wait to tell Landis. Maybe we can finally have a little time to ourselves?"

"I'm sure he'd love that."

Minutes later, they were boarding the plane. The good news: Solomon had managed to secure a direct, non-stop flight to South Bend. The bad news: it would take sixteen hours.

As the plane lifted off, Hecate leaned back in her seat, the hum of the engines lulling her into a sleepy daze. She promised herself she wouldn't let any disturbing dreams creep in this time. But as always, the universe had other plans.

***

Hecate found herself on the edge of a balcony looking out over a dark and broken landscape. She recognized immediately where she was, only everything was different, dead even. She was back home, atop the Hesburg Library, on the deck of the Fourteenth Floor, a place that existed separate from reality.

The campus below her, once rich and proud, had crumbled to ruins. She looked around and saw that the rest of the world had fallen prey to the same catastrophe. A heavy blanket of sadness settled over her, cold and suffocating.

She heard soft footsteps behind her and turned around to find her dream lover approaching. Without a word, he cupped her face in his hands, his lips claiming hers in a kiss that made her forget everything. Her body melted against him, lost in the heat of his touch.

After a long moment, he pulled away.

It took a moment for her to find her voice. Then the sadness returned, and she looked at him. "What happened here?"

He responded, "The inevitable. Man is always destined to destroy what he creates. It's in his nature."

"So, everyone's dead?"

"Not everyone, but most."

"Solomon? Landis?"

For a brief, chilling moment, his eyes flickered red before returning to their usual depth. "Yes," he answered, the word hanging between them like a stone.

She looked down sadly, "What now?"

He took her hand in his and lifted her chin with his other, "Just because everything is dead now, it doesn't mean it can't be rebuilt."

The first rays of the sun peeked over the horizon, casting a golden light that touched everything in its path. The light seemed to carry with it a quiet promise, a flicker of hope in the broken world around her. "With you as my queen, we can remake this world into the glory that it's supposed to be."

Hecate looked at him in shock, "Queen?"

"Yes, my love, my chosen one. All you have to do is say the word, and you shall be exalted to my side, and we will rule the world together."

She blinked, caught in a mixture of disbelief and fear. "But why me?"

He laughed at her, "Because you are perfect in every way, sweet Hecate. You just don't see it. You don't believe in yourself like I do. But you will. You have power inside you — power that you've only begun to tap into. What more could a man ask for?"

He brought her close to him, so that he engulfed her. As he held her tight, her eyes grew tired, and she closed them, drifting back into the darkness. She heard his name, "Azazel", whispered along the wind as she succumbed to unconsciousness.

***

When Hecate stirred awake, a jolt of disorientation hit her. She blinked, her mind slow to catch up with reality, and found that they were already halfway through their flight. It felt as though she had only just closed her eyes moments ago, lost in some fleeting dream.

Her gaze drifted to Solomon beside her, and she was struck by the sight of him, peacefully asleep. It was the first time she'd seen him like this—his normally sharp features softened. She had caught him napping a few times, even snoring once, and often found him meditating, but he had always given her the impression that sleep was unnecessary for him. That he had transcended it somehow, evolved beyond the need for rest.

Her unease deepened as she looked around the cabin. Every other passenger was asleep as well, their heads tilted back, their bodies slumped in the uncomfortably still air. Then she noticed the black tendrils of smoke rising from each person's head, curling in the air like dark serpents. They coalesced above them, twisting together into a mass of writhing shadows that clung to the ceiling.

A violent tremor passed through the darkness, and Hecate's heart seized in her chest as another tendril shot toward her. It wrapped around her arm like a vise, its touch searing her skin with a blistering heat. Her breath caught in her throat, and she screamed, her voice cutting through the thick silence of the plane.

As her voice echoed through the plane, each passenger stood from their seat and looked at her through glowing white eyes, Solomon included. They pointed their fingers at her and opened their mouths in a ghoulish cry reminiscent of a scene from Invasion of the Body Snatchers, only Hecate had nowhere to run. Seconds later, they converged on her, a grotesque tide of twisted souls intent on pulling her under.

****

Hecate jolted awake, her body trembling with the remnants of a nightmare. Her heart raced as she wiped her face and arms frantically, as if trying to escape from the grasp of something unseen. Solomon, undisturbed by her movements, continued to snore softly beside her.

It wasn't long before a rush of déjà vu hit her like a heavy wave, dragging her back into the vivid memory of her dream. Not just the one she had just woken from—the other one, the one before that. The one where the world had crumbled, lifeless, into ruins.

She turned to her side, irritated to find an old woman staring at her with an expression of distant horror, as though Hecate carried some unseen plague. With a huff of annoyance, Hecate flipped her off, and the woman, unamused, returned her attention to the pages of SkyMall, pretending to find the bizarre, useless merchandise somehow interesting.

Solomon finally stirred, his face contorting in mild confusion as he shifted toward her. "Wow, I must've been exhausted," he murmured. "I rarely sleep like that."

Hecate turned to him with a concerned expression on her

face. "Where have I heard the name Azazel before?"

The words hung in the air for a long moment, and Solomon's brow furrowed. There was a flicker of concern in his eyes. "Where did you hear that name?"

"I saw him in my dreams," Hecate replied. "I've seen him a couple of times."

Solomon's silence stretched on, causing Hecate to shift uncomfortably in her seat. "Why? What's wrong?" she pressed.

His eyes darkened, his lips drawing into a thin line. "You've heard that name before... because Azazel is one of the kings of Hell."

Hecate froze. "Why is a king of Hell visiting me in my dreams?"

The tension in Solomon's face deepened, his jaw tightening as he leaned forward. "I don't know. It shouldn't be possible. He's been imprisoned for two thousand years. He shouldn't have the power to do that."

"What do you mean?" she asked, a chill crawling up her spine.

"A long time ago, a rift opened between our world and Hell," he began, his voice low and distant, like the words had been buried for a long time. "Before I could seal it, seventy-two demons slithered through, wreaking havoc. Azazel was chief among them. Over time, I tracked each one down, bound them into vessels. I was planning to return them to the pit... safely. But Azazel..." His voice faltered.

Hecate absorbed his words in silence for a moment. "He wants out," she said, her voice barely a whisper. "And for some reason, he wants me."

Solomon's arm slipped around her, pulling her close. "Don't worry about him," he said, his voice steady. "There's no way he can escape. The vessel he's trapped in is protected and hidden where no one can find it."

But as Hecate closed her eyes, Azazel's image returned to her. His mesmerizing green eyes. His crooked smile. The strength of his embrace. His name echoed in her mind, louder now, almost as if it was inside her.

She looked up at Solomon, her eyes laced with fear. "Are you sure?"

"Yes, I'm sure," Solomon replied, but she could see the flicker of doubt in his eyes.

The rest of the flight passed in a heavy silence. Neither of them spoke, each lost in their own thoughts. When the plane finally touched down, the announcement came that electronic devices could be turned on, and Hecate immediately checked her phone for any word from Landis.

Nothing.

She felt Solomon's gaze on her, the words he was about to speak hanging in the air, but her hard stare silenced him. She knew what he was going to say. It wasn't what she needed to hear right now.

"I know what you're going to say," she muttered. "But right now, I just want to go home. I want to lie down in my own bed."

Solomon nodded. "Sounds like a good idea."

The taxi ride back to campus was uneventful. They were both exhausted, their minds heavy with unspoken fears, as they exited the cab in front of the library. A shiver ran down Hecate's spine as she looked up at the familiar building, her thoughts drifting back to the dreamscape she couldn't escape.

The campus was nearly deserted at this late hour. They walked around the building to the side entrance, slipping into the secret elevator that would take them to the basement.

On their way, they passed a few students, all grinning like the world was fine. It irritated her. *What the hell are they so happy about?* she thought bitterly.

She dragged her luggage down the hall to her room, each step feeling heavier than the last. If her suitcase hadn't had wheels, she might've just left it behind. It felt like an anchor. Finally, she reached her door and swung it open, but what she saw inside made everything else disappear.

Landis stood there, waiting for her. Before she could even process it, she dropped her suitcase and rushed into his arms, her legs locking around him as he held her tightly.

After a moment, she pulled back, her face contorted in a mix of relief and frustration. "You shithead!" she exclaimed, punching him lightly in the arm. "Why didn't you call me?"

Landis pulled his phone out of his pocket and showed it to her with a sheepish grin. The screen was shattered. "I kind of had a little accident... and I haven't had a chance to replace it."

Hecate stared at him for a second, stunned. Then she laughed. "How in the hell did you do that?"

"Remember the surprise I told you about?" He winked, and Hecate blinked, her memory struggling to catch up.

"I was bending down to pick it up, and I tripped," he admitted with a grin. "Landed right on my phone."

Hecate chuckled, shaking her head. "Okay, now you have to spill it. What's this big surprise that ended up costing you a new phone?"

Before Landis could answer, a soft meow interrupted her. She turned, startled to see a black cat sitting by the door, staring at her with large yellow eyes.

"Hecate, this is Abaddon," Landis said with a wide smile.

Hecate kneeled down, her eyes wide with disbelief, and as her fingers brushed against the feline's fur, it purred loudly, rubbing its head against her hand.

"She likes you," Landis said with a soft laugh.

Tears welled in Hecate's eyes as she scooped Abaddon into her arms, holding the cat close.

"She's perfect," Hecate whispered as she nestled her nose across Abaddon's soft fur.

Jezebeth sauntered through the front door, her arms flung wide as though she owned the place. "Honey, I'm home!" she called out. "Oh, wait. My mistake. I forgot. He can't answer you, Little Mouse. But don't worry, I'll be sure to send him your regards in Hell when I see him," she added with a grin that could curdle blood.

Her laughter filled the room, a cackle so dark and malicious that it echoed off the walls.

"Nice to see you amuse yourself so much, demon," Gideon remarked flatly.

Jezebeth spun on her heel, her eyes narrowing into slits as she scowled at him. "Oh, come on, lighten up," she sneered. "Let's have some fun before the real party starts. You know what you need? To get laid. A little piece of ass might loosen that stick up your ass."

With a confident swagger, she approached him, her fingers brushing against his chest before sliding lower. "I'm game if you are," she purred, her lips curling into a smile that was pure poison.

Then, turning her attention to Tarek, her grin grew even more wicked. "Better yet, why don't I play with your little boy-toy here for a while? I bet I could make him squeal like a little girl."

Gideon's patience was stretching thin, but he held it together, knowing the risk of losing his cool in front of her. She was a volatile force—one of the most feared demons in Hell. You never knew what she might do next.

He changed the subject quickly. "Who's the 'Little Mouse' you were referring to?"

Every time Jezebeth smiled, it was like the mask of a madwoman slipping into place. That same deranged grin twisted her face now, sending a chill through Gideon. "Oh, Little Mouse?" she mused, her voice dripping with venom. "That would be Helena Thompson, of course. You remember her, don't you? She was strong at first, but that didn't last long. After I raped and beat her in ways you can't even begin to imagine—repeatedly, inside her own mind—she broke. Now, all that's left is a whimper. A little speck of what used to be. Now, she's just a little mouse'."

She glided over to Tarek, her eyes glinting with something dark, something hungry. "Here, let's give you a little demonstration," she said, placing his trembling hands gently on the sides of her head. Her eyes locked onto his, a sickly sweetness dripping from her words. "Listen closely."

Tarek hesitated, his heart hammering in his chest, but he obeyed, closing his eyes and pressing his palms to her skull. At first, there was nothing but an eerie silence, but then, slowly, a sound filtered into his mind—scratching, distant, agonized wails that seemed to crawl from the depths of a nightmare. Faintly, a voice whimpered, "Please... help me."

It was a voice stripped of hope, a sound so broken and pleading that it made Tarek's stomach churn. The words felt hollow, like a final cry from the very edge of despair, knowing there was no one left to save her. When he pulled his hands away, his body trembled with the weight of what he'd heard, but no words came.

Jezebeth watched him with a satisfied glint in her eye. "See? I told you," she said, her tone smug. "Nothing left but a little mouse."

Gideon cleared his throat. "Just make sure you do your part when the time comes."

Jezebeth's lips twisted into a cruel smile. "Oh, don't worry about me, Sweet Cheeks," she purred. "You just be ready to pick up the pieces when it's done. And believe me," she leaned in closer, her breath cold against his ear, "it's going to get messy."

***

Hecate slowly stirred from her sleep, her body stiff and disoriented. She blinked her eyes open, noticing Abaddon curled up beside her, purring softly. But Landis was gone. The bed beside her was cold and empty. The clock on the wall read a little past six.

Still in her pajamas, Hecate shuffled down the hallway, cradling the black cat in her arms. As she neared the main room, she heard the sound of whispering. She couldn't make out the words, but the voices were unmistakable. Solomon's low, steady tone, followed by the sharp edge of Landis's voice, both speaking urgently, about something that clearly didn't concern her.

A crisp voice slithered into her mind. *They're keeping secrets from you.*

Hecate froze in her tracks. She glanced down at Abaddon, her heart pounding. "Was that you?" she whispered.

Abaddon blinked up at her, her green eyes glowing softly in the dim light. A soft meow escaped her. *It's our secret.*

Don't worry, I'll keep you safe.

Hecate shook her head in disbelief. It seemed every day brought a new twist, a fresh layer of madness, and today was no different. The feeling of being out of control clawed at her. But she couldn't ignore the gnawing sensation that something was wrong.

With slow, deliberate steps, she crept closer to the main room, straining to hear more.

"I don't like it," Landis said, his voice low but filled with tension. "You know how she's going to react."

Solomon's response was calm but heavy with something unspoken. "I know, but this is different. If everything goes according to plan, she'll never know."

That was enough. Hecate's patience snapped. Without thinking, she stormed into the room, her voice sharp and cutting through the silence. "What the fuck is going on here? I thought we agreed—no more secrets!"

Landis's eyes shot wide open in panic. "Oh, shit," he muttered under his breath.

Solomon was quick to react, but there was no hiding the tension in his voice. "Listen, Hecate, it's not what you think."

Hecate's eyes narrowed, fire and fury swirling within them. "Then tell me what it is."

Landis hesitated. His voice cracked when he spoke, "It's about your mother."

The words hit Hecate like a punch to the gut. Her stomach lurched, and her heart thudded painfully in her chest. "What about my mother?" Her voice trembled as she tried to hold back the storm brewing within her.

Solomon stepped forward, reaching for her arm, but she yanked it away, her gaze burning with a fury he hadn't expected. "I think it would be better if we talked in private," he said tensely.

"Why? So you can hide more from me? So you can keep playing your fucking games, Solomon?" Her voice rose, frustration twisting with betrayal. She turned to Landis. "And you're in on this too?"

Landis's eyes softened, pleading with her, but there was nothing in his expression that could erase the hurt. "That's not true, Hecate," he said softly, glancing at Solomon. The older man gave a subtle nod. "Why don't we go back to your room? We'll tell you everything."

The silence that followed was suffocating. Hecate's breath quickened, her mind racing, and the tension hung in the air like a storm cloud on the verge of breaking.

After a lingering silence, Hecate finally relented, her footsteps echoing down the corridor as she turned away. Solomon and Landis trailed in her wake, burdened with the impending confrontation that promised nothing but pain and heartache.

CHAPTER 22

Solomon stepped out of the car, his boots clicking against the pavement as he made his way toward the front steps. Hecate sat frozen in the passenger seat, her heart pounding in her chest. The weight of what they were about to face settled like a stone in her stomach. After a long moment, she gathered herself, slamming the car door behind her as she rushed up the steps to catch up with him.

She grabbed his arm just as he reached for the door. Her voice trembled as she spoke, "Are you sure about this?"

Solomon turned to face her, his expression unreadable, the gravity in his eyes cutting through her like a knife. "I told you," he said, his voice quiet but firm, "we should've let someone else take this case."

Tears welled up in Hecate's eyes, her voice choking on her words, "But... that's my mother in there. There's no way she's possessed. She can't be. She's been a God-fearing woman her whole life. There has to be some kind of mistake. Please, tell me it's all just a big mistake?"

Solomon's gaze softened. "It's no mistake, Hecate. The Church has been watching her for a while now. They've confirmed it. She's... changed."

Her mind raced, her thoughts swirling with confusion and guilt. She couldn't make sense of it. How could this happen? Was there something she missed? Had she not been there enough? Had she not been the daughter she should have been? If only she had shown more compassion, been more present, maybe—just maybe—she could have stopped this.

But deep down, she knew. She couldn't have stopped it. There was nothing she could have done.

Hecate wiped the tears from her eyes, swallowing hard as she steadied her breath. "Okay," she finally said. "Let's get started. But... please, Solomon. Promise me you'll do everything you can. Promise me that nothing will happen to her."

Solomon paused, looking at her for a moment longer, his gaze full of an emotion she couldn't quite read. Then, with a quiet sigh, he gave a slow nod. "I promise." His voice was steady, but inside, his mind churned with a thousand unspoken fears. He had no idea if he could keep that promise, but he'd be damned if he didn't try with every ounce of himself.

***

A soft, breathless squeal slipped from Jezebeth's lips. "They're here! Time to get this party started!" Her eyes gleamed with a wicked, hungry excitement as she squirmed against the restraints.

Gideon moved around the room with practiced precision, tying her arms and legs to the bedposts. His movements were efficient, but his eyes never wavered from her, the weight of his words cold and calculating. "Just make sure you do your part, demon."

Jezebeth tilted her head, her smile a venomous curve of

pleasure. "Oh, don't worry about me, Gideon. Everything will go exactly as planned, as long as you leave your little boy-toy here to keep me company." She let her gaze drift toward Tarek, a flicker of amusement lighting up her dark eyes.

Tarek shifted uncomfortably, his nerves stretched thin as the air between him and Jezebeth crackled with the promise of violence. He wasn't thrilled about staying in the same room as her, but he knew the role he had to play. "Just keep your distance," he muttered, his voice edged with unease.

Jezebeth merely chuckled—a low, chilling sound that sent a shiver up his spine.

"I'll leave you two alone then," Gideon said. "It's probably a good idea that Solomon doesn't see me here."

Before he left, Jezebeth blew him a slow, mocking kiss. "I'll see you in Hell, Gideon. In fact, I'll be waiting with open arms and open legs."

Gideon grunted, the sound laced with annoyance and something deeper—a fear he wouldn't acknowledge. With a swift motion, he turned and left, retreating to one of the other bedrooms.

As the door clicked shut, Tarek positioned himself by the door, his eyes never leaving Jezebeth's calculating gaze. The tension in the room was thick, charged with a twisted sense of anticipation, and neither of them knew which side of the storm would break first.

***

They moved through the house, the air thick with tension, until they reached the back bedroom. As the door creaked open, Hecate hesitated, turning her gaze away from the bed, afraid of what she might find. Then her mother's voice pierced the stillness like a knife, sending a chill crawling up her spine. "What's the matter, dear? Don't you want to give mommy a kiss?"

Hecate's breath caught in her throat. Slowly, she turned, her heart pounding in her chest as she faced the horror she had feared. Helena, once the embodiment of warmth and kindness, was unrecognizable. Her wrists, raw and burned, were cruelly bound to the bed frame, while boils and lesions covered her once-beautiful face and arms. A sickly stream of milky pus oozed from her body, pooling onto the bloodstained sheets. Her eyes—wild, feral, unseeing—glinted with madness, and a serpentine tongue slithered from her mouth, dripping with venom.

Jezebeth's voice slithered from the shadows, taunting. "Maybe if you'd bothered to visit me once in a while, you filthy little bitch, this wouldn't have happened."

"Don't listen to her," Solomon warned. "It's the demon speaking."

The twisted form of Helena let out a mocking laugh, her head tilting with a sinister grin. "Ah, Solomon, I was wondering when I'd get to see you again. Still trying to pretend you're some holy man, I see."

Solomon's eyes narrowed. "You have the advantage, demon. You seem to know me, but I don't know you. What name do you go by?"

Jezebeth's laugh was sharp, a rasping sound that made Hecate's skin crawl. She recoiled. The pain of seeing her mother's suffering was nearly too much to bear. "You're not going to trick me that easily, Prophet. Maybe you should ask my seventy-two brothers who you so kindly imprisoned so long ago. I'm sure they'd be eager to help."

Solomon's jaw clenched, his mind racing. "Is that what this is about? The resurgence of your kind?"

A cruel smirk curled on Jezebeth's lips. "Eventually, Prophet, you'll meet your end—and when you do, they'll all be free. You thought you could bury the truth by planting that fake chest in the lake, fooling the Babylonians while you hid the real one away. But we know where it is, and it's only a matter of time before we open it and unleash destruction on the world."

A flicker of fear crossed Solomon's face, but he steeled himself, pushing the fear back down. "Enough! Time for you to return to the hole you crawled out of."

Jezebeth's gaze flickered toward Hecate, the cruelty in her eyes fading into something softer, more vulnerable. "Help me, Hecate. I need you. I don't think I can hold on much longer."

The pitiful plea tore at Hecate's heart, and tears spilled down her cheeks. "Mom! Just stay strong! We'll save you."

But in an instant, the demon's hold on Helena snapped back, the transformation vicious and sudden. The voice that emerged was guttural, mocking. "Ha! You think you can save her, you little fucking whore? You're weak and pathetic! In the end, she'll die, like so many others before her."

Solomon yelled, "I said, enough!" Then he began reciting the ritual in earnest, sensing that time was running short.

The air crackled as Helena's body twisted, the demon's resistance thrashing against Solomon's incantation. Helena's back arched unnaturally, her body straining against the ropes. Then, with a horrifying lurch, her legs floated upward, her body twisting until she hung upside down, her head bent backward like a grotesque mockery of a crucifix. The ropes tore free as her head spun around with an unholy snap.

"Azazel sends his best!" Jezebeth cackled, her head turned backward to face Hecate with insane delight. "Now, let's see you fix this!"

The horror unfolded in slow motion. With a sickening crack, Helena's body slammed into the bed, her neck snapping with brutal force. The rest of her body followed, the skin stretching and tearing, the ligaments pulling until her head was ripped from her shoulders. It bounced once, landing at Hecate's feet with a cruel, mocking smile still frozen on its lips.

"See, told you," the severed head whispered before it fell silent, the final vestiges of life snuffed out. From the body, a black cloud of smoke billowed, disappearing into the floor, leaving nothing but the stench of decay.

The room was silent, save for the sickening drip of bodily fluids onto the floor. Stunned and motionless, Hecate could barely comprehend the madness she had just witnessed. Her sobs broke the stillness, a raw, broken wail of grief as she crumpled to the floor, her heart shattered into jagged pieces.

Tarek, shaken to his core, glanced at Solomon, his eyes wide with horror. Solomon's response was a brief nod toward the door. With a silent agreement, Tarek turned and left the room, quietly closing the door behind him.

Solomon moved toward Hecate, his steps slow, deliberate, as he kneeled beside her. His hand hovered over her shoulder, unsure of how to comfort the shattered girl before him. "I'm so sorry, Hecate."

For a long moment, Hecate didn't respond. Then she slowly lifted her head, her eyes cold—icy with something darker than pain. Her voice was a quiet, venomous whisper. "This is all your fault. If you had told me everything, we could've stopped this. But instead, you kept your secrets, like you always do."

Solomon felt the sting of her words, the weight of her anger, but he knew it was the grief speaking. "I know you're hurting, but I did everything I could. I tried to save her."

"Liar!" she spat, her voice full of fury. "You did nothing. Now she's dead."

Before he could respond, she surged to her feet, her movements frantic, desperate. She ran toward the door, pausing only to cast one last, seething look over her shoulder. "I swear to God, Solomon, you'll pay for this."

CHAPTER 23

Tarek moved down the block, his mind reeling from the nightmare he had just witnessed. When he reached Gideon's car, the door swung open, and he collapsed into the passenger seat. He couldn't shake the images that played in his mind like a twisted movie reel.

Gideon turned to him, his gaze sharp, demanding. "Well? What happened?"

Tarek swallowed hard. "I've never seen anything like it. The demon changed in seconds. By the time Solomon and the girl walked in, her skin was covered in sores that leaked puss and blood. It was like she'd been tied there for months. And she—she made burn marks appear on her wrists and ankles, like she was tortured."

Gideon's expression darkened, but he stayed calm. "And then?"

"They started the ritual," Tarek continued, his voice shaky. "Jezebeth played her part like a damn actress, leading Solomon on. But just when he thought he could save her, she… she sacrificed the woman. It was the most gruesome thing I've ever seen. By the time I left, the girl was on the floor, crying uncontrollably."

"Good," Gideon said, his tone cold. "If this plays out the way I think it will, Hecate will blame Solomon and turn on him. We need to be there to pick up the pieces."

Tarek leaned back in the seat, staring out the window. "He was rattled when Jezebeth mentioned the imprisoned demons."

"So the legend is true," Gideon mused. "The real chest wasn't discovered by the Babylonians all those centuries ago. That means he still has it hidden. That's been Azazel's plan all along. We need to find out where he's hiding it."

Tarek's gaze shifted to Gideon, confusion still thick in his mind. "What do you want me to do?"

Gideon met his eyes with a look that was both calculating and determined. "Get close to Hecate. Become her friend, her confidant, her lover, if you have to. Do whatever it takes. I'm working on a plan—something big. If it goes right, we'll get everything we want. And maybe even a little personal revenge, too."

Tarek nodded, understanding his role, but it didn't sit well with him. Still, he couldn't ignore the pull of the mission. He got out of the car and made his way back to the house, where he sat on the front porch, waiting for the storm to arrive.

He heard the sound of footsteps before he saw her. Hecate stormed out of the house, grief radiating from her like a dark cloud. Tarek quickly wiped the shock from his face and replaced it with a look of genuine terror. She nearly tripped over him as she rushed past.

"I'm sorry," she muttered through her tears, barely seeing him as she continued her frenzied march down the walkway.

Tarek stood and followed her, his voice tentative. "Are you going to be okay?"

She didn't answer at first, the weight of her anguish pressing down on her. Then she stopped and slumped against the car, her sobs racking her body. "I don't know," she whispered, her voice breaking.

Tarek kneeled beside her. "Do you have somewhere to go?"

Her gaze went blank, like she hadn't even considered that. The thought of going back to campus with Solomon there was unbearable. And Landis—his loyalties tied to Solomon—she couldn't go to him either. Just hours ago, her world had seemed full of hope, full of light. She had love, she had dreams. Now, all of that had been shattered. How could she move forward from this?

"I guess… I don't really have anywhere to go," she said softly, her voice distant.

Tarek took a breath and pulled out his phone, making a quick call. A minute later, Gideon's car pulled up in front of them.

"I have a place you can stay tonight, until we figure things out," Tarek said.

Hecate hesitated for a moment, torn between distrust and the desperate need to escape. Finally, she climbed into the backseat, and Tarek followed her in. As the door clicked shut, he turned to her, his tone steady.

"Hecate, this is Gideon. He's been my mentor for a while. I consider him like a father to me."

Gideon turned in his seat, offering her a warm but somber smile. "Pleased to meet you, Hecate. Tarek gave me a brief rundown on the phone. I'm truly sorry for your loss."

Hecate nodded numbly, her eyes unfocused, her mind still reeling from the events.

Gideon's voice softened. "If you'd like, you can stay with us for the night. In the morning, we can figure out what comes next."

Hecate eyed him warily, suspicion etched on her face. She

studied him for a moment.

"I promise you," Gideon said, a hint of humor creeping into his voice despite the gravity of the situation, "we're not serial killers or anything."

"Whatever," Hecate muttered, exhaustion lining her words. "I just need to get away from here."

"I understand," Gideon replied, his expression kind as he shifted the car into gear. He glanced into the rear-view mirror as he drove away, a subtle smile forming when he saw Solomon exiting the house.

The game was just beginning.

***

Solomon bolted out of the house, his heart pounding as he called after Hecate, "Hecate, wait!" But his words were swallowed by the roar of the engine as the car disappeared into the night.

Feeling frustrated and helpless, he pulled out his phone with trembling hands, dialing Landis's number. As the line rang, he replayed the events over and over in his mind, trying to find the turning point, that one moment where he could've changed everything. Could he have saved her mother? Could he have stopped the demon before the savage horror claimed her life ?

His gut told him that there was something darker, something far more sinister at play. His instincts told him it was Azazel. It had to be. The Prince of Hell, ever patient, had been stretching his claws beyond the confines of his prison, manipulating events from the shadows. And somehow, Hecate had become the unwilling key in his scheme.

After a few rings, Landis answered. All Solomon could say was, "I couldn't stop it."

"Couldn't stop what?" Landis asked.

Slowly and deliberately, Solomon recounted every agonizing moment of the terrible ordeal, his voice breaking down as he recounted the words Hecate had spoken to him before she ran away.

For a long moment, silence reigned on both ends of the line, before Landis said, "You've got to do everything you can to get her back, Solomon. Promise me you'll get her back."

A heavy sigh escaped Solomon's lips as he forced himself not to make another promise this night that he wouldn't be able to keep.

He hung up, his hand tightening around the phone. After a moment, he dialed Hecate's number and it went straight to voice-mail, though he wasn't surprised. He had likely become the last person on Earth she wanted to hear from.

Winning her back, earning her trust again, was going to be difficult. But he had no choice. He had to try. For her. For them.

CHAPTER 24

Hecate stood frozen, her mind struggling to process the nightmare unfolding at her feet. The head of her mother, Helena, now severed from her body, came to rest with a sickening thud on the floor. The horror of it all was overwhelming. One moment, Helena was alive, her voice trembling with desperation, pleading for salvation. And in the blink of an eye, she was gone. In that instant, the floodgates opened, memories—both bitter and sweet—rushed into Hecate's mind, but it was the crushing weight of regret that anchored her. Her mother had died without hearing a single word of repentance.

"Oh, don't look so surprised," Solomon said. "You knew this was always a possibility."

"How can you say that?" Hecate's voice cracked.

"Give it a rest, Hecate," Solomon scoffed. "This was always a possibility. You knew what we were up against."

"But you promised me she'd be okay!"

"I said what I had to say." Solomon's gaze was cold, unwavering. "You of all people should understand—there are no guarantees in this line of work. Her death? It was inevitable. It was the only way to rid the world of the evil that had corrupted her."

"How can you be so... cold? You act like her life meant nothing to you!" Hecate snapped.

"In the grand scheme of things," Solomon said sharply, "it didn't. It was a simple exchange: one life for many."

Hecate's anger flared like a storm unleashed. "I guess I finally get to see you for what you really are—an egotistical, self-absorbed, judgmental asshole!"

"Get off your high horse, Hecate!" Solomon sneered. "What's done is done. You can't change the past. It's time to move on."

Her hands trembled with fury as she raised them, summoning energy that crackled in the air. She was done with words. "You'll pay for what you've done, you fucking bastard!" she spat.

A beam of raw, unbridled power shot from her palms, aimed straight for Solomon, but he vanished into thin air just before impact. Her heart sank as she found herself staring at the empty space where he had been.

From behind her, a voice slithered through air. "Don't be surprised by Solomon's actions. He's always been quick to condemn others, while holding himself to a far more lenient standard."

Hecate whirled around, her breath catching in her throat as she faced Azazel. "You act like you know him," she said, her voice laced with disbelief.

"Yes," Azazel replied with a knowing smile, "I do. We have a... complicated history."

Hecate's shoulders slumped as exhaustion and sorrow washed over her. "All this time, I thought he was different. He gave me hope, a new life, and then he ripped it all away... like I never mattered at all."

Azazel's eyes softened. "I'm sorry you had to go through

that to see who he really was. But just know this: I would never turn my back on you like that. If you were mine, I'd treat you like a queen for the rest of my days."

Hecate's eyes flickered with doubt. "What about Landis?" she asked .

Azazel's lips curled into a stiff smile. "Landis? He's no different than Solomon. Charming smile, pleasant face... but the truth? He comes from a long line of darkness. It's only a matter of time before his true nature shows."

She looked up at him. "How do I know you're not just telling me what I want to hear? How do I know I can trust you?"

Azazel stepped forward and gathered her into his arms with surprising tenderness. "Search your heart, Hecate," he whispered into her ear. "You know the truth."

***

When Hecate opened her eyes, she found herself in an unfamiliar room, the soft, worn sheets of a small bed beneath her. She was at the back of a house, the one Gideon had brought them to. She wasn't sure she could trust him, and the discovery that he was a Catholic priest only deepened her doubts. Yet, despite the questions swirling in her mind, nothing had happened so far to suggest he was anything but what he claimed to be.

She turned onto her side, her gaze fixed on the wall as tears blurred her vision. So much had happened in such a short time. It felt as though she had lost everything, with no clear path forward. The sharpest ache, however, was the realization that she would never get the chance to say "I'm sorry." Her mother was gone, forever.

She fought to push the scene from her mind, to block out

the agony that clung to her like a shroud. But her efforts were futile. The memory looped relentlessly, replaying her mother's death again and again, each time ending the same way—with Solomon's failure, the broken promise that had cost her everything.

A soft knock at the door broke through her grief, offering a brief reprieve. Hecate didn't want to talk to anyone—not now, not with everything she was feeling—but she couldn't bear the solitude, either. She needed the distraction.

"Come in," she murmured, her voice barely above a whisper.

Tarek stepped into the room, closing the door behind him, and sat at the foot of the bed. "Are you doing okay?" he asked softly.

Hecate rolled onto her back, staring at the ceiling, but didn't respond.

"Look," Tarek said after a pause, "I'm not gonna feed you any bullshit about talking it out or opening up. I figure you'll deal with everything your own way. But, I do know one thing: you're gonna need to eat at some point. And if you're hungry, we've got breakfast ready downstairs."

Hecate gave a small nod as Tarek stood up and left, the sound of his footsteps fading down the hall. She sat up slowly, her body stiff from sleep and grief. She scanned the room, trying to place where she was. The whole escape had been a blur—she couldn't remember the direction they had taken after leaving her house. South? Maybe. But what if she was trapped by another evil person? What if this was all a set-up, another cage?

Stop it, Hecate, she thought. *You're going to drive yourself insane.*

The only way out was to face the present. She had to stop looking over her shoulder. Slowly, she stood up and opened the door.

A long hallway stretched before her, the floorboards creaking underfoot. Doors lined each side, and at the far end, a staircase led down to the lower floor. It didn't take long for her to recognize where she was—some sort of dorm, sponsored by the Church for wayward children. It felt eerily familiar, like the time Solomon had first taken her in. The whole situation mirrored that moment in unsettling ways.

She shook her head, trying to dispel the rising sense of déjà vu. As her fingers brushed the cool banister, a voice suddenly whispered in her mind: *I hope you're okay. Remember, I'm here to protect you.*

"Abaddon?" she whispered.

Yes.

How am I going to get through this? I don't know what to do...

Trust those you're with. I know who they are, and they will help you get your revenge.

Revenge? Hecate was startled at the thought. *I don't want revenge. I just want to move on.*

But you do want revenge, Abaddon's voice insisted. *You said so yourself. You told Solomon he would pay. And he will. He failed you, betrayed you. He must be punished. If not, he'll keep doing this to others. You're not the first he's hurt.*

There have been others? she asked in shock.

Countless others.

I don't know what to say? He just seemed so... different. I never imagined anything like this.

Get your strength back, Abaddon replied in a soft reassuring voice. *Then come find me. We'll figure it out together.*

With that, Hecate descended the stairs, her mind swirling with confusion and doubt. What was she supposed to do? How could she trust anyone?

The dining area came into view as she reached the bottom,

and her breath caught in her throat. A long banquet table stretched across the room, surrounded by a motley group of boys and girls of various ages. They ate ravenously, their faces smeared with dirt and hunger, each bite as though it might be their last. The sight was both heartbreaking and familiar. These were the lost, the broken—kids who had been chewed up by life and spit back out, their innocence long gone.

Hecate's heart tightened in her chest. She'd been there before, after the deaths of her father and sister. She had found herself at rock bottom, just as they had. And now, it seemed, she was back again.

"Ah, Hecate," Gideon's voice rang out from the head of the table. "I'm glad you decided to join us. Please, have a seat."

There was only one empty chair, conveniently placed next to Tarek. Hecate hesitated before sitting down, trying to be as inconspicuous as possible. To her relief, the kids around her didn't seem to care much about her arrival. They continued to focus on their breakfast, the occasional whispering among them being the only sign of curiosity.

The food before her was simple—scrambled eggs, bacon, sausage, hash browns. But seeing how the others devoured it with such fervor, as though it might've been their only meal in days, Hecate felt out of place. She felt like a queen in a palace, indulging in a feast while they fought for scraps.

After she ate, feeling both full and yet empty, Tarek spoke again, his voice low and serious. "So, Hecate, Gideon and I have been talking, and we just want you to know that whatever you need to do, we're here to help."

Hecate thought for a moment, then said simply, "I need to get my cat."

CHAPTER 25

Solomon stood frozen in the middle of the street, his eyes locked on the taillights of the car as it carried Hecate away. He could feel every rush of emotion pulsing through her—anger, sorrow, rage, and for the first time in a long while, fear gripped him. A fear that gnawed at him, deeper than anything he had ever felt before.

He knew the devastation a tragedy like this could bring. He had seen it, felt it in others, and now, as he watched Hecate slip further from his grasp, he feared the darkness that would consume her. It was a darkness from which he doubted she could ever return.

Solomon's mind raced. He had already felt Azazel's power firsthand, knew the depth of the demon's wickedness. He had spent countless decades monitoring Azazel's prison, aware that even the smallest misstep could have catastrophic consequences. Now, that misstep had come, and it was tied to Hecate.

He climbed into his car and started the engine, the hum of the motor doing little to calm the storm inside his mind. As he drove through the streets of South Bend, each turn felt like a moment lost, each minute passing as a heavy reminder of how little control he had over what was unfolding. What had he missed? Who had set these events into motion? He had an idea, but it did little to ease his dread.

Instead of heading to his private quarters on the campus—a secluded wing of the Snite Museum, a place hidden from the public—he turned the car toward the library. He had to see Uriel.

The Archangel was waiting for him as the elevator doors opened, his face etched with concern. "There isn't much time, Solomon. You must save the girl before it's too late."

Solomon's heart twisted, and for the first time in eons, a tear slipped from his eye. "I fear it already is. Her mother's death shattered her, and now she's sinking into a darkness from which she may never escape."

"You must try, Solomon," Uriel pressed. "If she falls into the wrong hands, she could become the very thing we feared the most."

Solomon met Uriel's gaze. "Landis is our only hope. We must pray that their love can break through the darkness."

"Then we must put our faith in the boy," Uriel said quietly.

Solomon nodded, his voice low. "I believe Azazel is waking."

"I've felt it too," Uriel confirmed.

"My gut tells me that Gideon is at the heart of this," Solomon murmured.

"If that's true, then we must be prepared for anything."

Solomon exhaled slowly. "Use all your resources to uncover Gideon's game. I'll find Landis. We have to fix what's broken."

With a final, understanding look, Uriel turned back to the main room, and Solomon descended to the basement. The weight of what lay ahead crushed down on him. He had no idea what the future held, but one thing was certain—it wouldn't be easy. Landis had become a dear friend, an adopted son even, and he prayed that this tragedy wouldn't ruin their relationship as well.

When Solomon arrived in the great room, Landis was pacing near the elevator, his nerves as raw as Solomon's. The moment Solomon stepped off the elevator, Landis rushed to him.

"Any news?" Landis asked.

Solomon shook his head. "Not yet. But Uriel's working on it. I'm sure she'll turn up soon. I'm heading out to canvas the area. I might be able to pick up her trail."

"What do you want me to do?"

"Stay here," Solomon instructed. "If she shows up, you'll be the first to know. But you need to understand, she's in a fragile state right now. She's not the same person."

Landis didn't like the idea of staying behind. He felt helpless, torn between wanting to find her and knowing that Solomon was right. If Hecate did return, she would need him here, not out looking for her.

Solomon's voice grew dark, "We have to be careful. I believe Gideon is behind all of this."

A flicker of thought crossed Landis's mind—a terrifying possibility—that perhaps Gideon had somehow been involved in the accident that killed his parents. It was as though they were caught in some vast, invisible web, its threads tightening around them.

"Yeah," Solomon said. "I've been thinking the same thing."

Landis shot him a sharp look. "Stop reading my mind!"

Solomon gave a wry smile. "I'm sorry. I was lost in my own thoughts and couldn't help myself."

After Solomon left, Landis went to Hecate's room and laid down on her bed, hoping for some peace. It didn't come. Abaddon leaped onto the bed beside him, curling up close to his side, her presence calming him for a brief moment before he finally drifted off to sleep.

***

As soon as he was fully asleep, Abaddon slipped away. She reappeared moments later, silently shadowing Solomon as he entered the Snite Museum. She moved like a whisper, unnoticed as she passed through the door just before it closed.

Inside, Solomon walked purposefully through the museum, passing exhibits that seemed to vanish behind him. He reached a door marked 'Authorized Personnel Only' and paused. He inserted a key into a panel on the wall, and with a soft hum, a small door slid open. Pressing his thumb against the glass, Solomon waited for the soft click of the lock before turning the handle. Once again, Abaddon slipped through just behind him, invisible and silent.

The room beyond was small, a secret hidden from the world. Abaddon watched Solomon pause, his eyes scanning the space, his mind reaching out. For a moment, she felt his presence, his awareness brushing against her hidden form. Then, with a flick of his hand, he turned to face a blank wall. His right hand extended, and as he whispered a few words, the ring on his finger began to glow. With a twist, the ring's face emitted a soft light that turned the wall into a shimmering portal.

The moment before the portal closed, Abaddon glimpsed the other side. It was enough to know what was waiting there.

Abaddon whisked herself away once more and reappeared in Hecate's room. Landis stirred slightly when she jumped back on the bed before he drifted back off to sleep. She nestled in next to him, purring softly.

CHAPTER 26

Hecate hid in the shadows holding her breath as she waited for the right moment. Finally, the side door creaked open and she slipped inside, moving silently toward the elevator. She pressed the button for the basement, the soft hum of the elevator echoing in the small space as she descended.

She vowed that this would be the last time she saw this place. The cold walls that had started to feel like home now felt like prison bars. Betrayal burned at her heart.

When she entered her room, the unexpected sight of Landis lying on her bed stunned her. She froze, confusion flickering through her as Abaddon leaped gracefully from the mattress, padding toward her. Hecate quietly scooped her up into her arms.

Her fingers tightened around Abaddon's soft fur, but as her feet moved toward the door, Landis's voice broke through the silence, "Hecate? Where are you going?"

She stiffened. "I didn't want to wake you," she muttered, unable to meet his gaze.

Hecate could feel him behind her, the heat of his body just a breath away. Without another word, Landis wrapped his arms around her, pulling her into him. His embrace was strong and familiar—something that should have been comforting, but all it did was deepen the emptiness inside her.

Abaddon jumped from her arms and padded to the side, leaving Landis to hold her tighter, as if he could hold her together, but she was already shattering.

The tears came, fierce and unrelenting. She let them flow, her body shaking in his arms, but even in her sorrow, something in her stirred, something cold and unforgiving.

After what felt like forever, she pulled away, wiping her eyes. "I have to go," she whispered. "I don't want Solomon to see me."

"Why not?" he asked.

Hecate shook her head, her voice brittle. "I think he's done enough already."

He reached for her, his hands pleading. "Don't be like that. You act like it was his fault?"

"You weren't there! He just stood there watching her die, like he didn't care. Like he was paralyzed. He just watched as the demon violently killed her!" Her hands trembled as she clenched her fists. "He did nothing!"

Landis's face tightened. "I think you're overreacting, Hecate. I'm sure he did everything he could."

Her fury exploded. "Don't you dare tell me I'm overreacting! You have no idea what it felt like! You weren't there!"

Landis flinched. "Hecate, I didn't mean it like that."

"It doesn't matter how you meant it. You said it," she spat. "I can't be around him. I won't. And I doubt I'll ever fucking forgive him."

Landis stared at her, his expression a mixture of sadness and disbelief. "So, what does that mean for us?"

Hecate looked at him coldly. He no longer resembled the

man she had come to love. She now saw him as an enemy. Solomon's partner-in-crime. In the blink of an eye, her love had turned to hatred. "It means we're done," she said flatly.

She turned away, cradling Abaddon in her arms as she walked out of his life forever.

***

Gideon sank into the bed, exhausted. His foster children, with their endless whining and needy behavior, had drained him. The act of playing caretaker was tiresome, but it served the greater purpose, feeding the darkness he had been sworn to.

Just as he began to slip into the quiet comfort of sleep, the doorbell rang. A groan escaped his lips before he focused, stretching his senses out to meet the visitor. A smile tugged at the corners of his lips when he saw who it was.

He moved quickly to the front door and opened it to reveal Hecate, her face streaked with tears, her eyes red and raw. She held Abaddon close to her, tucked tightly in her arms as if she were the only anchor she had left in the world.

"Can I stay here?" She asked softly. Her voice was fragile, barely a whisper.

Gideon didn't hesitate. His arm encircled her gently, leading her inside. "Of course, my dear. For as long as you need."

He guided her upstairs to the room she had stayed in the night before, his mind already working, turning over the pieces of his Master's plan.

"I'm just downstairs, first door to the right, if you need anything," he said.

She nodded slightly before he closed the door behind her. Alone in the hallway, his thoughts began to swirl, pulling him deeper into the labyrinth of schemes he was orchestrating. There was much to be done, and Hecate's arrival was only another thread in the tangled web.

He returned to his own room, but sleep eluded him. Instead, he took a seat in the chair across from the bed, his posture upright as he closed his eyes, sinking into meditation.

A few moments passed, the quiet broken only by the soft purring of a cat. Gideon opened his eyes and saw Abaddon sitting before him. The feline regarded him with a strange, almost knowing stare.

He leaned forward, studying the cat more intently. "Well, what do we have here?" he asked curiously. "Does she know what you really are?"

Abaddon responded with a soft meow, her mouth opening as a long, serpentine tentacle shot from her throat, connecting with Gideon's forehead.

Pain lanced through his skull, sharp and sudden, and he cried out, but it wasn't the physical pain that shook him. No, it was the rush of images—flashes, memories, raw and violent—that flooded his mind. The boy's parents, both dead. The brutal death of Hecate's mother at the hands of Jezebeth. Solomon, venturing through a portal, glimpsing a forbidden world beyond. And then—the prison. Azazel's prison. Hidden, but not for long.

The vision faded as Abaddon released her grip, the cat sitting back down, her purring steady and satisfied. Gideon sat still for a moment, processing the flood of information. His lips curled into a slow smile.

"Thank you, friend," he said with a dark smile.

Another soft meow, and Abaddon vanished, slipping back into the shadows like a wisp of smoke.

Gideon didn't waste a second. He grabbed his phone, his fingers dialing quickly. The phone rang twice before

Victoria's voice answered, cool and expectant.

"It's time," Gideon said with an excited edge to his voice. "Here's what we need to do..."

PART TWO: LIES

CHAPTER 1

Sometimes you have to wade through hellfire before you find your way back to heaven. Andrew knew that truth intimately as he stood watching Priscilla, the glow of the late afternoon sun casting a halo around her hair. Memories clawed at the edges of his mind—dark, suffocating memories of the chaos they had endured. The aftermath of Vizibir's destruction had been more than devastation; it had been a descent into madness orchestrated by Gideon. That man had wielded his power like a blade, slicing through the remnants of Andrew's life with relentless precision.

Ex-communication from the Church was only the beginning. What followed was an onslaught of criminal charges, accusations built on intricate webs of lies. Andrew could still feel the cold sweat of those nights, the gnawing dread as each trial brought him closer to ruin. If not for Solomon's intervention, Andrew knew he would have been imprisoned, condemned to an endless void. In the end, all charges were dropped.

Now, as Andrew breathed in the warm, jasmine-scented air of their new home, he felt the fragile stirrings of hope. Life had given him a second chance, a chance he held onto with fierce determination. And Priscilla was at the heart of it all. Through every torment and shadow, she had stood by him, an unwavering light. Her loyalty only deepened the love that surged within him, a love he once thought would be smothered by grief.

Their decision to start over had been mutual. They abandoned the suffocating chaos of the city, seeking solace in the embrace of Palm Springs—a place where days bled into sun-drenched evenings and time moved without urgency. Here, they could be ordinary, unmarked by the past. They even adopted a German Shepherd puppy, Buddy, whose boundless energy filled their days with laughter. For the first time in years, life seemed to promise peace.

Grace, too, found her place nearby. She took an apartment in Palm Desert, the distance between her and Priscilla now measured in minutes instead of miles. Yet despite the new start, a hint of regret twisted in Grace's chest, tied to the memory of Matthew. She couldn't deny the spark that had kindled between them, but fear of commitment, of exposing herself to more loss, kept her at arm's length. So, she chose the safe path and plunged herself into her studies at COD's drama program, where the theater offered her a stage to craft a semblance of normalcy.

They all made the same mistake—thinking their lives could ever be normal.

***

Andrew held Priscilla's hand tightly as they walked out of Mario's, the soft glow of the restaurant's lights casting warm reflections on the wet pavement. The air was cool and tinged with the rich scents of pasta and garlic, remnants of an evening that filled more than just their stomachs—it soothed their souls. "That was nice," Andrew said, holding the car door open for her. "We should come here more often."

Priscilla eased into the passenger seat with a small laugh. "Yeah, but next time, let's skip the appetizers. I'm so stuffed, I can barely move."

Andrew chuckled as he shut the door and walked around to the driver's side. Just as his hand reached for the handle, a shadow swept across the horizon, skimming the edges of twilight with an unsettling presence. It was subtle, a shiver in the air, but it lodged in his gut like a lead weight.

As he slid into the driver's seat, Priscilla immediately noticed that something was off. "What's wrong?" she asked.

He looked up, his eyes narrowing at the dimming sky. "I don't know. For a moment, I just felt... something. It's gone now."

Priscilla raised an eyebrow, trying to break the tension with a wry smile. "Did you just feel a disturbance in the force?"

Andrew laughed. "How long have you been waiting to use that line?"

"Let me see... how long have we been back together?"

He leaned in, touching his lips to hers tenderly. "Not long enough," he murmured.

But the moment shattered when Priscilla's gaze snapped past him, eyes wide and face pale. She was staring out the windshield at something that wasn't there moments before— a little girl standing a few yards away, framed by the dim wash of the street lamps. Her hair was dark and tangled, cascading around a white dress cinched at the waist with a red ribbon. In her tiny hand, she clutched a single black rose. Her smile was unnatural, stretched too wide, as she lifted the flower as though offering a gift.

"What's wrong?" Andrew asked, following her gaze. The second his voice broke the silence, the girl blinked out of existence, leaving only the black rose lying on the pavement like a silent warning.

Priscilla turned to him, her voice shaking. "Take me home."

He didn't hesitate, slamming the car into gear and peeling away from the curb. The tires screeched as he pushed the speed limit, the tension in the air coiling tighter with each passing second. They burst through the door of their house, locking it behind them, as if thin wood and steel could keep out what lurked beyond.

"What do you need me to do?" Andrew asked urgently.

Priscilla's eyes darted around the room, calculating. "Pour salt along every door and window while I work on a spell to protect us."

Without another word, Andrew raced to the kitchen, yanking the salt box from the pantry. The grains spilled and scattered as he dashed from one frame to the next, whispering a prayer he couldn't remember learning.

Priscilla kneeled on the living room floor, chalk in hand, sketching intricate symbols with practiced precision. She was nearly finished when a chill crept up her spine, and the room filled with the sound of scraping. A rasping noise brushed against the window—soft, methodical. The kind of sound that made the hairs on the back of her neck stand on end. There were no trees near the house. No wind. Yet, the sound persisted.

Then the doorknob rattled.

Priscilla's blood turned to ice. Slowly, she looked up, eyes fixed on the front door as it shuddered in its frame. The noise stopped, replaced by silence that was somehow worse. A thick black mist seeped through the crack at the base, curling and shifting until it took form—a figure more nightmare than man. It stood seven feet tall, cloaked in darkness with spindly arms that ended in glistening claws. Beneath the hood, nothing but a deep, malevolent void hissed and crackled.

Andrew burst into the room, skidding to a halt as the creature lunged at him. The thing's claws wrapped around his throat in an iron grip, and it lowered its head, snarling inches from his face. Moonlight poured in, casting a cold light over its grotesque features—a twisted face with a mouth full of jagged teeth and eyes that glowed like embers. Saliva dripped onto Andrew's cheek as he gasped for air.

"Andrew!" Priscilla cried as she rushed forward, a silver knife clutched in her hand. But before the blade found its mark, the creature pivoted, seizing her with its other clawed hand. It squeezed, cutting off her scream as spots danced in her vision.

The front door banged open, and a commanding voice split the tension. "Wait!"

Victoria strode in, a flicker of amusement in her eyes sharp as broken glass. The Strigoi loosened its hold but kept them both firmly pinned.

Victoria's gaze slid to Priscilla, her expression softening into a mockery of affection as she reached out and touched her sister's face. "It's good to see you, *petite sis*. I've missed you."

Priscilla's voice came out in a strained whisper. "Victoria... I should've known you'd crawl back from Hell someday."

A wicked smile curled Victoria's lips. "So, how do you like the new me?"

A memory sliced through Priscilla's mind, one so vivid it stole her breath—it was a day twenty-five years in the past, stained with betrayal and blood. The day her sister turned against them all; the day Priscilla drove that very same dagger into Victoria's belly to stop her madness.

Victoria reached down, plucking the knife from the floor, its silver blade glinting under the moon's watchful eye. "This blade feels familiar," she mused, running a thumb over the edge. "And now, after all these years, I finally get to repay the favor."

Priscilla's eyes narrowed. "You brought all of that down on yourself, Victoria."

"Oh, I wasn't implying that everything was your fault. I admit I was a little hot-headed back then. That didn't mean you had to kill me, though."

"You murdered our mother!" Priscilla's voice shook with fury. "You deserved to die."

Victoria's eyes flashed. "That old hag got what was coming to her. Always praising you, never me. She never respected who I was or what I could become."

"Because she saw the darkness in you," Priscilla spat. "The darkness everyone else saw."

Victoria's smile was all teeth. "And I became it. Thanks to you, I met Azazel. And let me tell you, being remade was glorious."

Her gaze drifted to Andrew. "And since we're sharing old stories... Gideon sends his regards."

Victoria stepped closer to Priscilla, her voice turning cold. "Before I repay you for what you did to me, I need you to tell me one thing: where's that little bitch of a daughter of yours?"

CHAPTER 2

No matter how hard Grace tried, the words refused to come alive. Each line she practiced felt brittle and empty. It didn't help that she'd never had much patience for Shakespeare, and rehearsing *Romeo and Juliet* only made her focus slip further. With auditions just a week away, she knew she wasn't ready.

Her study partner, Jessica, a perky little sophomore who had just recently changed her major to theater, tossed her script onto the chair next to her, "Come on, Grace! You're better than this. What gives?"

Grace sighed. "I don't know. Maybe it's just that Shakespeare fucking sucks?"

Jessica laughed. "Don't give me that. You've nailed Shakespeare before. There's something else, isn't there?"

Grace was silent for a moment. She hadn't let anyone in since she'd left Matthew behind and moved to California—not even her parents. But Jessica had become a friend, the kind who saw right through her. "It's... his name is Matthew," she admitted at last.

Jessica's eyes sparkled. "I knew it! It's always a boy. Spill, now. I want every detail."

Grace managed a small smile. "There's not much to tell.

We went through something big together. I think we both felt it, but then I got scared. Moving here felt easier than facing it. But he's been on my mind ever since."

"So call him, already!"

"I've tried, a thousand times." Grace admitted.

"And?"

"Every time, I hang up before he can answer."

Jessica stared at Grace wide-eyed. "Are you shitting me? You're probably the most fearless chick I've ever met. Hard to picture you afraid of anything."

"You haven't met Matthew," Grace murmured, a bittersweet smile touching her lips.

Jessica's grin widened. "He must be something special."

A big smile crossed Grace's lips, "Yeah, he's pretty special."

Her smile quickly disappeared when she suddenly felt dizzy and fell out of her chair onto the floor. Jessica jumped over to help her. "Grace? Are you okay?"

Jessica helped her sit up, and saw that she was shaking visibly. "What's wrong, Grace?"

Grace looked at her, trembling with fear. "It's my parents. Something's happened."

Jessica was stunned. "How do you know that?"

"It's... it's a feeling. I need to go. Now." Grace pushed herself up, wobbling dangerously.

"You're in no condition to drive," Jessica said firmly. "I'll take you."

"Are you sure? It could be—"

"Dangerous?" Jessica smiled bravely. "What are friends for, if not a little danger?"

The early November darkness had swallowed the Valley by the time they rushed outside, Daylight Savings Time claiming the light by five o'clock. Each step felt like trudging through quicksand, fear clutching at Grace's chest. She'd had premonitions before, but never like this—never this consuming, this physically draining. Death had a way of leaving more than corpses; it claimed a piece of those left behind. And now, Death's shadow tightened around her, suffocating.

Tears welled up in her eyes as the feeling of dread sank deeper into her bones. Jessica shot her worried glances as they hurried to the car. "Maybe it's not as bad as you think?" Jessica said hopefully as she started the engine. "Maybe they're just hurt. Maybe—"

"They're gone." Grace's voice cracked, and she knew it was true.

Jessica floored the gas, the car streaking through dim-lit streets—Monterey, Dinah Shore, then onto the road to Palm Springs. It was only a twenty-minute drive, but every tick of the clock stretched into an eternity. To her, it felt like twenty hours.

They screeched to a halt in front of the condo. Everything looked normal, eerily so. No lights, no noise. Lifeless.

Grace swallowed hard, trying to steady her breathing. "Wait here," she said.

Jessica opened her mouth to protest, then clamped it shut and nodded.

Grace stepped up to the door, heart thundering. Eyes closed, she focused like her mother had taught her, trying to feel her presence. For a fleeting moment, a whisper touched her mind, then vanished.

The doorknob turned easily under her hand. The scent hit first—coppery, thick. Then she saw them: her father crumpled on the floor, throat torn open; her mother beside him, a knife embedded deep in her stomach.

"Mom! Dad!" The words barely left her lips when a voice,

low and mocking, shattered the silence.

"I knew you'd come, eventually."

Whipping around, Grace met Victoria's eyes, cold as winter's edge. "You did this?"

Victoria sauntered closer, lips curved in a cruel smile. "Not all by myself." She nodded, and from the shadows, the Strigoi stepped forward, its eyes glinting with hunger.

"It's nothing personal," Victoria added, pausing, eyes narrowing. "Actually, that's a lie. Your mother had it coming."

Grace's blood ran cold. "You're Victoria... you're supposed to be dead."

Victoria's laugh was sharp, cutting. "Oh, Grace. You should know by now that dead doesn't always mean gone."

Grace's voice shook. "Are you here to kill me, too?"

"Eventually. But for now, we need you alive."

The Strigoi lunged. Reflexes took over, and Grace dove forward, snatching the knife from her mother's stomach. She thrust it upward, catching the creature's chest with the silver blade. It let out a shriek before crumbling to dust.

Panting, Grace turned to Victoria, her eyes burning with savage fury. "You'll pay for this, you—"

Victoria dodged Grace's swing, but not before the knife bit into her arm, drawing a hiss of pain. Quickly, she ran from the house, disappearing into the night.

Grace raced outside, heart hammering. Jessica's car came into view, and with it, a fresh horror when she saw Jessica slumped forward, blood smeared across the window.

"No..."

She yanked open the door. Jessica's eyes fluttered, mouth moving soundlessly. Her throat had been slashed from ear to ear.

Tears flooded Grace's vision. "Don't talk. I'll get help.

You'll be okay."

Jessica managed a slight nod before a shuddering cough sprayed blood across her lips. The light faded from her eyes with a last, panicked breath.

A siren wailed in the distance. Grace scrambled for her phone, dialing with shaking hands. The call connected on the second ring.

"Matthew, I need you!" she sobbed. "Something terrible's happened!"

CHAPTER 3

Matthew watched as the final customer stepped out, and Chuck twisted the lock behind them. For a moment, a sharp throb ran through his finger. Glancing at the ring, its gem hidden beneath a layer of black nail polish, he noticed a faint glow leaking from its edges before dimming away.

Demons were everywhere—he'd learned that the hard way. But they weren't all out for blood. Most wandered aimlessly, finding delight in sowing chaos, wearing their human guises like costumes. The ring, once a beacon flaring endlessly, had been muted out of sheer exhaustion; he couldn't chase every threat. And besides, he was trying to bury the past, though the ache made it clear he didn't truly want to.

But that was the real problem. He was hopelessly and completely obsessed. Every time he closed his eyes, Grace was the only thing he saw, and it hurt that she didn't feel the same way. Sure, they had felt a little spark between them, but it was apparent that her feelings weren't as strong as his.

He sighed and walked back to his department so he could finish recovering the area and be ready for business tomorrow

"Shit!" he said as he rounded a corner and found multiple boxes of products scattered on the floor, each one opened up, and white Styrofoam pieces dotting the floor. Two floor lamps and a table lamp were the victims of the careless shopper who had desecrated their packaging. "Can't these damn customers learn how to pick up after themselves?"

As he was trying to put the Styrofoam puzzles back together, while struggling to keep the magnetized remnants that floated through the air from sticking to him, a young kid named Billy rounded the corner. "You need a hand there?" he asked.

Matthew nodded, "Sure. I don't know why people can't just fucking leave things alone? There's a damn display already put together right in front of them! Makes you wonder what their house looks like?"

"I hear ya," Billy said, as he bent down to help.

Suddenly, the ring on Matthew's hand pulsed, a rapid heartbeat of light. The nail polish cracked under the intensity, illuminating the gem. He looked up, meeting Billy's eyes and the knowing smirk that spread across his face.

"Well, I guess the cat's out of the bag now," Billy said.

Matthew stood up slowly and backed away. As he did so, Destiny, a pixie-haired cashier, walked up behind him, eyes flicking between them. The ring blazed brighter.

"Not you too?" Matthew whispered.

Destiny frowned at Billy. "Nice going, Shithead. This was supposed to be a surprise. I should've known you'd fuck it up."

Billy shrugged. "Not my fault."

Chuck's footsteps echoed as he advanced, the trio closing in. His expression was icy. "Don't look at me," Destiny snapped. "Blame your boy here."

Matthew's chest tightened. "Chuck? Man, this really sucks.

I liked you."

"Strictly business, Matthew," Chuck said flatly. "Nothing personal."

"Feels pretty personal to me."

Chuck's eyes narrowed. "Well, regardless of how you feel. Enjoy your last few minutes alive."

Instinct immediately took over. Matthew twisted the ring's stone, aiming it at Chuck. A streak of energy slammed into his chest, sending him crashing into Billy and Destiny. The maneuver gave Matthew a chance to run to the end of the aisle, but that was as far as he could get before the trio regrouped and started coming after him. He turned the ring again and pointed it at the floor a few feet in front of him. "Here goes nothing," he said.

The floor immediately started to buckle. A second later, the twenty-foot-high racking began to sway. He heard Billy yell 'Fuck!' just before the whole aisle collapsed on them. Then he watched as the whole store came tumbling down like a giant set of Dominoes.

Quickly, he ran toward the front door, only to realize it was locked and Chuck had the key. The reinforced glass was too thick for him to break, and he had already used the ring twice for the day. His only escape was through the emergency exit near the back of the store.

As he ran toward the door his ring started glowing again. He looked down to find that the black covering he had used was flecked off, and the stone was glowing brighter than ever. He pressed the center to hide his location.

He slowed down as he got close to the exit and peered through the glass. At first, he couldn't see anything through the darkness, then slowly, a figure emerged around the side of the building.

Matthew cursed when he saw the beast, "Fuck me!"

It was the same insect demon he had encountered when he had first met Andrew, and knew first-hand how destructive it was. Then he watched in horror as it proceeded to demolish every vehicle in the parking lot, including his beloved Mustang.

His heart sank, not just because of the car, but the presence of the demons meant something bigger was going on. And his fear was that it concerned Grace somehow.

Matthew waited by the door, crouching down low to keep from being spotted. After nearly twenty minutes, the demon drifted away.

He had planned to wait a few extra minutes to make sure the coast was clear before he opened the emergency door and set the alarm off. But a loud crash, followed by a series of moans coming from the direction of the collapsed fixtures, told him that someone had survived.

Matthew slammed the emergency door open and burst through the opening. The siren blared loudly into the night as he fled the store, running across the parking lot as fast as he could.

A half-mile later, he stopped, gasping for breath. He was standing in front of a 7-Eleven with no idea what to do next. He was pretty sure that if he went back home, he'd have a welcoming committee waiting for him.

Then his phone started buzzing. He pulled it from his pocket and answered it as soon as he saw the caller ID on the screen. "Grace? Are you okay?"

CHAPTER 4

Hecate rolled over in bed, fingers brushing against Abaddon's fur. The cat responded with a low purr.

"Morning," she whispered, her voice brittle from lack of sleep. "Hope you slept better than I did."

A soft voice whispered through her mind, *Good morning.*

Hecate stopped, her fingers pausing mid-stroke. "What are you?"

Besides a friend? Some call me an elemental, others a demon. But that's just the label for what they don't understand. I am an old soul, and I've been searching for someone like you for a long time.

"Me?" she asked curiously. "Why me?"

Because you're special, Hecate.

She scoffed. "Special. Right. Gee, where the fuck have I heard that before?"

Not for your power, Abaddon said. *It's your heart that gives you strength. You feel everything with a rawness most can't fathom.*

"I call that a curse," Hecate muttered, eyes clouding with old memories.

A chuckle rippled through her mind, *That's what being an Empath is. It's both a blessing and a curse.*

"Well, sometimes I wish I could just turn it off."

Instead of trying to turn it off, learn to wield it. Feed off of it. Use it to your advantage.

Hecate rolled her eyes. "Now you sound like everyone else trying to tell me how to use my powers."

I'm sorry, Abaddon's tone softened. *I didn't mean to push.*

Hecate sighed, dragging her hand through her tangled hair. "It's fine. I guess I'm just not in a good place right now."

You're entitled to it. What Solomon did—Abaddon's thought darkened—*it was unspeakable. He should pay for his sins. Do you know he's been deceiving you all along?*

Her heart skipped a beat. "What are you talking about?"

Everything. He's kept secrets from you since the beginning.

"What kind of secrets?" she whispered.

Have you heard about the demons he's imprisoned?

A flash of her mother's possessed eyes seared her vision, the suffocating memory of that day gnawing at her soul. She swallowed hard. "Not until the day my mom died."

That's because he used their power, siphoning their life force for his rituals. He never sent their souls to Hell; he trapped them. That's how he's survived all these years.

Hecate was at a loss for words. All this time she had assumed that his longevity was because of some spiritual awakening, or some mystical ritual he had discovered. She never would've guessed he was the same kind of monster he professed to hunt.

But now... now, the truth bared its fangs. "How do you know all this?" she managed.

Because one of the demons he bound was my maker.

"Azazel," she whispered, the name tainted with an odd mixture of reverence and fear. "Did he send you to me?"

No, Abaddon replied. *Finding you was pure fate. And I'm grateful for it. I think we could be more than allies, Hecate. We could be friends.*

A small smile stretched across Hecate's lips as she nestled closer to the cat. Doubt crept in, cold and unwelcome, but a sliver of warmth nestled beside it. Security. Something she hadn't felt in ages. "Me too," she admitted softly.

A knock on the door interrupted their conversation. Hecate was silent for a second, hoping the person would go away. They didn't.

"Who is it?" Her voice cracked.

"It's me, Tarek."

She wasn't in the mood for visitors, but Tarek had been there to help her through the nightmare. "Come in," she finally said.

The door creaked open, and Tarek's eyes roamed the room. "Were you just talking to someone?" he asked curiously.

Hecate grinned. "Just a video on my phone."

You can trust him, Abaddon murmured, *but not yet.*

"Gotcha," Tarek said, smiling as he stepped inside. "Gideon said you were here, so I thought I'd check if you needed anything."

She started to shake her head, but felt her stomach rumble. "Actually, I could use some food."

Tarek nodded. "Breakfast is in an hour, but I could sneak you something now if you're desperate."

She laughed lightly, a sound that hadn't passed her lips for a while. "I can wait. I don't want you getting in trouble."

"Suit yourself," he said, backing out. "See you soon."

The door clicked shut. Abaddon's voice slithered back into her head, *He's kind of cute. I think he likes you*

Hecate snorted. "That's the last thing I need. After Landis, I'm done with guys for a while."

Landis was a liar, Abaddon's voice turned harsh. *He'd say anything to protect Solomon.*

"I really thought he was different," she whispered, the memory slicing deep.

I know. I'm sorry.

A long silence stretched before she added, "Tarek is kind of cute, though."

Moments later, she dragged herself to the bathroom. Her reflection glared back at her, gaunt and weary. She gripped the sink, the sadness unfurling inside her like a storm as she thought about her mother. She'd never get the chance to make up for all the shit she had caused. The ache of her mother's loss twisted her insides until she felt hollow. She also realized that she was utterly and completely alone.

Suddenly, her mirror image shimmered. A shadow formed behind her, his eyes shining like molten gold. Azazel's voice caressed her ear, his breath searing her skin. "You are never alone," he whispered as his fingertips grazed her shoulders, solid and real.

She shivered at the sensation. When she spun around, his eyes held her spellbound. "I am here for you, my beauty. Waiting. Longing. Let Abaddon guide you. Trust Gideon and Tarek to lead you. Find me, my love."

And then, he was gone, the vision evaporating like mist.

***

Gideon's phone vibrated, and when he answered, Victoria's voice came through, ragged and strained, "Gideon? I need help."

His grip on the phone tightened. "What happened?" he demanded.

"The girl escaped."

Gideon's anger raged. "How in the hell did that happen? Didn't you have the Strigoi with you?"

"I did." Her breath rasped like she was fighting for air. "She caught us off-guard, Gideon. Killed him with a silver dagger. Then she sliced me with it. I barely made it out alive."

"And the others?"

"They're not an issue anymore. Andrew and Priscilla are dead," she spat out. "I gutted my sister myself."

Gideon closed his eyes, a slow, satisfied smile curving his lips. *Finally, a step forward.*

"But the silver…" Victoria's voice wavered, pain soaking through every word. "It's killing me."

There was a pause, then Gideon's tone shifted. "Send me your coordinates. I'll dispatch someone to assist you."

Then he turned off his phone. He had no plans to send help. She was a loose end that needed to be tied. Her recklessness and underestimation of Grace was an inconvenience, but he knew that eventually she'd lead them to Matthew. And then he, in turn, would lead them to Solomon.

CHAPTER 5

Solomon stood at the top of Liberty Tower, the weight of the world pressing down on him as the first hints of dawn crept across the horizon. The air was thick with the chill of the early morning, and the city of South Bend stretched out before him, bathed in shadows and muted light. At twenty-five stories high, the tower loomed like a sentinel, the tallest in the city, offering a bird's-eye view of the sprawling urban landscape. It was his favorite place to visit when he wanted to reflect on the miracles of life. It was also his place of solitude when his soul was hurting.

And this morning, his heart was heavy, burdened by the weight of a loss he couldn't quite bear. His thoughts circled like vultures, relentless and unforgiving. He replayed the events in his mind over and over, each time searching for a sign that he could've done something different, something better. But every time, the conclusion was the same—he had done all he could, and it hadn't been enough.

He closed his eyes, feeling the breeze tug at his hair, and let the silence wash over him. He couldn't shake the feeling of betrayal that gnawed at his insides; that he had let her down when she had needed him the most. She had become the closest thing to a daughter in over two thousand years. Now, he feared that he had lost her forever. Worse still, he knew how fragile she was, making her vulnerable to forces far darker than he had ever imagined. The thought of her being prey to such evil was like a dagger to his heart.

As the weight of it all pressed down on him, the ring of his cell phone shattered the stillness, dragging him back to the present. His heart skipped when he saw the caller ID.

"Matthew? Is everything okay?" Solomon asked worriedly.

Desperation rang through Matthew's voice. "Solomon, I need help! It's Grace... she's in trouble!"

A cold knot twisted in Solomon's stomach. "What kind of trouble?"

"She was attacked. She said it was Priscilla's sister."

The thought sent a chill through him. Solomon's worst fears were beginning to take shape.

Matthew's voice faltered, before he continued, "And Solomon... Andrew and Priscilla... they're dead."

Solomon felt the world around him disappear and he fell to his knees. His vision blurred as the tears started to flow. He had considered Andrew a brother in every sense of the word, and Priscilla, a sister. Now they were gone.

A minute passed before Matthew's voice broke through the silence. "Solomon? Are you there?"

"Yes," Solomon whispered. "I'm here. Just... shaken."

"I know," Matthew replied. "But we need to get to Grace. We need to move fast."

"Where are you?" Solomon asked.

"I'm outside a 7-Eleven near Indianapolis."

"Indianapolis?" Solomon asked in confusion. "What are you doing there?"

"I moved her a few months ago after my lease was up. Trying to start fresh."

"Okay," Solomon said. "I'll get the first flight out. I should be there within a couple of hours. Is Grace still in Palm Springs?"

"Yeah... but I don't know where exactly. After the attack, she ran. She's hiding from the authorities."

"Smart," Solomon murmured, his mind already racing. "If you contact her again, tell her to get a burner phone. Something untraceable. She needs to give you her location, and fast."

"I will," Matthew said desperately. "Please hurry, Solomon. I can't lose her too."

"I'll do my best, Matthew. I swear."

The line went dead, and Solomon stared at the phone in his hand. His chest tightened as he stood, wiping away the last of his tears.

***

Grace burst through the front door, her breath coming in ragged gasps as she skidded across the hardwood floor. Panic clawed at her insides, urging her to move faster, to get as far away as possible. Her eyes darted wildly around the room, searching, desperately. The air was thick with the acrid stench of blood, but she forced herself to ignore it, her focus narrowing in on the kitchen counter. There, at last, she found the keys to her parent's car.

Her fingers shook as she snatched them up, a faint metallic clink echoing in the silence. But just as she turned to bolt for the garage, a small, trembling figure waddled into the room.

Buddy.

The little sausage of a puppy looked up at her with wide, innocent eyes. Despite everything, he was alive. How, she couldn't begin to fathom. But when he whimpered, stumbling toward her on shaky legs, Grace's heart cracked wide open.

"Shit," she whispered, scooping him up without a second thought, clutching him to her chest. She wasn't about to leave him behind—not now, not after everything.

With Buddy safely tucked under her arm, Grace darted into the garage, the sound of her pounding heart almost drowning out the distant sirens wailing closer. She threw open the door to the red Mercedes, praying it would start, praying she could get away before the rest of the world came crashing down around her.

The engine roared to life, and she slammed the pedal to the floor, tires screeching against the pavement. A gnawing sense of dread lingered in the back of her mind. She knew the cops wouldn't believe her—hell, she didn't believe herself half the time. A demon vampire, an evil sorceress? It sounded like something out of a nightmare. But it was real, all of it.

She pushed the car to the limit, weaving through the complex, careful not to draw attention, until she finally broke free onto Ramon Road. The road stretched out before her like an endless, desolate path, but she didn't stop, couldn't stop. She needed to get far away. To put miles between herself and the nightmare that had destroyed everything.

Without thinking, her hands gripped the wheel tighter as she turned left onto Gene Autry. She wasn't sure where she was going—her mind a blur of fear and frantic thoughts—but the familiar sign for Wet'N'Wild flickered into view.

The water park had been shut down for over a year, now a hollowed-out shell of its former self. The perfect place to hide. It wasn't just abandoned; it was forgotten. And right now, she needed forgotten.

Grace cut the headlights, the darkness swallowing the car as she snaked along the side of the park, coming to a stop at the rear. She parked in the shadows, just beneath the gnarled branches of a tree, where no one could see, tucking Buddy snuggly in the back seat, where he immediately curled up and went to sleep. The air was thick with the scent of dust and neglect as she slipped out of the car, her shoes crunching softly on the gravel. She gripped a crowbar tightly in her hand, the metal cold and reassuring, as she approached the boarded-up entrance.

"Well, shit," she muttered, her voice barely a whisper, as she surveyed the barricade. The park, once a place of laughter and screams, now stood silent and abandoned. She needed a way in.

She found a loose board at the bottom corner. Her fingers dug into the gap, prying the wood away with a strength born of desperation. The board gave with a sharp crack, and she squeezed herself through the narrow opening, pushing through the dark into the eerie quiet of the forgotten park.

Her heart raced as she kept low, eyes darting around the abandoned rides and empty pools, wondering if she'd have to run again at a moment's notice.

But she didn't see him. The homeless man, sitting quietly in the far corner, his ragged clothes blending into the shadows, a smile curling at the corners of his lips. He watched her, his gaze steady and unnervingly calm, as she disappeared into the park.

Grace never noticed the smile—never saw the shadow that followed her as she scurried deeper into the darkness.

Landis sat alone in the booth at Bob Evan's, the familiar hum of the restaurant around him doing little to quiet the storm brewing inside his mind. His fork clinked aimlessly against the plate, pushing the food around as if in a futile attempt to convince himself he had any appetite left. He had hoped that coming here, to his usual haunt, would lift his spirits. It hadn't. A few bites in, and the hunger that had gnawed at him all afternoon was gone—swallowed by the weight of the thoughts that churned inside his skull.

He picked up his phone and stared at the screen, desperately hoping for a message from Hecate. But there was nothing. He put the phone down, a sigh escaping his lips, but before the silence could fully swallow him, a voice interrupted.

"You okay?" Janet asked warmly. She topped off his coffee with a practiced hand, her eyes scanning him with a kind of familiarity only years of serving could bring.

"Yeah," Landis lied, his words heavy as if they had been pulled from the deepest part of him.

Janet wasn't buying it. "You expect me to believe that?" she asked, raising an eyebrow, her lips curling slightly in a skeptical smile.

Landis couldn't help but let a flicker of a smile escape. Janet had been his waitress for nearly two years, and in that time, she'd seen through every mask he'd tried to wear. She knew him better than anyone, maybe even better than he knew himself.

"Can't get anything by you, can I?" he asked, his voice a little softer now.

"Nope," she smiled widely. "And whatever it is, it'll get better. Always does."

"I sure hope so," he muttered, but his heart wasn't in it.

"Well, if you need anything, Hun, I'm here for you."

"Thanks, Janet," he said, his voice barely above a whisper.

She nodded, turning away to plate her next customer's meal, her movement graceful and efficient. Landis took a sip from his coffee, its warmth a temporary comfort, but as he set the cup down, a feeling prickled at the back of his neck. Eyes. Watching him.

He looked up to see a trio of young adults about his age sitting at a nearby table. The woman, her dark hair sharp against the glow of the overhead lights, stared at him with an unsettling intensity.

Landis shifted uneasily under their gaze. The woman glanced away for a moment, tapping something into her phone, but then she was back, her eyes locked onto his once more. The others noticed and followed suit. They weren't being subtle.

Minutes passed, the air growing heavier with the tension between them. Then, without warning, the trio stood, tossed a couple of bills onto the table, and walked out. No words exchanged, just a stiff, deliberate exit. It made Landis feel... wrong.

It's nothing, Landis. Just your mind playing tricks, he tried to convince himself.

He took another sip of coffee and tried to let the past drift away for a moment. It didn't work. He couldn't stop thinking about her.

After looking at his phone one last time, he sighed and got up, following the creepy groups example and throwing a twenty on the table before leaving.

His mind was a roller-coaster as he got into his car. Part of him felt like he needed to talk to someone and get his feelings out in the open. The other part thought he should just keep to himself and let his feelings pass. In the end, he just turned on the car and started driving, hoping the universe would hit him with some form of inspiration.

Minutes passed. He wasn't sure where he was going, only that he couldn't stay still. Then, as the streets blurred past him, his phone buzzed in the passenger seat. He glanced at the screen. It was a message from Hecate: *Meet me at the bowling alley. 8 tonight. We need to talk.*

A wave of something—relief? Hope?—flooded through him. He quickly typed out a reply, his fingers shaking slightly. He couldn't help but wonder why the bowling alley. It seemed so… out of place, so unlike her. But then he remembered. Their first actual date had been there.

The day crawled on as he ran errands, distracting himself with mundane tasks in an attempt to pass the time. A watched pot never boils, and if he stared at the clock too long, it would only make the minutes stretch into hours.

As the sun began its slow descent, the sky heavy with clouds, Landis parked his car in front of Chippewa Bowl. The first sprinkle of rain dotting his windshield felt like fate.

He stepped out of his car with a smile, determined not to let the weather affect his mood, but as he walked toward the entrance, something in his gut twisted. He saw them. The same trio from the restaurant.

There is no fucking way that this is a coincidence.

He tried to walk past them, but the girl spoke up, her voice cutting through the air like a shard of ice.

"Hey guys, look! It's the creep from the restaurant."

Landis froze. His heart thudded in his chest, and before he could move, one of the guys was standing in front of him, blocking his path.

"Well, shit!" the guy sneered, his voice dripping with venom. "Did you see the way he was looking at you, Shawna? Like you were just another item on the menu?"

Landis opened his mouth to defend himself, but the second guy stepped forward, shoving a finger into Landis's chest. "Is that true, freak? Were you checking out my woman?"

"Listen," Landis said, his hands held up in a defensive gesture, "I don't know what you're talking about!"

The first guy's grin widened. "Oh, so now you're calling us liars?"

"That's not what I—"

Suddenly, the second guy pulled a knife from his pocket, the blade gleaming in the dim light of the parking lot lights. "How about we cut those pretty eyes of yours out so you can't look at women like that anymore?"

Panic surged through Landis. He took a step back, his back hitting the parked car behind him. His heart raced, but he wasn't about to back down.

The girl circled behind him, grabbing his hair with a force that sent a sharp jolt of pain through his scalp. His vision blurred, his body tensing as he saw the change in their eyes— their pupils blackened, the smirks twisting into something darker, something demonic.

He twisted out of her grip and knocked the blade from the

guy's hand, sending it clattering to the ground just as a roll of thunder split the sky. The storm had arrived. But Landis knew the danger he faced tonight wouldn't pass with the rain.

***

She's almost ready, Abaddon whispered in Gideon's mind while Hecate was in the bathroom.

Good, Gideon replied, his mind already working on his plan. *I have an idea that'll turn her completely against them. Can you get me her phone?*

Abaddon grabbed the device off the bed with a swift motion and vanished. She reappeared a moment later in Gideon's room, the phone delicately clutched in her mouth.

"Impressive," Gideon said, glancing up at her.

Abaddon set the phone on the bed beside him. Gideon wasted no time; he picked it up and typed a message, pretending to be Hecate. When he finished, he handed the phone back to her. "Find a way to break it, just in case."

She snatched the phone from his hand and disappeared, materializing on the bed a minute before Hecate emerged from the bathroom.

Feigning a tired feline stretch, Abaddon pushed the phone off the bed and sent it crashing to the floor. *I'm so sorry, Hecate! I forgot it was there.*

Hecate quickly retrieved the phone from the floor like she was trying to avoid the five-second rule. Except the rule doesn't apply to non-consumable inanimate objects. When she looked at the device, she was sad to see that the screen was shattered.

"Damn," she muttered, eyeing the broken device. "Well, that sucks."

I'm sure Gideon can get you a new one, Abaddon said meekly.

"I hope so," Hecate replied, trying to hide her frustration.

A soft knock came from the door. "Breakfast is ready, Hecate, if you're still hungry," Tarek's voice called through.

"I'll be down in a minute," she answered.

She heard his footsteps withdrawing and waited for a minute before getting up. *Time to go be the outcast again,* she thought. Then she scooped up Abaddon and headed downstairs.

She was surprised to find only Gideon and Tarek in the dining room. "Where is everyone else?"

"Most of them are busy," Gideon answered casually. "Running errands, working, you know how it is."

"Oh, right. I guess that makes sense," she said, settling into a seat.

"I hope you like omelets?" Tarek asked as he set a plate in front of her. Covered in melted cheese and sprinkled with green peppers and onions, it looked almost too perfect, like something straight out of a food magazine.

"Wow," she said, her eyes widening. "Impressive."

"Tarek's quite the chef," Gideon added. "I think he's missed his true calling."

Tarek waved off the compliment. "I just like to eat. To eat, you've got to cook. Simple math." He chuckled, taking a bite of his own omelet, one topped with cheese and mushrooms. He turned to Hecate. "Speaking of food, we're getting a group together tonight at the bowling alley. You should come join us."

Hecate hesitated, a brief flash of the past passing through her mind. The memory of her and Landis on their first date, at this same bowling alley, was still fresh. She had tried to bury it—at least for now, until she figured everything out.

It'll be fun, Abaddon whispered. *You could use a little fun, right?*

"Okay," Hecate said tentatively. "But I should warn you, I'm a pretty good bowler."

Tarek smiled. "Is that so? Well, I'm not too bad myself, if I do say so."

"Is that a challenge?" she asked, a playful glint in her eyes.

"Maybe?" Tarek grinned.

She smiled back. "Challenge accepted."

Then she turned to Gideon with puppy-dog eyes. "I have a problem, though," she said, holding up her phone. "Is there any way you can help me get a new one?"

Gideon raised an eyebrow. "Why, what happened to it?"

Hecate glanced down at Abaddon, who looked up at her with wide, innocent eyes and let out a soft meow.

Gideon chuckled. "We'll go to the mall later and see what we can do."

"Thanks," she said in relief.

The trip to the mall turned out to be more than just a quick phone replacement. After stopping by the Verizon store to take care of the insurance and get Hecate a new phone, Gideon insisted they hit a few other stores for new clothes. Hecate protested at first, but when she realized that buying new clothes meant she wouldn't have to go back to campus to collect her things—things that could easily be replaced—she relented.

By the end of it, Tarek was holding a mountain of shopping bags. "How did I get appointed bellhop duty?" he grumbled.

"Because you're a gentleman," Hecate teased.

"I don't know about that," he replied, but there was a hint of a smile in his voice.

"But I can tell."

Gideon gave him a sly smile that went unnoticed by her.

As they continued through the walkway, a group of three kids approached them, all approximately their same age. Tarek went to greet them, giving them each a frat-boy like hug, while being a little colder toward the girl. He led the trio back toward Hecate and Gideon.

"Hey, Hecate," Tarek said, "This is Darius, his brother Oscar, and their sister Shawna."

"Nice to meet you," Hecate said, smiling.

Shawna just kind of nodded as she looked Hecate up and down.

"How do you two know each other?" Hecate asked, eyeing Tarek curiously.

"We were friends in high school," Darius explained, grinning. "Tarek was... a handful back then."

"Hey, speak for yourself," Tarek said, feigning offense. "Anyway, we're heading to the bowling alley tonight. You should come join us."

Shawna glanced at her brothers and shrugged. "Sure."

"Awesome. See you at eight," Tarek said as they started to walk away.

"Bye, Gideon," Shawna called over her shoulder.

Gideon gave a casual wave, a smile playing at the corners of his lips.

"You know them?" Hecate asked once they were out of earshot.

"Yeah," Gideon answered. "I haven't seen them in a while. They used to run with a rough crowd. A real trio of hellions, if you ask me. But they've probably changed by now. I hope, anyway."

"Well, I changed," Tarek said, grinning. "Thanks to you."

Gideon raised an eyebrow but didn't say anything.

Their shopping trip finally came to an end, and they rushed back to the car just as the sky darkened and the first thunderclaps echoed in the distance. As they pulled into the parking lot of Chippewa Bowl, the rain began, the first drops splattering onto the windshield.

As they got out of the car, Hecate was stunned to see Landis there, struggling with the kids she had met at the mall only hours before.

Her heart dropped into her stomach as she watched him shove Shawna to the ground, then kick Darius in the groin. Oscar lunged forward to defend his brother, but Landis twisted away and thrust the blade forward. Oscar fell, clutching his stomach as the blood pooled beneath him.

Darius and Shawna screamed in horror as Landis backed away, still gripping the knife.

"My God, Landis!" Hecate cried, her voice cracking. "What have you done?"

Landis stared at her, vacant and lost, before letting the knife fall to the ground.

CHAPTER 7

The shadows engulfed Grace as she darted into the abandoned park, the weight of desolation pressing in around her. The air reeked of stagnant water and decay, the remnants of a once-vibrant place now suffocated by filth and neglect. She had been here before, but now it was different—eerie, silent, as though the park itself had given up.

She quietly found a secluded corner, hidden away from the main area, where any passing officer might find her, should they come across her car and start poking around. Then she turned on her phone and texted Matthew. As she waited for a response, she sat there refusing to give in to the grief that pounded on her soul like a prison inmate clamoring for his release.

A minute later, Matthew responded with a quick text: *Where are you? Hope you're okay? Be safe.*

She exhaled a shaky breath and typed back, *Yeah, I'm okay. Hiding out. Wet'N'Wild. Please hurry!*

I'm trying.

The brief exchange left her feeling both comforted and further alone. Her heart drummed against her chest, grief clawing at her insides like a beast eager to break free. She pushed the feeling aside, focusing on staying safe.

Suddenly, the sharp sound of movement sliced through the quiet. Grace's breath caught in her throat. Fear surged, sharper than before. She quickly powered off her phone, her senses heightened as the oppressive silence seemed to stretch, suffocating. Her eyes darted around, seeking any sign of movement.

Then came a swift blur of fur. A cat, its eyes wide and wild, darted in front of her, chasing something small and frantic. Grace's heart skipped, a startled cry escaping her before she could stifle it. The cat pounced, snatching up its prize, and vanished into the darkness beyond. She let out a nervous laugh, embarrassed at her own reaction.

But just as the tension began to fade, a voice sliced through the stillness, freezing her in place. "I don't get many visitors anymore, not since they boarded the place up like that."

Grace turned around slowly. An old man stood there, his appearance ragged, his long beard matted and unkempt, his missing teeth exposed in a twisted grin.

She forced a smile, trying to mask her fear. "I'm sorry," she muttered, glancing around. "I didn't realize anyone else was here."

The man's smile grew, something dark flickering in his eyes. "It's okay, dearie," he said, his voice almost gentle, but with a glint of something unholy lurking beneath. "I can use the company."

Grace's instincts screamed. Something about him felt off—wrong. She took a cautious step back. "I was just looking for somewhere quiet. Didn't mean to disturb you. I'll go."

Before she could make her escape, the man lunged, his movements impossibly fast. "Nonsense!" His voice was almost gleeful. "We're just getting acquainted. Besides, it's been a minute since I've eaten."

The air around him shifted. His skin pulled tight over bone, his beard vanished, and his teeth elongated into sharp fangs. His eyes flared bright yellow, glowing with an otherworldly hunger. The air grew thick with sulfur as he howled, a sickening cloud of poison swirling around her.

Grace fell to the ground instinctively, the noxious fumes burning her lungs. She scrambled to her feet and bolted, desperation fueling her every step. The park, once a place of fun, had become her personal nightmare. She raced for the row of shops near the entrance, her breath coming in ragged gasps.

All the doors were locked, every window boarded up. She was trapped. Her mind raced for any way out. Her eyes fell on the small building at the center of the park, where the lazy river used to flow, and found the door to the small building still hanging ajar. Her pulse quickened, and without hesitation, she dove inside, slamming the door behind her. The lock was broken, and her legs pressed against the door, holding it shut as best she could.

Seconds later, the door began to tremble. A voice, low and chilling, slipped through the cracks. "Come on, Grace. I'm hungry," it crooned. "I just wanna eat."

She gritted her teeth as panic flooded through her. "How do you know my name?"

The demon chuckled darkly. "Oh, you're a legend, sweetie. That little stunt you pulled with the Strigoi? Word's spreading fast. Everyone wants a taste. Looks like I'll be the one to take the first bite."

Grace's fingers fumbled around for something she could use as a weapon. Anything to keep this thing at bay. Her hand closed around the handle of a broom, its wood rough beneath her grip. But before she could brace herself, the door gave way, and the demon crashed through.

The broom handle came up instinctively, and in one swift motion, Grace shoved it into the demon's stomach. It grunted, its twisted face contorting in pain. For a moment, the world seemed to freeze, but then, with a sickening laugh, it staggered back, wiping blood from its lips.

"You'll have to do better than that, you fucking whore."

Before she could react, the demon shrieked, a sound that tore through the night. A response echoed back from somewhere in the distance, a chorus of howls that made her blood run cold.

Grace didn't hesitate. She yanked the broom out of its stomach and drove it upward through its chin, the wood splintering as it pierced its skull. Black blood exploded from the wound, spraying in all directions. The demon's body jerked, then fell lifeless to the ground.

"Take that, you piece of shit!" she spat.

But the howls of other monstrosities filled the air, closer now, maddening in their intensity. She knew she only had minutes before she was overrun.

Matthew's thirst hit him like a hammer once the call with Solomon ended. With a low groan, he pushed open the door to the convenience store, the cool air inside offering a brief respite from the oppressive heat outside. As he scoured the rows of beverages, his phone buzzed in his pocket. He pulled it out to see a text from Grace, letting him know where she was hiding. After a quick reply, he slid it back in his pocket, trying to ignore the rising tension in his gut.

While he was still perusing the beverage coolers, a police car pulled up. The officer, a short and squat guy with a balding head, eyed him suspiciously as he walked into the store.

Then the ring on his finger started to glow.

Matthew's gaze darted around, his heart rate spiking. The small store, crammed with customers, felt suffocating. There was the cashier, a couple of teenagers, a gang of bikers by the beer aisle, a frazzled woman with pink hair—hell, the demon could be anyone. It was easier when the monsters were obvious. When they had scales or fangs. When you could see them coming.

A tug on his arm broke his thoughts. He looked down, his

pulse hammering in his throat, to see a little girl standing beside him, wide-eyed and innocent. *Shit*, he thought. *Not the little girl. She can't be more than four years old.*

"Can you help me, Mister?" she asked in a small voice. "I think something's wrong with my mommy."

Matthew's stomach churned as his eyes shifted toward the back of the store. He saw the woman—her body sprawled on the floor, a pool of blood slowly expanding around her head. His instincts screamed at him to walk away, to turn around and pretend he hadn't seen a thing.

But the girl's hand was still gripping his sleeve, tugging him forward.

He followed her slowly down the aisle. He knew he shouldn't be here, shouldn't be looking. But something about the innocence in the girl's eyes compelled him.

And then he saw it. A scene straight out of 'Alien'.

The woman's eyes were lifeless, her body still, but there was a sickening writhing beneath her skin, her stomach distending unnaturally as something inside her struggled to break free. The tearing sound was grotesque, a sickeningly wet noise as a clawed hand breached her stomach, tearing through flesh and fabric alike.

Matthew stumbled backward, his mouth dry, his mind reeling.

He tried to back away from the scene, but the little girl was there, looking up at him with sad eyes. "Aren't you going to help her?" she asked.

He was tongue-tied. What could he say to her under the circumstances? *Sorry, kid, your mom is fucked?*

The little girl's voice was suddenly sharp, cutting through his horror. Black eyes had replaced her sad ones, and the girl now reeked of evil and hatred. Her voice dropped into something guttural. "What the fuck are you going to do, you dumb shit?"

The air in the store seemed to freeze as he stood there, stunned, trapped between the little girl's soulless stare and the horrifying spectacle in front of him. The woman's body convulsed violently, and the nightmare emerged—a creature with reptilian features, its head larger than its body, yellow eyes glowing with hunger. Its mouth was full of jagged teeth, and its lower half was like a squid's, its tentacles flapping eagerly, tipped with sharp barbs.

It screeched, a horrendous sound that made Matthew's blood run cold. Before he could react, the creature lunged, its spindly limbs scraping the floor like a spider's legs, tapping eerily as it closed in on him.

But then, just as the creature was about to pounce, a gunshot rang out. The demon exploded in a shower of blood and viscera, its shriek cut short.

Matthew whipped around to see the officer standing there, his gun aimed steadily. The officer's lips curled into a grin. "Sorry, little lady," he said coldly, his gaze flicking to the girl. "This one's mine."

The girl blinked, her expression flickering for a second— her eyes still black, but a hint of pleading in them. She tried her best to give him the sad, puppy-dog eyes, but he wasn't buying it. He pulled the trigger and put a bullet in her brain.

The rest of the store was eerily silent. Matthew's stomach twisted as he watched the officer calmly scan the room. No one looked shocked. No one seemed disturbed by the carnage unfolding before them. They all just stood there, as if this were a regular part of their day.

The officer's gaze shifted over the remaining customers. "Anyone else want to question my authority?" he asked, his voice low and dangerous.

There was no response. None dared to speak up.

"Good," the officer muttered. "Then I suggest you get the hell out of here before you end up like her."

One by one, the remaining customers filed out of the store, each casting hardened glares at Matthew and the officer as they left. All that remained were the cashier and the stock boy, standing behind the counter, frozen. The officer glanced at them, unfazed.

"That means you too," he said.

When neither moved, he didn't hesitate. With two quick shots, he dropped them both.

Matthew stood there in stunned silence, his mind struggling to comprehend the sheer brutality of what he'd just witnessed. Even after everything he had been through, nothing had prepared him for this.

The officer holstered his gun and slid his arm around Matthew's shoulders, guiding him toward the door. "Name's Pascal," he said casually. "Solomon sent me. Figured you might need a hand before he could get here."

Matthew looked down at his hand in confusion, realizing that the ring was still glowing fiercely. "But... you're a demon!"

Pascal nodded without missing a beat. "Yep."

"And you're friends with Solomon?"

Pascal's grin widened. "Friends? Nah. More like mutual respect."

He motioned toward the door. "Time to hit the road. Won't be long before more of 'em show up, and they're not gonna be happy."

Matthew followed, his head spinning with confusion, fear, and disbelief. As they reached the car, Pascal threw him a sideways glance. "How's that little honey-biscuit of yours doing, by the way?"

CHAPTER 9

"But they attacked me first, Officer!" Landis pleaded, his voice cracking as the officer yanked him by the arm, slamming him into the back of the squad car. He glanced out the window, his heart sinking when he saw Hecate standing there in the rain, her face frozen in pure terror. The look in her eyes was a silent goodbye—the last piece of hope he'd clung to, now shattered forever.

How had everything changed so quickly? They had been happy—he'd believed they were truly in love, that they'd had a future together. Yet, in an instant, it had all been ripped away, and he couldn't even comprehend why.

Then he saw Gideon. Of course, it was him. The twisted man responsible for all of this, the one pulling the strings. Landis's mind raced as he desperately tried to reach Solomon. But the storm raging inside was too loud for his voice to penetrate.

Landis's chest tightened as he watched Gideon lead Hecate away from the scene. She didn't look back. No final words. No last touch. Just gone. And then another man appeared beside them—a face he almost recognized, but it didn't matter. They vanished, leaving Landis alone in the car, the weight of the world crashing down on him.

The officer climbed into the front seat and turned the ignition key, the engine roaring to life. Landis's gaze shifted to the ambulance where Oscar's body was being loaded in, a casualty of whatever demonic plot had been set in motion. That Oscar had been possessed when he attacked didn't matter. Landis knew no one would believe him. They'd see him as the killer. The one who murdered an innocent man, all because Gideon, with his dark agenda, was playing games that could end the world.

The officer adjusted his rear-view mirror, catching Landis's eye. "You okay back there, kid?" The question felt more like a threat, his voice low and tinged with malice.

Then the officer turned his head and Landis froze. The man's mouth stretched wide, impossibly wide, revealing two glaring eyes inside his throat that locked on Landis with a gaze that dripped with hunger.

A wave of panic surged through Landis. He tried to push himself out of his body, desperately attempting to reach Solomon, but as his soul left his body, a black, ethereal hand shot out of the officer's throat and wrapped around his neck, yanking him back into his physical form.

"Not happening, pretty boy," the officer growled. "No one's coming to save you."

Landis's breath caught in his throat as the black hand squeezed harder, sending a burst of darkness through him and knocking him unconscious.

When he regained consciousness, the car was still moving, but the city was far behind them. They were heading east on Ireland Road, the surroundings growing sparse, with wide fields stretching out on either side.

The officer turned onto a narrow road, the wheels kicking up dirt as they bounced over the uneven terrain. He stopped after a short drive, then climbed out of the car, leaving Landis to wonder what fresh hell awaited him.

The officer opened the back door, his grin stretching wide as he ordered Landis out. "Okay, out you go."

Landis hesitated, his body shaking, but the officer's hand shot out, grabbing him by the arm and yanking him forcefully from the car. "I said get your fucking ass out here!"

The wet ground seemed to swallow his feet as Landis stumbled out of the car. The officer opened his mouth again, and the voice from within spoke, deep and distorted. "Any last words?"

Landis's mind screamed for Solomon, his heart racing as he tried to reach out. One final attempt, one last plea for help. But again, that black hand reached out and seized him, its grip like ice, choking the life from him.

The officer's body shimmered, the flesh seeming to fall away, crumbling like an empty husk. The officer was gone. In his place, towering above him, stood a shadow demon—tall and spindly, with a grotesque head that seemed too large for its thin body. Its mouth stretched across most of its face, filled with jagged teeth, and it let out a bone-shaking roar that sent a chill straight to Landis's soul.

Before Landis could even move, the demon bent down, its massive jaws snapping open, engulfing him whole, swallowing him in the darkness.

CHAPTER 10

The cries of the beasts grew louder, echoing through the air, and Grace's heart raced. She could feel the walls closing in and knew time was running out. To anyone else, the calls would've seemed like the cackling of crows, a common sound in the desert. But Grace knew better. These weren't ordinary birds—they were something far worse. She couldn't pinpoint the exact threat drawing closer, but she wasn't sticking around to find out.

She scrambled toward the entrance, her breath coming in quick gasps as she wedged herself back under the loose board. A sharp sting of pain shot through her as a rusted nail caught her left arm, tearing through the skin and leaving a bloody trail in its wake. She howled in agony, but didn't stop. "Great, just great," she muttered between clenched teeth. "Now, on top of everything else, I've got to worry about tetanus, too."

The wind picked up, sending sand and grit cutting into her face with each step. She bent low, fighting the sting in her eyes, forcing herself to focus on the twenty yards between her and her vehicle. When she finally reached it, the sight nearly stopped her heart—her tires were shredded, torn to pieces by whatever had passed through.

A shiver rushed through her as she opened the door, fearing the sight she might find. She was relieved when she found Buddy still alive, whimpering and shaking in the back seat. Gently, she scooped up the animal and held him to her, trying to calm him down, even while her own fears threatened to consume her in the midst of the nightmare she found herself in.

Her level of terror grew even higher when she reached into her back pocket for her phone and found it missing. Realizing that she must've dropped it when the demon first attacked, she had no choice but to venture back into the park to find it. Without it, there would be no way Matthew would find her once he arrived, if he arrived at all.

She quelled that fear quickly, refusing to give into the doomsday thoughts that threatened to overtake her. He would come for her. She knew it. She believed it. She had to.

As the cries of the beasts grew louder, more frantic, she returned to the entrance, careful to avoid the same nail that had already injured her. Her mind raced as she hurried to the corner where she'd first called Matthew, Buddy bouncing in her arms as she ran. Her phone was nowhere to be found.

She sprinted toward the center of the park, passed the dead demon's body on her way to the storage building. Inside, the darkness swallowed her, but she kept moving, her fingers brushing over shelves and tools in a frantic search until she saw a faint glimmer of light. She snatched her phone up, pressing the button, and a faint sigh of relief escaped her lips when the screen flickered to life.

The cries grew even louder, impossibly close. Her heart pounded, and she knew she was out of time. But she had to find somewhere better to hide. She shone the phone's light around, scanning the room, and her eyes landed on a screwdriver lying among deflated rafts and forgotten paddles. She grabbed it and sprinted toward the food shops at the front of the park.

The Mexican food stand, the one that used to serve tacos and burritos, was her only option. Her hands trembled as she worked the screwdriver into the lock, frustration mounting when it wouldn't budge. With a growl, she jammed the edge of the tool into the door-frame, pushing with all her might until she felt the satisfying give of the lock. The door creaked open, and a rush of stale air slapped her in the face.

The place reeked of rot—the former operator who failed to clean the place thoroughly before they left, leaving behind a colony of bacteria that had festered in the desert heat, filling the air with a noxious cloud. Grace quickly pulled her shirt over her nose, gritting her teeth against the stench as she slipped inside. Even Buddy whined and squirmed from the stench.

Just as she moved to close the door behind her, a shadow passed overhead. Her eyes shot to the sky, and she saw a murder of crows soaring over the wall, their black wings slicing through the air with eerie precision. They landed near the entrance, and before she could react, they began to merge, twisting and writhing, until a single figure towered above her —nearly seven feet tall, with limbs like twisted branches and a sharp, beaked face.

A cry echoed from the creature, its voice jagged and unnatural, and it turned its piercing black eyes toward Grace.

She slammed the door shut, backing into the darkened interior, her phone's weak light flickering as she scanned the room for something—anything—to use as a weapon. But it was empty, save for the dust and decay. The screwdriver was all she had, and it wouldn't save her. Hell, she could've had a rocket launcher and it wouldn't have done any good.

She shoved Buddy toward the corner of the shop as the door burst open with a deafening crack, and the demon surged inside—a writhing mass of feathers and flesh. It shrieked as it lunged toward her.

Grace froze, her heart pounding as the creature bent down, bringing its face to hers. She saw the true depth of evil in the beast's eyes—the twisted, unnatural angles of its body, the hundreds of crows that made up its monstrous form, all still living, breathing, and glaring at her with hunger.

The demon suddenly split apart, and in an instant, she was consumed by a swarm of crows. Their wings battered her, their beaks tearing at her skin, their cries deafening as they enveloped her, devouring her whole.

A minute later, the birds flew into the night sky, squawking triumphantly as they disappeared into the darkness. Grace was gone.

Hecate kept her eyes fixed on the road ahead as Gideon drove through the town, the landscape blurring by as she tried to piece together the shattered fragments of her heart. The weight of the past few days pressed down on her, each moment more suffocating than the last. Landis's indifferent reaction to her mother's death still stung like an open wound, but it was his blind defense of Solomon that cut deepest. She had held onto the faint hope that, somehow, they would find their way back to each other—rekindle the love that had once burned between them. Now she understood. That flame was extinguished for good.

A few minutes of silence passed before Tarek's voice broke through the quiet. "You okay, up there, Hecate?"

She didn't respond immediately, her mind still swirling with tangled thoughts. Instead, she just gave a soft grunt.

Through the rear-view mirror, Gideon glanced at Tarek, his eyes narrowing slightly. Tarek nodded once, then the two men began speaking in unison, their words barely above a whisper, the cadence eerie and unnatural. Hecate's lips curled into a sharp laugh before she could even stop herself.

Gideon's brow furrowed. "What's so funny?"

"Men... life... everything!" she replied, her tone raw with bitter amusement.

She held her hand up in front of her face, eyes wide in feigned wonder as she waved it through the air, her fingers tracing invisible patterns like she was in the midst of a psychedelic dream. "Wow, look at that! I've never seen colors like this before. Can you guys see it too?" Her voice held a childlike curiosity, but there was a wildness behind her eyes.

Before either man could answer, Hecate twisted around in her seat and fixed her gaze on Tarek. "I wanna get drunk. Do you wanna go get drunk?"

Tarek raised an eyebrow, his lips curling into a half-smile. "Sure. Where to?"

She pouted, leaning forward as if weighing the decision. "Not sure. Somewhere fun, though."

He thought for a moment. "I know a place. Gets pretty crazy."

Gideon chuckled softly from the front seat. "You can drop me off at home on the way."

Hecate shot him a look over her shoulder. "You don't wanna join us?"

"No. I'm too old for that now. I'd just be a third wheel."

Hecate shrugged. "Suit yourself."

A few minutes later, they pulled up in front of Club Fever, only to find it closed for renovations.

"Well, shit. I was just here a couple of months ago," Tarek muttered, sounding genuinely apologetic. "I didn't know, Hecate. I'm sorry."

She stared at the closed doors for a moment, disappointment flickering across her face before she softened. With a grin, she grabbed Tarek's hand, pulling him closer to her. "Maybe we can have our own little party, then?"

Without warning, she kissed him hard, her lips urgent and

demanding. Tarek responded in kind, their passion igniting like a wildfire. When they finally pulled apart, breathless, he put the car in drive, and a few miles later, they arrived at a small house tucked away in the shadows.

Tarek led her toward the door, and Hecate craned her neck, looking up at the sky. The rain had turned into a light drizzle, and she held out her hand, catching the droplets, laughing with childish delight at the sensation.

Tarek chuckled, opening the door to the house and watching her dance inside. He couldn't help but smile at the spell they'd cast—it was working, just as planned. Her inhibitions had melted away, and now she was his. But he needed to be careful. He needed to finish what he'd started before the effects wore off.

As soon as the door clicked shut behind them, he pulled her into his arms, kissing her deeply. She responded eagerly, her hands wandering, exploring every inch of him, pulling him closer.

When her hand found his crotch, he grinned and pulled back, his breath heavy. "Let's take this to the bedroom," he said as he scooped her up effortlessly and carried her into the next room.

He threw her onto the bed, pinning her arms above her head with a force that sent a jolt of excitement through her. He trailed his tongue down her neck, across her chest, each touch sending shivers of pleasure through her body until she was gasping for more.

"I'll be back," he said and turned toward the bathroom, but not before throwing her one last hungry glance.

"Don't be gone too long," she purred. "I'm ready to get this party started."

He smirked. "Don't worry. You'll get more than you can handle."

"We'll see about that," Hecate replied with a devilish grin.

In the bathroom, Tarek stared at his reflection in the mirror, his body trembling slightly. He breathed deeply, focusing as the incantation began. "Attenrobendum eos, ad consiendrum, ad ligandum eos, potiter et sovendum, et ad, congregontum eos, corem me."

His body convulsed as Azazel took hold of him. When Tarek gazed back at his reflection, it wasn't his own face staring back. For a brief moment, Azazel's eyes glinted in the mirror, then Tarek returned, with something dark, lingering beneath the surface.

Naked, he strode back into the room, his eyes locking onto Hecate. He pulled her into his embrace, undressing her with heated intensity, his lips trailing fire along her skin, moving up her thigh, across her stomach, circling her breasts before capturing her mouth in a deep, consuming kiss.

"Give yourself to me, Hecate," he whispered against her lips.

Her eyes fluttered open and her breath caught in her throat when she saw Azazel's face before her, straddling her like a ghost from a nightmare. For a moment, she thought she was still dreaming. But no—it was real. He was real.

"Give yourself to me, wholly and completely," he murmured, his voice a velvet promise. "You will never be alone again. You will feel strength like you've never known. Rule by my side and become the queen you were always meant to be."

Hecate stared into his eyes, his words reverberating in her mind, sinking deep into her soul. She grabbed his head and pulled him to her, kissing him with a ferocity born of desperation and desire. Her legs wrapped around his waist, pulling him closer, tightening herself against him. She was done being weak. Done being lost. It was time for a change.

Their lovemaking became frantic and urgent fever pitch, until Azazel's teeth sank into her neck with a savage hunger. He drank from her deeply, the sensation sharp and terrible, as he drained her of life until the darkness consumed her.

After he pulled away, with her life force nearly gone, he muttered words in a language older than time, and expelled a stream of black liquid into her mouth. She choked, gasping as it burned through her, and then agony wracked her body. Her back arched as she screamed, the transformation ripping through her like wildfire.

Then, as the world spun into oblivion, she collapsed onto the bed, slipping into unconsciousness.

Azazel bent down and kissed her gently on the forehead, his voice soft and tender. "Sleep now, my queen. When you awaken, there will be much for you to do."

CHAPTER 12

Solomon sped toward the airport, an icy dread gnawing at him. Landis was unreachable, his phone ringing endlessly with no answer. Hecate was gone, swallowed by the chaos that had been set in motion. And now, Matthew and Grace were in danger, fighting for their lives. All of it traced back to one man—the one who was unmaking everything Solomon had fought to protect.

His mind raced, calculating the worst-case scenario. Gideon was on the verge of breaking the seal, and if that happened, Hell itself would follow. Every ounce of Solomon's focus turned to one thing: stopping Gideon before it was too late. He had to find Matthew. He had to save Grace. If his instincts were right, Pascal would be his only chance. He wasn't thrilled to work with the demon, but desperate times demanded desperate measures. And if Gideon was planning what Solomon feared, Matthew's ring would be the only weapon left to avert the apocalypse.

As he neared the airport, the ring on his finger pulsed—faster, harder, with a warning that made his gut twist. He couldn't shake the feeling that something was horribly wrong. The world seemed to be teetering on the edge of some unspeakable precipice.

Ignoring the usual protocols, Solomon circled around to the back of the airport, entering a restricted area with a practiced swipe of a keypad. The gate groaned open, and he slid through, pulling into a small parking garage. He slipped through a service entrance and into the concourse, moving like a shadow. He found his gate and stood in the corner out of sight, waiting for the call to board.

Once the other passengers had boarded, Solomon approached the gate agent. She smiled at him, scanning his boarding pass without hesitation.

"Enjoy your trip, Solomon," she said cheerfully.

Her voice sent a ripple through him, a feeling of something wrong simmering beneath the surface. He nodded and made his way down the ramp and into the cabin. It was first-class—a luxury he rarely indulged in, but it felt like a necessity now. The fewer eyes on him, the better.

The moment he settled into his seat, he felt it. The stares. Twenty-two eyes fixed on him. A mix of middle-aged men, a couple of young adults, and a little girl—maybe six, with pink ribbons in her hair. Each of them locked onto him, their eyes gleaming with malice. Their smiles, twisted and cruel, sent a shiver down his spine.

Just as he made to stand, the flight attendant, a woman with an unsettling calm in her eyes, stopped him.

"Now, now, Solomon," she said with a smile that didn't reach her eyes. "You know the rules. Stay seated until we've reached the desired altitude."

A voice crackled over the intercom, smooth and sinister.

"Ladies and gentlemen, my name is Angrboda, and I'm your chief flight attendant this wonderful evening. Welcome aboard Hellish Airlines, flight 666, non-stop service to Hell and back. Our flight time will be six hours and sixty-six minutes. Altitude: six hundred sixty-six thousand feet. Ground speed: six hundred sixty-six miles per hour."

The words settled into Solomon's mind like ice. His worst fears were beginning to take shape.

"At this time," Angrboda continued, "please ensure your seat backs and tray tables are in their upright position, and all torture devices are properly fastened. Weapons must be set aside until instructed otherwise. Violators will be eliminated on the spot. Thank you, and enjoy your flight."

The sudden clank of metal echoed in the cabin. Solomon's eyes darted around, watching as the passengers—each with bloodied knives and cleavers—placed their weapons on the floor at their feet. Even the little girl, with her flowery dress and innocent face, gently set down a long knife beside her.

The warning bell rang. The plane began to taxi, its engines roaring to life as it accelerated down the runway. Solomon's pulse drummed in his ears. His survival instincts screamed at him to act—but he was trapped, surrounded.

Once they were airborne, the voice of Angrboda returned, "Attention, passengers," she said, her tone chilling. "We will be reaching optimal altitude soon. At that time, feel free to kill or maim as you see fit. Just remember—Solomon is our main target."

Solomon's chest tightened. This wasn't just a flight. It was a trap, and he was the prey.

"First-class will have first crack at the heretic," Angrboda continued, "and if he survives, business-class will get their turn. Finally, economy class will have their chance. As always, thank you for flying Hellish Airlines. Happy hunting."

The bell rang again, and with a collective, feral roar, the demons lunged at him. Solomon knew he didn't have much time. The last thing he thought before the onslaught began was that this was far from over. Not by a long shot.

***

Solomon severed the psychic link with the clay golem, the decoy he had crafted with painstaking precision. It had cost him time, effort, and a considerable amount of energy—resources he couldn't afford to waste. But this wasn't about the golem anymore. It was about survival. And right now, survival meant making hard choices. He wasn't new to death—he'd danced with it before, and likely would again—but today, he wasn't ready to embrace it. Not just yet.

As his consciousness pulled away from the lifeless construct, he could almost feel the fury radiating from the demons while they hammered at the golem's clay body. Their claws sank deep into its fragile form, but the little girl demon with the twisted grin was the most satisfying to watch. Solomon smirked at the thought, savoring the fleeting victory. The link was severed just in time. They were still clueless, thrashing against the empty shell while he slipped away undetected.

He shifted his focus to the present, turning his attention to the pilot of the small Cessna, the steady hum of the engines vibrating through the cabin. Solomon signaled him to change course, redirecting the plane onto the pre-arranged route they had discussed earlier.

He leaned his head against the cold window, watching the sprawling city below shrink into a blur of lights and shadows. The gnawing sense of urgency crawled through him—something in the air, something unseen, was telling him that time was slipping through his fingers like sand. And the worst part was that he didn't know if he'd have enough to make it count.

CHAPTER 13

A thunderous drumbeat echoed in Hecate's skull, a relentless pounding that seemed to tear at her insides while an invisible weight crushed her chest. She fought to pry her eyes open, her body screaming in protest. When she finally opened her eyes, she found Abaddon purring contentedly inches away from her face.

Hello, Abaddon said. *How are you feeling?*

"Like I got run over by a fucking truck," Hecate rasped. She blinked hard, trying to focus. The familiar surroundings of her room greeted her vision, but the disorientation still lingered. "How did I get here?"

What do you remember?

Hecate exhaled slowly, trying to piece together the fragments of the previous night. Her thoughts were a tangled mess, fleeting images flashing before her eyes. But slowly, the memories began to fuse together. Her heart raced as she recalled the chaos. Her voice trembled, "I remember Landis... and the knife... there was so much blood. How could he do something like that?"

What about after that?

After that, things were still a blur. "I remember... getting in the car with Gideon and Tarek... then dropping Gideon off... after that..." She trailed off, unable to recall more.

Then, in a sudden, violent jolt, Azazel's image flashed into her mind as a wave of pain exploded through her body. A thousand needles dug into her flesh, each one piercing deeper than the last, as though her organs were being set on fire. The scream that tore from her lips sounded like the very fabric of her soul was unraveling.

Abaddon opened her mouth and her tentacles curled around Hecate's head, anchoring her in place. *Don't resist, Hecate. Let it flow through you.*

"What's happening to me?" Hecate cried out.

You're changing. Abaddon's voice was gentle, but firm. *When you gave yourself to Azazel, you surrendered everything— body and soul. You're becoming what you were always meant to be.*

A soft hum vibrated through the air as Abaddon closed her eyes. The high-pitched sound filled the space around them, and in its wake, a wave of dark and electric blue energy swirled through the room, enveloping both of them. Through Abaddon's healing song, Hecate's pain began to ease, but the transformation continued—her bones stretched, her organs twisted, her very being bent and reshaped from the inside out.

Then, in a heartbeat, the room disappeared, and she was standing in the middle of a barren wasteland. The earth beneath her feet was cracked and split, like the dying remnants of a shattered world. The air hung heavy and cold, and a stark loneliness seeped into her bones.

A voice, familiar yet haunting, broke through the silence. "Don't be afraid, Hecate. I'm here for you."

Hecate turned around and saw the figure standing before her, her dark skin glowing against the desolate backdrop, wearing a flowing silk gown that billowed around her like a storm. She smiled softly, a warmth in her eyes that felt like home.

"Abaddon?" Hecate whispered.

Abaddon nodded.

"Where am I?"

Abaddon stepped closer. "We're in your head."

Hecate's gaze swept the desolate landscape, her heart sinking. Was this what was left of her soul? "Is this it?" she murmured. "Is this all that remains of me?"

Abaddon's touch was gentle as she cupped Hecate's face, guiding her to meet her gaze. "Oh, Hecate, you've been hurt so many times, betrayed until you've lost the very essence of who you are. But I'm here to help you reclaim it. To remind you of your birthright."

Without warning, Abaddon leaned in, pressing her lips to Hecate's. At first, Hecate stiffened, unsure, but then—something inside her shifted. She surrendered, melting into the kiss as it ignited a fire deep within her.

When the kiss ended, Abaddon pulled away. "Look around you now."

Hecate's eyes flew open in shock. The wasteland was gone. In its place, a lush, vibrant landscape stretched before her, the once-barren earth now teeming with life. Birds flitted through the air, singing, while animals darted between the bushes, as if the world itself had come alive just for her.

"Wow," Hecate gasped. "Did you do this?"

Abaddon smiled. "No, you did. This is your mind. I'm just here to guide you."

"Well, I'd say you helped alright."

"We're not done yet," Abaddon replied. "Look over there."

Hecate followed her gaze and saw a massive volcano rising against the sky, its dark summit etched against the horizon. "What is that?" she asked.

"That's your final destination," Abaddon said. "The place where you will be truly reborn."

Before Hecate could respond, Abaddon turned and began walking toward the volcano. After some hesitation, Hecate followed, her heart pounding in her chest as they drew closer to the base, the ground beneath their feet pulsing with the energy of the molten core.

Minutes later, they stood on the edge of the volcano, staring down at the bubbling pool of lava below. The air was thick with ash swirling around them like dark snow.

"Now what?" Hecate asked, her voice barely a whisper.

"Now you give yourself over completely," Abaddon's eyes locked with hers. "Let go of everything that has hurt you. Let the fire purify you. Become something beautiful, something feared."

"How do I do that?" Hecate asked, her voice trembling.

Abaddon smiled gently. "I think you already know the answer."

Hecate's gaze dropped to the pool of lava below her. Fear seized her, paralyzing her in place. Even knowing this was all happening in her mind, the terror coursing through her was raw and real.

"Don't be afraid, Hecate. It'll be over quickly. I promise. You'll thank me later."

Hecate turned to look at Abaddon, seeking reassurance. What she saw left her breathless. Abaddon's beauty, her love, radiated with such intensity that it gave Hecate the strength she desperately needed.

Taking a deep breath, Hecate steeled herself. Without another thought, she flung herself over the edge of the volcano, her body plunging toward the lava below. The heat seared her skin, her flesh blistering and peeling away as she fell. She screamed, her body dying in an agonizing instant.

Then there was nothing. Only darkness and silence.

But then, power surged through her—filling every fiber of her being. Her flesh reformed, reborn, stronger than ever before. With a force she couldn't fully comprehend, she shot upwards, her black wings unfurling, cutting through the air like a blade.

As she landed before Abaddon, her wings folded behind her, her skin returning to its normal hue, though now marked with the streak of silver through her hair and the mark on her ankle—Azazel's mark.

"How do you feel?" Abaddon asked.

Hecate grinned, her excitement nearly bursting through her. "Like I've never felt before. I feel incredible."

"You should feel honored. Azazel only grants power to those who truly deserve it."

Hecate glanced at the mark on her ankle, feeling the weight of it. She was bound to Azazel, and she would do whatever it took to prove her worth.

"What now?" she asked.

"Now you wake up," Abaddon replied, "and you make them all pay. For everything they've done to you."

Hecate's smile widened. "I like the sound of that."

CHAPTER 14

They had just driven away from the convenience store when a massive shadow swept across the sky. Pascal slammed his foot on the accelerator, pushing the car to its limits, weaving through traffic as cautiously as he could. When they'd gone about a quarter-mile, the shadow split, revealing a flock of black birds that dove toward the building like a deadly swarm. Matthew knew, without a doubt, that they would've torn him apart if it weren't for the demon's interference.

But that led to an uncomfortable realization. How much could he trust this demon, even though he was supposedly aligned with Solomon? He trusted Solomon—mostly—but sometimes the demon's methods felt... off.

"Hold on!" Pascal barked suddenly, jerking the wheel hard to the right.

Matthew's fingers gripped the door handle as the car veered sharply onto a side street. "What's going on?" he asked.

Pascal's voice was grim. "I think we've got a couple tailing us. Need to get off the main roads before we're spotted."

"Aren't we supposed to be meeting Solomon at the airport?" Matthew asked nervously.

"Soon. But there's a detour we have to make first."

"We don't have time for detours! Grace is in danger!"

"Relax, kiddo," Pascal muttered, his voice smooth as ever. "I'll get you to your girl. But we've gotta handle this first. Otherwise, we're not going anywhere."

Matthew clenched his fists. He was at Pascal's mercy, and the demon knew it. Regardless of whether Solomon felt he was trustworthy or not, Matthew knew he better keep his guard up.

After a tense few minutes, Pascal pulled into an old parking garage in the heart of downtown. He drove deep into the shadowed corners and shut off the engine, leaving them in the suffocating silence.

Time crawled by, thick and heavy. Pascal's breath was shallow as he waited for any signs of danger. The minutes stretched on, each one making Matthew's frustration boil hotter. He was losing precious time that could mean the difference between life and death for Grace.

Just as Matthew thought the coast was clear, Pascal reached for the ignition—only to freeze. A single glance into the rear-view mirror made his blood run cold. A dozen demon birds swooped down, their black wings cutting through the air.

"Shit!" Pascal hissed, ducking down into his seat.

Matthew immediately followed suit and hunkered down as low as he could go, hoping that they wouldn't be found. They stayed like that for what felt like an eternity, waiting, praying the creatures would lose interest. Nearly twenty minutes later, Pascal's hand slid toward the ignition again, turning the key with barely a sound. Slowly, cautiously, he pulled the car out of the garage and back into the darkened streets.

The moon was only a tiny sliver of itself as Matthew

looked out through the windshield, making the night darker than usual. That darkness weighed on him even more. "So, where are we going?" he asked anxiously.

Pascal's response was quick, almost too casual. "We're going to see an old friend of mine. He's the only one who can get you to your woman in time."

Matthew's stomach twisted. "What do you mean?"

"You'll never make it there in time by flying. Your honey-biscuit won't last that long. I've got intel—what's coming for her isn't just a couple of goons. They're sending something much nastier."

Matthew's blood ran cold. "Gideon," he muttered, his fists tightening. "I knew it. We should've taken him out when we had the chance."

"Gideon's a real dickwad alright," Pascal retorted, "but he's just a pawn in a much bigger game. Doesn't even realize it. This goes straight to the top, all the way to Azazel."

"Azazel?" Matthew replied with a mixture of confusion and disbelief in his voice. "The Demon-Prince?"

Pascal's voice dropped. "Yeah. The big A. The one who wants to destroy the world and make it his playground."

Matthew snickered, "Of course he does. Isn't that always what these pieces of shit want?"

"My suggestion is that you not allow that to happen. Sure, I may be a demon, but I happen to like this world, and would prefer to keep it the way it is."

Matthew raised an eyebrow. "Speaking of demons, how did you end up working with Solomon?"

Pascal chuckled darkly. "That's a story for another time. Let's just say it involves Azazel and a whole mess of demons. A lot of demons."

"You helped Solomon imprison them?" Matthew asked, his mind racing. "Why?"

"As I said, I like this world the way it is, and they were all going to fuck it up," Pascal answered bluntly. "I have a personal stake in this. Because if those demons get free? We're all screwed, If what's happening now is their breakout plan, I'm as good as dead. And 'dead' for me is a lot worse than it is for you."

Matthew grew silent as he thought about Pascal's words. He was beginning to have a deeper appreciation for the demon. Plus, he had a feeling he was going to need all the help he could get to save Grace.

A few minutes later, they pulled up to an old, decrepit house on the west side of Haughville—the roughest part of Indianapolis. The kind of place you avoided if you had any sense of self-preservation.

"Wait here," Pascal ordered, stepping out of the car. "And don't do anything stupid."

Before Matthew could respond, Pascal closed the door and walked up to the house. That he had his gun drawn didn't fill Matthew with confidence in the situation. Neither did the gunshots he heard a few minutes later.

Matthew was just about to get out of the squad car when he saw a figure running down the street toward him. Dawn was just barely starting to creep up the horizon, peeling the black away and turning the sky into a dark gray, allowing him to see that it was a woman being chased by a group of four guys, each one laughing and howling in response to the lady's screams. As they drew nearer, his ring started glowing brightly.

"Fuck me!" Matthew exclaimed. "Not again! I don't have time for this shit!"

"Help me, please!" the lady shouted as she raced up to the car and started pounding on the window. Her eyes held a desperate look as she pleaded with Matthew. Her blond hair had a streak of blood running through it that started near her forehead and ran down to her ear, and a flurry of bruises covered her face and arms. He knew that the men chasing her caused her pain.

Against his better judgement, Matthew opened his door and jumped out just as the four men approached. They stopped short of the vehicle, regarding him suspiciously. Dressed in various garments that didn't really go together—like a bunch of patchwork quilts that had been randomly assembled by someone who was colorblind—each one was in his twenties, and each one had a gleam in his eyes begging for a fight.

The one closest to Matthew, tall and skinny, with a long stride, sauntered forward, chuckling, with a weird click in his speech, "Miren lo que tenemos aquí, chicos... un héroe!"

When the other three guys started laughing, the same click resonated in their voices, and together they sounded more like a chorus of insects than the thugs standing before him.

He pointed his finger in Matthew's chest, "Is that what you are, amigo, a hero?"

Matthew held his arms up in defense and backed away from the guy, "Look, I don't know what your deal is with this girl, but I know that real men don't hit women."

The guy's eyes burned with anger, "I don't think you realize who you're messing with, amigo."

Matthew replied, "Oh, I know exactly who I'm messing with. Just another group of demon thugs acting like dicks."

The guy raised his hand to attack Matthew and then froze when he saw the glowing ring on Matthew's finger. "Well, I'll be damned, Francesca! You were right."

"See? Told you he was the one," the woman said with a grin that made Matthew's skin crawl. "You should listen to me a little more often." But as she spoke, her form began to shift. Her human body distorted into something grotesque—a monstrous, centipede-like creature, her mandibles snapping as she lunged at him.

As he recovered from her attack, the four men had transformed themselves into the same insect demons. Silently, he cursed himself. He should've known better. *Pascal's not going to be happy,* he thought bitterly.

Almost immediately, he was surrounded as the group skittered along the pavement, encircling him. He knew that if he was to survive, he needed to get them in a group so he could use his ring effectively.

A plan came to mind. A stupid plan, but still a plan. He started running down the street and fell to the ground, acting like he had tripped. Immediately, three of the demons pounced on him. As they converged, he twisted the face on his ring and a fireball shot out. Their screeches echoed in the air as their bodies burned.

The two demons that were left split up, making it harder to fend off their attacks. While one rushed at him from the front, the other slashed at him from the rear. He cried out as a pair of claws raked down his back.

With a growl, he adjusted the ring once more and shot a bolt of lightning, disintegrating one demon in a flash of green slime.

The last demon—the female who had initiated the deadly charade—sprang on him from behind, this time ramming her mandibles into his neck. Then he felt a tube pierce his flesh as the creature sucked furiously.

Matthew twisted desperately to dislodge the demon, but its strength was too much. Finally, he slammed himself backward onto the ground, putting his full weight on the creature. It was enough to knock the wind out of it so that it released its grasp.

Weak and staggered from the attack, Matthew managed to adjust his ring once more and shot a beam of energy at the demon, raising it high in the air before he brought it crashing back to the earth head-first. The impact snapped its neck instantly.

Gasping, bloodied and drained, Matthew heard Pascal's voice from the porch of the house. "I thought I told you to stay in the car?!"

Matthew slowly turned around to see Pascal walking toward him holding a pillowcase with something squirming around inside.

Pascal looked around to see the demon corpses lining the street, then saw the wounds that Matthew had sustained. "I also told you not to do anything stupid."

Matthew looked at him weakly, "I'm sorry?"

Then his body shuddered, he closed his eyes, and fell to the ground.

CHAPTER 15

Hecate woke up feeling strong and energized. For the first time in a long time, an air of optimism surrounded her. The weight of her past seemed to lift, and a smile tugged at the corners of her mouth as she recalled the dream that had triggered this change. It had been vivid and surreal, but it had left her feeling alive.

Then she felt something sharp against her tongue. She spat instinctively, and a warm trickle of blood ran down her chin. Panic flared through her brain as she bolted from the bed and scrambled toward the bathroom.

She flicked on the light and froze in front of the mirror. The reflection staring back at her was a stranger's. Her skin had transformed, now a pale, almost translucent alabaster, giving her the appearance of a delicate porcelain doll. Her fangs—long and sharp—protruded from the corners of her mouth. And her eyes were no longer human but eerily feline, glowing with an unnatural gleam.

"What the fuck happened to me?" she cried out in horror.

Abaddon, always there, always watching, appeared on the vanity, her lithe form perched gracefully. *What do you mean?* the voice echoed in Hecate's mind, calm and unbothered.

"What do I mean?" Hecate snapped, eyes wide with panic. "Look at me! I'm a freak!"

No, Abaddon countered smoothly, *you're more beautiful than you ever were. You're perfect. A goddess.*

Hecate was unsure whether to be offended or flattered. "How did this happen?"

Don't you remember your dream?

"I thought it was just a dream..." Hecate's words faltered. "I didn't know it was real."

It's very real, Abaddon replied calmly. *And now you're more powerful than you ever imagined. It's time to usher in a new age.*

"New age?" Hecate echoed, disbelief lacing her tone. "How am I supposed to face the world like this?"

Just close your eyes. Picture yourself as you were. It's a simple glamor spell. You can do it easily.

Hecate squeezed her eyes shut, picturing her former self, trying to focus on the familiar. When she opened them, the reflection in the mirror had changed—her human appearance restored. It wasn't much, but it was a start.

"Well, that helps a little," she muttered, running her fingers through her now-normal hair. She was much more toned than she had been before; her breasts fuller, her hips rounder; her ass firmer. Then a memory from the dream flared again. She felt a thrill rising within her. "Does that mean—?"

Yes, Abaddon said with a note of pride.

Hecate flexed her shoulders, and with a soft, almost imperceptible sound, a pair of large, black bat-like wings unfurled from her back, stretching wide. The wings were strong, powerful, and unsettling in their beauty.

"Can I... fly?" she asked, her voice barely a whisper, her hands trembling as she touched the sleek feathers.

Like the dark angel himself.

Suddenly, Tarek was standing in the doorway with a

shocked look on his face. Hecate quickly used the glamor trick, but it was too late. He had already seen her.

"Uh... sorry," he stammered. "I knocked, but no one answered. Is this a bad time?"

Hecate's glare was venomous. "If you tell anyone what you saw, I'll rip your throat out."

Tarek's face instantly grew pale. "I didn't see anything," he whispered fearfully.

"Good," Hecate said coolly, her voice low and dangerous. "Now, what's so urgent that you thought it was okay to come into my room uninvited?"

"Gideon wants to see us downstairs," Tarek replied.

With a dismissive humph, Hecate pushed past him, Abaddon hopping down from the vanity to follow at her heels. As she passed him, Tarek's voice came from behind, awkward but sincere, "Is it weird that I thought it was kinda hot?"

Hecate froze in her tracks, glancing over her shoulder. Her icy gaze lingered for a moment before softening, as a thought crept into her mind that Tarek might become a useful tool for her later.

"Oh, and he said to bring your cat," Tarek added.

"The 'cat' has a name," Hecate corrected sharply. "Her name is Abaddon."

Tarek wisely fell silent, choosing not to pursue the subject further.

Downstairs, they found Gideon seated at the dining table reading the newspaper. He glanced up at Hecate, studying her for a long moment before speaking.

"Show me," he demanded.

Hecate blinked, confused. "What do you mean?"

He knows, Abaddon said.

Hecate sighed, clearly irritated. "Fine. Just don't start with the wisecracks, old man."

She shrugged her shoulders, and with a fluid motion, her wings unfolded once more, stretching wide as they filled the room. She also withdrew the glamor spell, showing him her true form.

"Wow!" Gideon exclaimed, his eyes widening in genuine awe. "Consider me impressed. These new enhancements will ensure our success as we lead the world into a new age."

Hecate closed her wings with a flick of her wrists and settled into a chair. "And what does that have to do with Solomon?"

Gideon leaned back, tapping his fingers together. "We think we know where the chest holding Azazel and the rest of them is. And that's where you come in. We've got the bait, and we need you to set the trap."

Hecate's mind raced, and she leaned forward, a wild measure of excitement flashing in her eyes. This was bigger than she had anticipated, and she was ready to do her part.

CHAPTER 16

As soon as the plane's wheels hit the tarmac, Solomon powered on his phone, and the screen lit up with a text from Pascal: *Call me ASAP. We have a problem!*

Solomon called him back immediately. Pascal picked up on the first ring.

"What's the problem?" Solomon asked urgently.

"Your dumbass boy here doesn't listen. That's what the problem is," Pascal replied. "He's in awful shape right now."

"What happened?"

"I told him to stay in the car while I took care of some business. When I came back, the ground was littered with Lamia bodies. Apparently, one of them bit him before he killed it."

"That's not good. Meet me in twenty minutes."

"I'd say we've got Fifteen. He's barely hanging on."

"I'll be there. Just keep him alive."

The call ended as the plane taxied toward the private hangar. Solomon immediately sprinted toward the waiting black car. As soon as he was inside, the engine roared to life, and he peeled out onto the road, making another call.

The voice that answered sounded smooth and almost too

friendly. Solomon knew better. He'd made a deal with the witch in the past, and he feared the price may be coming due.

"Well, well, well. Solomon," Morgan's voice purred through the phone. "How nice of you to call. You must be desperate."

"You could say that," Solomon replied.

There was a brief silence on the line before Morgan's mocking laugh echoed. "Is the mighty Solomon asking for help? This ought to be good. What makes you think I'll help you?"

Solomon's voice remained steady, but he knew this conversation would cost him. "Don't forget, I saved your life from Reverend Parris in 1692. You'd be dust if it weren't for me."

Morgan scoffed. "Parris was a fool. I could've turned him into a toad with a snap of my fingers."

"True," Solomon agreed, "but then he'd have won, and more of your sisters would have died."

There was a long pause, and then Morgan grumbled, "Fine, fine. What is it you need?"

"A friend of mine was bitten by a Lamia. He's dying. I need the antidote to the poison."

"Well, that's unfortunate for him," Morgan said with a twisted smile in her voice. "I bet he's in a lot of agony right now."

Solomon's patience was running thin. "Do you have the antidote or not?"

"Of course I have it," Morgan replied. "But it's going to cost you. You owe me, Solomon, and I expect you to pay up when I call."

Solomon took a deep breath. "Fine. But know this—Gideon's trying to open the seal to free Azazel. If that happens, no one, not even you, will be safe."

Morgan fell silent for a moment before responding, "That changes things. You'll still pay your debt, though, Solomon, or I'll collect in ways you won't like."

The line clicked off, and within seconds, a small vial of blue liquid appeared on the seat beside him. Solomon exhaled in relief, but his mind was racing. He hoped he wasn't too late.

When Solomon arrived at the abandoned farmhouse, the lack of Pascal's car had him briefly concerned. But then the headlights of an approaching vehicle eased his worry.

As Pascal's car rolled to a stop beside him, Solomon quickly moved to the back door, where the two of them carefully pulled Matthew's unconscious body from the car. The sight that greeted him made his stomach twist. Matthew's skin was an unnatural gray, his lips were cracked and blue, and his body trembled violently as the poison spread through his veins.

"Tip his head up," Solomon ordered.

He uncorked the vial and poured the blue liquid carefully into Matthew's mouth. Then they waited.

At first, nothing seemed to change. But slowly, Matthew's color returned, and the tremors eased. After a few minutes, his eyes fluttered open.

"What happened?" Matthew asked weakly.

Pascal was the first to speak. "You didn't listen, and nearly got your ass killed. You're lucky to be alive."

Solomon silenced him with a glare.

"Now, I remember," Matthew said as he struggled for a second before sitting up. "Some girl was being chased down the street by a bunch of thugs that turned out to be some kind of insect demon-things."

"It was a set-up," Pascal said. "Lamia are tricky like that."

"And their poison is lethal," Solomon added. "We barely

got here in time, otherwise you would've been gone."

"You'd better listen next time, or I won't be here to save your ass," Pascal added harshly.

Matthew shot him a glare but remained silent. His mind was still reeling from the pain and confusion.

The dizziness hit him again, and he quickly sank back down. The gunshots rang in his memory. "What about those shots from the house? What was going on in there?"

Pascal's eyes widened. "Shit, I almost forgot."

He rushed to the car and returned moments later with a squirming bundle wrapped in cloth. The muffled cries and grunts from within made Solomon raise an eyebrow.

"What did you do this time, Pascal?" Solomon asked him.

Pascal replied, "The little fucker wouldn't cooperate, and I knew we were in a hurry, so I just persuaded him a little."

"Just open the bag, Pascal."

Pascal plopped the bag onto the ground and a little 'humph' sounded from inside. He untied the cord and immediately a tiny creature jumped out. Standing a little over a foot tall, with arms that dragged to the ground, and a long, beaked nose, the imp glared up at Pascal, "You half-witted little skunk-sniffer! I have half a mind to slap you back to the pit where you belong!"

Pascal replied, "You can try, Beaky!"

"That's enough!" Solomon interrupted.

The imp turned toward Solomon, "I'm sorry, Sam. Is this twit with you?"

"Yes, Rumple, he's with me. And I apologize for his lack of decorum. But I need your help."

"Why do you always do this to me, Sam? I'm retired, remember? I don't do magic anymore."

"I remember. I'm hoping you'll make an exception this one time."

"And why should I?"

"Because Gideon is up to his old tricks again."

"Gideon! You should've killed him when you had the chance. He's like a nasty rash on the ass of this world that won't go away."

"That's why I need your help. He's sent some of his demons after one of my friends and we need to get to her before they do."

Rumple looked over at Matthew, "I'm assuming she's more than just a friend to one of you?"

Matthew started blushing.

Rumple huffed and turned back to Solomon, "It's going to cost you."

"I figured as much," Solomon replied as he pulled an object from his pocket and handed it to the imp.

Rumple took the object and ran his tongue along the flat side of it and then closed his eyes to concentrate. A second later he opened them again with a big smile on his face, "The arrowhead that Hiawatha himself used to write his blood into the stone that would be the foundation to form the Iroquois Confederacy. Where did you find this?"

Solomon replied, "I've been holding onto it for the right moment. I assume you approve?"

Rumple turned to Pascal, "Did you know that the Green Goddess herself gave this to him so he could commune with nature?"

"You act like I give a shit?" Pascal responded.

Rumple glared and shook his head at Pascal before turning back to Solomon, "Okay, what do you need from me?"

"We need a portal to a water park in Palm Springs."

Rumple's eyes gleamed. "I know the place. Too bad it's boarded up now. I had some fun there back in the day."

Matthew looked confused. "You've been there?"

"Kid, I've been everywhere." Rumple grinned.

He reached for a stick tied to his belt and began tracing a counterclockwise circle in the air. Moments later, a portal cracked open before them, showing the empty, dilapidated water park.

Matthew stepped forward, with Solomon close behind.

"Be careful," Rumple called out. "Gideon's no joke."

"I will," Solomon said. "Thank you, Rumple. This is the last time, I swear."

Rumple smirked. "We'll see about that."

As they stepped through the portal, the doorway snapped shut behind them, and the imp turned back to Pascal.

Rumple turned to Pascal, "Aren't you going with them?"

Pascal replied, "Naw, this is their fight. I've already compromised myself enough as it is. I figure I should probably lie low for a while until this blows over."

"Yeah, that might not be a bad idea. Just make sure you keep your mitts away from me. Next time, I won't be quite so forgiving."

Pascal just laughed, and in the blink of an eye, the doorway vanished.

***

Matthew and Solomon emerged from the portal, their feet hitting the cracked sidewalk that bordered the long-abandoned water park. The moment they stepped through, the sky above, still caught in the unnatural tug of time, shifted abruptly from the early morning light to an impenetrable darkness, swallowing the faint glow of the city.

Solomon's gaze flicked to the corner of the parking lot where Andrew's old car sat, abandoned and forgotten. The sight hit him harder than he expected, a small pang of regret twisting in his gut. Beside him, Matthew turned on his phone, using the flashlight to pierce the void, and immediately froze when he saw the dark streaks of blood spattered across the pavement at the boarded-up entrance.

Quickly, they pried open the entrance and stepped into the park's forgotten ruins. Matthew's pulse quickened as they followed the trail of blood, each step heavier than the last, until they found themselves standing before a small taco shop. Its door, hanging crooked, stood ajar.

A putrid stench of death hit Matthew like a physical blow, thick and oppressive. His flashlight darted across the room, and as his worst fears coiled in his chest, the beam landed on something that froze him in place.

Amidst a pile of black feathers, matted and streaked with blood, lay a solitary cell phone. He knew instantly it was Grace's phone. A second later, they heard a soft whimper in the corner and turned to see a small dog curled up and shaking in terror.

Matthew dropped to his knees. The flashlight slipped from his grip, rolling across the ground as he let out a choked sob, his body shaking as he finally let the tears fall.

CHAPTER 17

It began as a faint whisper, a sound barely audible, like the wind carrying a voice from some distant place. It was soft, timid, lonely, as if a frightened child, lost in the dark, calling out for safety, terrified the boogeyman would get her.

At first, Victoria didn't recognize the voice that called her name. But then a memory surfaced, one she had buried deep within her, and when her name echoed through the air again, she knew. It was her sister. It was Priscilla, reaching out across the chasm of time and space.

"Victoria?" Priscilla's voice cracked, desperate. "Where are you?"

Victoria's eyes snapped open. She was lying face down on a dirt floor, her body heavy, the air thick with decay. She tried to push herself up, but something invisible held her down, a weight that wouldn't let go. She struggled again, and the side of her face tore free from the earth, skin peeling away with a sickening rip.

A swarm of maggots squirmed in the gaping wound, wriggling through her flesh, crawling into her mouth as she gagged in horror. Her skin, now shredded, lay scattered across the ground, covered in the same wriggling vermin.

A sharp cry tore from her throat as panic set in.

Then, from the shadows, she saw a figure approach—Priscilla. But not the Priscilla she had just killed, not the older version she had left behind. This was the younger Priscilla, the one from before, the one who had once been her best friend.

"Oh, Vic!" Priscilla gasped, rushing toward her with a sad look in her eyes. "You poor thing. You're a mess."

Victoria's voice was muffled as she tried to speak. She spat out a mouthful of maggots, forcing the words out with difficulty. "Priscilla! Thank God you're here. Can you help me?"

Priscilla's expression shifted. "That depends. Are you ready to help yourself first?"

For a moment, confusion clouded Victoria's thoughts. But then, the awful truth hit her. "I'm dead, aren't I? But... this didn't happen before. Why is it different this time?"

Priscilla's voice softened. "You put your faith in the wrong place, Vic. Gideon turned his back on you when you needed him most, and Azazel has found someone else to take your place. They don't need you anymore."

Victoria looked down, tears welling up in her eyes. "So... I'm lost for good now? I guess I deserve whatever I get."

Priscilla reached out and gently lifted Victoria's chin, her touch tender despite the maggots that still squirmed beneath her fingers. "That doesn't mean you're lost. I need you. Now, more than ever."

"But I betrayed you..." Victoria whispered, her voice breaking.

Priscilla smiled softly. "No matter what you've done, no matter the distance between us, I will always be your sister. And I will always love you."

Victoria looked down at the ground as she weighed the

full measure of betrayal she had cast on her sister. "I don't deserve your love."

Priscilla laughed lightly, brushing a stray lock of hair from Victoria's face. "That's not for you to decide, silly."

Without another word, Priscilla placed both hands on Victoria's face, ignoring the squirming creatures that clung to her skin. She closed her eyes, and a soft, glowing light began to flow down her arms, surrounding Victoria. The light pulsed, warm and soothing, as the torn, decayed skin on Victoria's face slowly began to heal. In moments, she was whole again.

Victoria blinked, disoriented by the sudden change. Her voice was barely above a whisper. "After everything I've done, after all the shit I put you through, you still helped me. Why?"

"I already told you, Vic. Maybe your brain's still a little scrambled, but you keep asking the same questions."

Victoria lowered her head, the weight of her actions crashing down on her once again. "I killed our parents, Sis! They're dead because of me!"

Priscilla paused. "You said it yourself—death isn't permanent, remember?"

Victoria's heart ached as she let the words settle. "Yeah, I remember. But now... I'm doomed to Hell for all eternity because of what I've done."

Priscilla shook her head. "Not necessarily."

Victoria looked at her in disbelief. "What do you mean?"

"There's still time. Time to make amends."

Victoria's shoulders slumped. "How could I ever make up for the horrors I've done? No one would ever forgive me."

Priscilla gently cupped Victoria's face. "Forgiveness doesn't come from you. It comes from the ones you've wronged. It's up to them, not you. But you need to remember how love really works. There was a time—long ago—when you felt that love. Try to remember what that felt like."

Victoria searched the depths of her soul, trying to push through the guilt and the darkness that had consumed her for so long. She struggled to reach back to a time when love had been a bright, unbreakable force in her life. It felt so far away —like a faint flicker of light, barely visible through the fog of regret. But as she focused, the light grew stronger, and soon she was running toward it, drawn by its warmth.

When she reached it, the love of her family, the ones she had betrayed, wrapped around her like a comforting embrace. The arms that had once been outstretched in anger were now open with forgiveness, offering her a place within their fold once again. For the first time in so long, she felt whole again.

Tears fell freely as she sank to her knees, overwhelmed. When she finally lifted her head, she looked at Priscilla. "What do you want me to do?"

Priscilla smiled. "I need you to save Grace."

***

Grace's awareness drifted back in fragments, each piece slipping into place like a puzzle she couldn't solve. Her memory returned in flashes—an agonizing swarm of demon-birds attacking, their wings flapping violently against her as their beaks tore into her skin, drawing blood. Their shrill cries pierced her ears as her body was assaulted from all sides. And then… nothing. Until now.

She tried to open her eyes, but the effort was futile. A heavy, suffocating weight seemed to press down on her head, a thick fabric that threatened to choke her. Her limbs felt bound, held in place by something tight—ropes, chains, something constricting her. Every movement sent pain shooting through her body, sharp and invasive like a thousand needles pricking her skin. She let out a muffled cry, the sound weak and strained.

Then she heard a voice she knew all too well. A voice that had haunted her.

"Well, well, well," Gideon said. "Looks like she's finally coming around."

A second voice, unfamiliar yet filled with venom, followed. "It's about fucking time!"

Grace's head was pulled forward, the motion dragging more agony through her body. The hood was removed, and as her vision cleared, the horror of her surroundings crashed into her. She was suspended above a bed of jagged daggers, their tips glinting with her own blood, poised just beneath her flesh. The chains that bound her wrists and ankles stretched across a sinister rack, and a cruel collar locked her head in place, forcing her to face the torment awaiting her. The air was thick with the scent of damp earth, and the muffled roar from a nearby waterfall echoed through the chamber.

Gideon crouched before her, his eyes gleaming with amusement. "Hello, Grace. It's good to see you again, though, I wish it were under better circumstances. How's your mom and dad? Oh, wait—I already know the answer to that."

Hatred and rage surged through Grace, and with what little strength she had left, she spat out her words. "Gideon, you son of a bitch. I swear you'll pay for this. Matthew and Solomon are on their way right now."

Hecate stepped forward, her presence cold and menacing. "That's exactly what we're hoping for, you pathetic little twit."

Grace's eyes flicked to Hecate, her psychic abilities breaking through the veil of the glamor spell masking her true form. "Who the hell are you supposed to be?" Grace sneered. "A Maleficent wanna-be?"

A look of shock flickered in Hecate's eyes at Grace's ability to see through her magic, but the surprise was brief. She glanced at Gideon, who gave her a subtle shake of his head. Tarek, standing by his side, said nothing, but his slight gesture spoke volumes.

"It's a long story," Gideon replied casually. "One for another time. Isn't that right, Grace? But, if things go as planned, we probably won't have the luxury of reminiscing in the future."

Hecate shrugged off his comment and stepped closer, her hands seizing Grace's shoulders with brutal force. She pushed down hard, driving the sharp tips of the daggers deeper into Grace's flesh. The pain was excruciating. Grace screamed, her body writhing against the cruel restraint.

"Right now, bitch," Hecate snapped, "I'm ready to split you wide open. But Gideon wants us to play a little game first. And you, my little piss-ant, are the bait. Now, I want you to meet a very special friend of mine."

Grace's mind was still reeling when she saw a feline figure pad forward from the shadows. Abaddon sat down in front of Grace, her head tilted slightly, as if amused. She meowed once, a soft, almost sweet sound—before her mouth opened wide and a thick, slimy tentacle shot forward, striking Grace in the forehead.

Hecate stroked the creature's head gently. "As you can see," she said cruelly, "Abaddon isn't your average cat. And believe me, she has a special talent for inflicting pain."

The moment the tentacle made contact, Grace felt her body go numb. It was as if her very life force was being drained from her, pulled through her skull by some unseen force. She fought, instinctively, but Abaddon's grip was unyielding, her strength overwhelming. Grace could only vaguely hear Hecate's voice, muffled as though she were underwater. "Don't worry, dear," Hecate said, the words curling into her mind like a dark promise. "She's not going to kill you... yet."

CHAPTER 18

Matthew sat slumped against the taco shop's wall, his head buried in his hands, and his eyes raw and swollen from crying. His chest ached with a heaviness he couldn't shake, the weight of words left unsaid, of feelings he'd never been able to express. He had never told Grace how he felt, and now he'd never have the chance. Regret clawed at him, bitter and unforgiving. He cursed himself for waiting too long, for holding back when the chance was right in front of him.

Solomon sat down beside him, trying to find some words of comfort, but he was hurting inside just as much. Grace had become family, and he had relished every second he had spent with her. He couldn't imagine a world without her in it. In his arms, he held the pudgy little dog that was the last remaining link to Grace.

As he ran his hands through the puppy's fur, trying to ground himself against his rising grief, his phone buzzed in his pocket. He left it in his pocket, not bothering to look at it, much less answer it. Eventually, the caller gave up. A minute later, it rang again.

Matthew looked at him and gave a small nod.

Solomon finally pulled his phone out and answered it

immediately when he saw who the caller was. "Hecate! I've been trying to reach you. Are you okay?"

"Oh, Solomon!" Hecate sobbed. "I need your help. I really fucked up!"

"What happened?"

"I don't know… everything happened so fast. After my mother's death, I wasn't thinking straight. Tarek took me to meet this guy named Gideon, and I thought he was going to help me. But I think he was just using me. And now Landis is gone! I can't find him anywhere! What am I going to do?"

"It'll be okay," Solomon replied. "Where are you now?"

There was a long pause before Hecate answered, her voice small and vulnerable. "I'm at Bob Evans near the campus. Solomon, I'm so sorry for everything. For how I treated you… Is there any way you can forgive me?"

Solomon's voice softened. "Oh, Hecate. There's nothing to forgive. You were hurting. There's no fault in that."

"Thank you," she whispered. "But Solomon, I think this Gideon guy is up to something. He has a girl here—her name is Grace, I think—and he said something about taking her to a place called Devil's Hole. Does that mean anything to you?"

Solomon's breath caught in his throat. He pulled the phone away from his ear and turned to Matthew, his voice low and urgent. "Grace is still alive."

Matthew leaped to his feet, his eyes wide and his hands trembling. "What? Where is she? What's going on?"

"It sounds like Gideon's holding her captive," Solomon replied. "And I know exactly what he's after."

He moved the phone back to his ear. "Are you sure you're okay, Hecate? He didn't hurt you, did he?"

"No," Hecate replied, her voice trembling. "I'm okay, just scared. I didn't know what I was getting into. Are you at the library? Can I come see you?"

"I'm a few hours away, unfortunately," Solomon said. "But I'll get a flight back as soon as I can, and we'll figure this out together."

"Please hurry," Hecate begged. "I don't know what he's capable of."

"I know exactly what he's capable of," Solomon muttered. "Stay hidden until I get there."

The call ended, and Solomon stood motionless for a moment, his thoughts a whirlwind. He knew he was walking straight into a trap—but the depth of it? He had no idea.

Meanwhile, Matthew was an absolute wreck standing beside him. He had gone from heartbreak and despair, to hope and worry in a matter of seconds. "Where is that fucking bastard keeping Grace?"

"Devil's Hole," Solomon said grimly.

"Devil's Hole? Where the hell is that?"

"It's a secret cave behind Niagara Falls," Solomon replied solemnly. "It's where I hid the chest containing the demons. I don't know how Gideon found out about it."

"We can ask him that when we catch his sorry ass," Matthew snapped. "But right now, we need to get there. Fast."

Solomon nodded. "I agree. And the quickest way is to get back to South Bend first."

Matthew was confused. "South Bend?"

"I have a portal there," Solomon explained. "It'll take us straight to Devil's Hole."

"Of course you do," Matthew muttered with a bitter chuckle.

Solomon sighed. "I need to make a few calls to try to get us some help and arrange a flight back."

After handing the puppy over to Matthew, Solomon stepped a few paces away and dialed Pascal's number, hoping for help once again.

The demon answered quickly. "Solomon? Didn't expect to hear from you so soon."

"It's worse than we thought," Solomon replied urgently. "Gideon already has Grace, and he's using her to get to me."

"Well, that can't be good," Pascal said dryly.

"He knows where the chest is hidden," Solomon continued. "I don't know how, but he knows."

"Don't look at me. I didn't tell him," Pascal shot back.

"No, I wasn't implying that," Solomon said quickly. "But if I'm going to confront him, I need all the help I can get. I was hoping I could count on you."

Pascal was silent for a moment. "Listen, Sam," he said slowly, "I'm glad I helped you with the kid, but I really don't want to get tangled up in this. I'm already in deep. If Azazel gets free and finds out, it's going to be a thousand times worse."

"That's exactly why I need you, Pascal," Solomon pleaded. "Together, we can make sure he doesn't get free."

There was another pause, then Pascal spoke, his tone final. "Sorry, pal. I've already paid my dues. I'm afraid you're on your own."

The line went dead.

Solomon stood there for a moment, staring at his phone, frustration boiling inside him. He understood Pascal's position, but that didn't make it any easier. He made another call, this time to Morgan—but the response was the same.

He turned to Matthew, his face grim. "Looks like we're on our own."

"That's actually how I prefer it," Matthew replied with a steely edge in his voice.

Solomon nodded. "Just stay on your toes. I don't think Gideon will send any more goons after us, but you never know."

***

Pascal hung up the phone, his gaze distant as his mind whirled.

Rumple's voice cut through the silence, "What was that all about?"

"It was Sam," Pascal muttered, still lost in thought. "Apparently, Gideon's got the kid's woman and is using her to force Sam into opening the demon chest and releasing Azazel."

Rumple's eyes widened. "We can't let that happen! If Azazel gets free, we're all screwed."

Pascal sighed, rubbing a hand over his face. "I've already told him—I'm not getting any deeper into this mess. Besides, Sam's strong enough to handle it himself. He doesn't need my help."

Rumple shot him a frustrated look. "Yeah, keep telling yourself that, pal."

***

Morgan sat on the couch, her eyes closed as she replayed Solomon's words over and over, trying to pierce through the fog of uncertainty that clouded her mind. The future stretched out before her like a blurred vision, frustratingly out of focus, leaving her grasping at fleeting glimpses of what might come. With a heavy sigh, she leaned back into the cushions, giving up for the moment.

Her thoughts were interrupted by a sharp and insistent knock at the door. Morgan's body tensed. She moved cautiously toward the door, her instincts already on edge.

Peering through the side window, she caught sight of a woman standing there, fidgeting with agitation. The stranger was draped in a long trench coat, the hood pulled low over her face, obscuring most of her features. There was something vaguely familiar about her.

Morgan swung the door open just enough to make sure she was ready for anything. "Can I help you?" she asked.

"Are you Morgan?" the woman asked, her voice shaky but urgent.

"Depends on who's asking."

Victoria hesitated for a moment, then pulled back her hood, revealing her face—a scar stretching down her right cheek, from ear to nose. The sight of it sent a wave of recognition crashing over Morgan, and the disgust in her gaze was immediate. "I know exactly who you are, wench. What the hell are you doing here?"

"Listen," Victoria said quickly, "I'm not here to cause trouble. I know you've heard a lot of bad things about me, but it was Gideon. He's the one behind everything. I swear it."

"You act like you had no choice," Morgan shot back.

"I'm not saying I'm innocent. Lord knows I've done my share of terrible things, but he tricked me. Seduced me with lies, made me do things I shouldn't have. Now I'm trying to make amends."

Morgan's eyes narrowed, and she gave a bitter laugh. "Yeah, good luck with that."

"I'm serious," Victoria insisted, stepping closer. "I need your help. Gideon's got my niece, and he's using her to get Solomon to release Azazel. I need to stop him. Please."

Morgan studied her for a moment. "From what I've heard, Azazel's the reason you're still breathing. You think he's going to let you undo his plans?"

Even though Victoria's eyes immediately flickered with regret, she stood firm. "I've changed. I'm trying to atone. I know I can't undo the past, but I have to try."

Morgan's expression softened for a brief second, but then she shook her head. "Sorry," she said, her voice cold and unwavering. "You've come to the wrong place. This is your fight, not mine."

Without another word, she closed the door with a firm and final click.

"Piece of cake," Hecate grinned after hanging up the phone. "He bought it, hook, line, and sinker."

"Easy now," Gideon cautioned. "Don't get cocky. Solomon's not some pawn you can toy with. He's smarter than that."

"I know, I know," Hecate said. "But trust me—when this goes down, he won't know what hit him."

"I hope you're right," Gideon muttered. "If something goes wrong, Azazel's wrath will be the least of your problems."

Tarek leaned forward. "So what's the plan, boss?"

Gideon let out a long breath, gathering his thoughts. "The plan's simple. Hecate's going to convince Solomon to lead her to his secret portal. Then, with Abaddon's magic, we'll slip through unnoticed and infiltrate his hidden chamber. Once inside, we'll use the ring to unlock the chest."

He paused, his eyes distant. "I can feel it. It's close—so close. But it's hidden. We'll need Abaddon's magic to reveal it."

Hecate's brow furrowed. "How am I supposed to get Abaddon into the chamber with me?"

Abaddon, who had been hovering nearby, released her

grip on Grace and, in a fluid motion, shrank down to the size of a coin. Hecate watched in amazement as her feline companion scurried up her hand, quickly gripping her finger with surprising strength. The tiny creature now looked like little more than an odd piece of jewelry.

Hecate smiled, marveling. *You never cease to amaze me, little friend.*

"Will Solomon see through my glamor?" she asked, turning back to Gideon.

"Under normal circumstances, I'd say yes," he replied. "But with Abaddon enhancing your powers, your true form should stay hidden. At least until you decide otherwise."

Hecate raised an eyebrow.

Abaddon's voice echoed in her mind, smooth and steady. *Don't worry about Solomon. He'll be too distracted to notice anything out of place.*

Hecate nodded. *I certainly hope so.*

She stood and looked at Gideon. "I need to get back before Solomon does. As soon as we're through the portal, be ready. I don't want anything fucking this up."

Gideon's lips curled into a cruel smile. "Oh, we'll be ready, alright."

Hecate crouched down in front of Grace, her fingers brushing the unconscious woman's cheek. "Such a pretty face. Too bad your brain's turned to mush. Oh well, you've got to crack a few eggs to make an omelet."

Her hand moved, and the blades embedded in Grace's flesh twisted once more, sending fresh droplets of blood spilling onto the cavern floor. But Grace didn't react. Her gaze remained vacant, hollow, her expression devoid of anything but emptiness.

Hecate's wings flared out behind her, the air humming with power as she crouched and then launched herself into the air. She rocketed through the cavern like a missile, slicing through the waterfall with an almost predatory speed.

I like this, she thought, exhilaration coursing through her veins.

Abaddon's voice was light, almost amused. *I knew you would.*

***

Grace's eyes fluttered open, and she found herself adrift in the infinite expanse of space. The only source of light was a distant star, faint and cold, casting a dim glow. As she gazed downward, the familiar curve of Earth came into view, a blue-and-green orb hanging in the black void.

Her body moved with sluggish, disconnected motions, each attempt to push herself forward met with failure. Desperation clawed at her chest as she struggled against the emptiness, longing for something—anything—that might offer her an escape. After moments that felt like an eternity, she slumped in defeat, her breath shaky as the tears flowed. She was alone. And in that solitude, every shred of hope slipped away.

Just as despair threatened to consume her, a subtle force began to draw her forward—gentle at first, like the tug of a distant string. It felt like a tractor beam, pulling her toward something unknown. Then, in the silence of her mind, she heard her parents' voices, soft but firm, guiding her: *Stay calm. Believe.*

Grace squeezed her eyes shut, surrendering her fear, her pain, her sorrow. She let go. And in that instant, a surge of energy swept through her like an unstoppable tide. She was pulled faster and faster, her descent accelerating until she felt as if she were plummeting to Earth, her body aflame as it re-entered the atmosphere. She screamed as her flesh burned, then began to disintegrate, but it was too late to stop.

Then, without warning, her descent halted abruptly. She floated above her own body, still trapped in Gideon's cruel snare. Before her, materialized the ethereal figures of her mother and father, their forms translucent but filled with a powerful warmth. In their hands, they held the silver cord that tethered her soul to her body. Their love radiated through her, and in that moment, Grace knew it was they who had brought her back from the brink of oblivion.

Slowly, she merged with her body, every part of her reawakening, whole once more.

Gideon suddenly paused, his eyes flicking toward her, a faint unease crossing his features. Grace held her position, her expression vacant, her body limp. Inside, however, a quiet thrill bubbled up. She smiled to herself, the smallest flicker of defiance lighting her heart. She remained perfectly still, playing the part of the brain-dead captive with impeccable precision.

You'll get yours, Gideon. This isn't over—not by a long shot.

CHAPTER 20

As soon as the plane came to a halt, Solomon and Matthew rushed down the ramp and out of the gate toward the waiting car.

"We got everything ready as fast as we could, Sam," Wendell, the Avis agent, said as they approached.

"You did fine, Wendell," Solomon replied, his eyes scanning the vehicle.

Then he saw the car—a cherry-red Volkswagen Beetle—and his eyebrows shot up in surprise.

"Sorry," Wendell said apologetically. "It was the only thing left. I grabbed it without thinking."

"It's fine. It'll get us where we need to go," Solomon said, though a chuckle tugged at the corner of his mouth.

After squeezing into the cramped car, they sped toward campus, veering onto Dixieway South. Minutes later, they pulled into the Bob Evans parking lot, immediately surrounded by the chaos of patrons rushing out in a panic.

Dodging the frantic customers, they entered the restaurant, the scene inside grimmer than Solomon had anticipated. At least a dozen people—both patrons and employees—lay motionless, blood pooling around them from gunshot wounds.

Solomon approached a woman crouched behind the hostess station. "What happened here?"

Her voice trembled. "It happened so fast... Three men just came in and started shooting."

"Are they still here?"

"I don't think so. After a couple minutes, they just... left. It makes no sense."

Solomon muttered under his breath, "It makes sense to me."

Turning to Matthew, he ordered, "Stay alert. Look for anything unusual."

Matthew gave him a dry look. "Like this is normal?"

"You know what I mean," Solomon said.

He moved swiftly, staying low, scanning the room until he spotted Hecate curled in a corner, shaking and crying.

When she saw him, her face twisted in relief. "Oh, Solomon! Thank god you're here!" she cried, collapsing into his arms.

"It's okay," he reassured, wrapping his arms around her. "You're safe now."

Hecate buried her face in his chest, her words muffled. "It was Gideon's men. I'm sure of it. One of them... I recognized him. He must've sent them after me."

Tears streamed down her face. "People are dead... because of me."

Solomon stroked her hair, his voice firm. "No, Hecate. It's not your fault. You couldn't have known."

The distant wail of sirens cut through the tension. "We need to go," Solomon said.

They met up with Matthew near the front, sprinting to the car. After a brief struggle, Matthew finally wedged himself into the backseat, allowing Hecate to sit up front. With a screech of tires, they pulled out of the parking lot just as the first police cars arrived.

Hecate's breathing had calmed by the time they hit the road. She glanced at the car's interior and raised an eyebrow. "Nice ride," she remarked with a faint smile. "I never took you for a sub-compact kind of guy."

Solomon snickered. "It was all they had."

She turned to Matthew. "I'm Hecate, by the way."

"Matthew," he replied tersely.

"So, you're the famous Matthew I've heard so much about?" Hecate teased.

Matthew shot a questioning glance at Solomon through the rear-view mirror.

"Don't worry," Solomon said with a mischievous glint in his eye. "I only told her the good parts."

Matthew kept his thoughts to himself as Hecate turned back to the front. For a split second, he thought he saw something strange with his ring, but when he glanced down, it appeared normal. The unease in his gut, however, lingered.

"So, what now?" Hecate asked, breaking the silence.

Solomon's tone was grim. "Now we finish this. Once and for all."

He slammed the gas pedal, speeding down Douglas Road until he hit the roundabout. Slowing just enough to navigate the turn, he floored it again, racing toward the campus. He screeched to a halt in front of the Snite Museum.

"What are we doing here?" Hecate asked.

"Hopefully stopping the apocalypse," Solomon replied. "Follow me."

He led the way into the museum, with Matthew and Hecate trailing close behind. They were forced to halt in the middle of a room, surrounded by a group of giggling elementary students on a field trip.

"Excuse us," Solomon said, his voice polite but urgent. "We'll be out of your way in just a moment."

The children chuckled, while their teachers shot them disapproving glares. Solomon quickly ushered them through an emergency exit, down a hallway, and to another door. After inserting a key and pressing his thumb to a scanner, the door creaked open, and he gestured for them to follow.

Once inside, Solomon turned to them. "Stand back," he ordered.

He raised his arm toward the blank wall across from them. As he touched the face of the ring to the stone, a portal shimmered into existence. Matthew noticed a faint smile tug at the corners of Hecate's lips as she watched.

"You two first," Solomon said. "The portal will close right after me."

Hecate was the first to move, stepping eagerly into the swirling vortex, with Matthew close behind. Solomon followed, and the portal snapped shut behind him.

They found themselves in a vast cavern, the air thick with the scent of damp earth. In the distance, Grace was chained to a stone wall. "Grace!" Matthew shouted, rushing forward, but as he did, he saw Gideon and another man approach her, their steps slow and deliberate.

"She can't hear you," Solomon said, his voice cold. "This section is sealed off by an invisible barrier."

Matthew extended his hand, pressing against the air, but stopped when his palm met solid resistance. He turned to Solomon. "We need to hurry."

Solomon nodded grimly. "We need to destroy the chest before Gideon can get to it."

Matthew's gaze narrowed. "Why didn't you destroy it earlier?"

"Destroying the chest just sends the demons back to Hell. I

was trying to keep them trapped forever."

"And now someone's threatening to kill someone you love to release them," Matthew muttered.

"I never meant for any of this to happen," Solomon replied softly.

Solomon kneeled and uttered a few words in Latin. "Tua secreta psalmorum ad me."

For a moment, the ground shimmered, and a large, golden chest appeared before him. It was ornate, covered in runes and angelic imagery, with a small indentation in the front— exactly the size of the stone in Solomon's ring.

"Okay, let's destroy it!" Matthew said quickly.

A voice suddenly echoed in his mind. *Matthew! Watch out! It's a trap!*

Abaddon's voice, low and silent, whispered in Hecate's ear. *It's time.*

"Yeah, about that," Hecate said with a wicked glint in her eye. She drew a dagger from her waist and thrust it into Solomon's stomach.

"No!" Matthew cried desperately.

Abaddon leaped from Hecate's finger, growing to her full size in an instant. Before Matthew could react, she unleashed a high-pitched shriek, and the invisible barrier around them shattered.

Gideon and Tarek surged forward, joining Hecate as she lifted the chest from the ground. Matthew rushed toward Gideon, but Abaddon's tentacle shot forward, slamming into his chest. He collapsed instantly, paralyzed.

"We need his ring to open the chest," Gideon said.

Blood poured from Solomon's mouth as he spoke, "You won't win, Gideon. Good will always triumph over evil."

Gideon chuckled darkly. "It seems to me that we've already won."

Hecate yanked Solomon's hand, pulling him to his feet. She grabbed his finger and sliced it off with a swift motion. The ring slid free, and she held it up, admiring it for a moment.

"Do you want to do the honors?" she asked, glancing at Gideon.

"You go ahead. You've earned it," he replied with a smile.

Solomon's voice trembled with desperation. "I beg you, don't do this. You don't know what you're about to release."

Hecate's lips curled into a bitter smile. "Oh, I know exactly what I'm doing."

She pressed the face of the ring to the chest. A moment later, the ground trembled, and the chest glowed an ominous red. The lid flew open, unleashing a burst of fiery energy that shot toward the rock ceiling.

A chorus of sinister howls and mocking laughter reverberated through the cavern. The end had begun.

When Grace saw Abaddon's slimy tentacle reaching for Matthew, something inside her snapped. She knew the horror he was about to face—the kind of suffering she couldn't bear to watch again, not when it was someone she cared about. Not when it was the man she could finally admit to herself she loved.

"No!" Her scream tore through the air, and it hit Abaddon with the force of a bullet. The demon staggered back, her grip on Matthew loosening just enough for him to collapse to the ground.

Instantly, the energy in the cavern shifted. Hecate's focus broke, and the chest slammed shut with a deafening thud, trapping the demons inside once more.

Gideon spun, fury burning in his eyes. Lightning crackled from his fingers, and he stalked toward Grace, his voice dripping with venom. "Apparently, the little kitten had one last roar in her. Now I think it's time to silence you for good."

He raised his arms, unleashing a bolt of lightning straight at her. But instead of striking Grace, the bolt collided with an invisible barrier, dissipating harmlessly.

Gideon's gaze flickered to Victoria, standing in defiance

beside them. His face darkened. "So, the traitor shows her face. Betraying your own blood, Victoria? That's not going to be forgotten."

Victoria's voice was cold and unyielding. "For the first time in my life, I'm on the right side. Too bad it took me betraying my own sister to see through the lies you've filled me with."

Gideon's lips curled into a malicious grin. "Then I guess it's time for you to join the others in death. This time for good."

Before he could strike, time froze. Morgan's power held everyone in place, suspended in a moment of stillness. Rumple appeared with a flash, using his magic to undo the chains binding Grace, keeping her floating above the blades below. He was moments from whisking her away when Hecate broke free from the time-stop, hurling a fireball that sent him crashing to the ground. In the chaos, Grace was pushed to safety, but Rumple lay unconscious.

As time resumed, Morgan dropped her spell, and Pascal raised his shotgun, firing at Hecate. She evaded most of the shot, but the impact still sent her flying back, slamming into the wall. The ring slipped from her grasp and skittered across the floor, coming to a stop just within Matthew's reach.

Struggling against Abaddon's paralyzing grip, Matthew crawled toward the ring. His hand was just inches from it when Hecate recovered, her wings unfurling as she lunged at him with claws bared, screeching like a banshee.

Matthew seized the ring, rolling to the side just as Morgan sent a surge of electricity, knocking Hecate out of the air.

"Put the rings together," Solomon rasped weakly, his voice barely above a whisper. Blood dripped from his lips as he coughed.

Matthew didn't hesitate. He grabbed the second ring and

slid it onto his finger, watching in awe as the two rings fused into one. He aimed the ring at the chest and released a fireball toward it. The explosion shook the cavern, and the ground trembled violently as the demons screamed in fury, sucked back into Hell in a blinding flash.

As the dust settled, the remnants of the explosion echoed through the cavern, and the ground shook with a final, bone-rattling tremor. Tarek dashed to Abaddon, and Gideon lifted Hecate, vanishing through a portal with a flick of his hand.

Pascal, his voice barely rising above the roar of the destruction, shouted, "Looks like they had the right idea. We need to get the hell out of here. Now!"

He turned to Rumple, who was slowly struggling to his feet, "You strong enough to get us to safety?"

Rumple nodded weakly, but before anyone could move, Morgan stepped forward. "I'll do it. Where to?"

Pascal glanced at Solomon, who was pale and near death. "We need to take him to Uriel. If anyone can save him, it'll be him."

"Hold hands," Morgan instructed. "We can't risk being separated."

"Do you know where to go?" Pascal asked.

"Yeah. Uriel and I may not always see eye-to-eye, but we have... an understanding," she replied, eyes narrowing as she focused on the task ahead.

"Well, whatever that means, just get us there, fast!" Pascal urged.

As soon as Matthew grasped onto Solomon's leg, Morgan closed her eyes. With the cave crumbling around them, the group vanished in an instant, reappearing in front of Uriel.

The Archangel, his eyes hidden behind his special glasses, immediately went to work. He switched the lenses furiously as he approached Solomon. "Oh, my," Uriel muttered. "This doesn't look good. Not good at all."

"Can you help him?" Matthew asked nervously.

Uriel gave him a quick, pained look. "I will try my best."

Removing his glasses, Uriel folded them away in his pocket, then placed his hands over Solomon's body. A series of phrases, part Latin and part Hebrew, escaped his lips as a soft blue glow enveloped Solomon. The group watched, silent, as the wound in Solomon's stomach began to close—only to suddenly stop. The light dimmed, and Uriel looked up with a grim expression.

Everyone knew. Solomon was dead.

***

Gideon's breath came in ragged gasps as he sprinted through the forest, his heart hammering in his chest. The trees seemed to close in on him, branches whipping at his face, tearing his skin open in jagged stripes. Blood flowed freely, staining the earth beneath him as he pushed forward, desperate to outrun the beast that pursued him. All around, the demon's deafening screech tore through the air, a sound that rattled his bones and shattered his mind.

In the distance, he spotted a small cabin atop a hill—his only hope, a fleeting beacon of sanctuary. Without a second thought, he changed direction, veering toward the structure.

The forest floor was a maze of obstacles. His foot sank into a small stream as he crossed it, and before he could regain his balance, a tree root seemed to lunge at him, tripping him into the muddy water. As soon as he hit the ground, invisible hands clamped down on his skull, dragging him under. Panic surged through him as he thrashed, fighting against the unseen force, until, with a violent gasp, he broke free, scrambling up the bank.

He didn't stop. His only thought was the cabin—safety, the last refuge. The cries of the demon grew louder, more insistent, and he pushed himself harder, his legs burning, his breath ragged as he covered the final stretch toward the door.

But just as hope was within his grasp, the earth before him split open with a deafening roar. He froze, eyes widening in terror as the white worm demon erupted from the ground, its massive form towering over him. Its round, razor-sharp mouth spun with unnatural speed, a whirlpool of teeth prepared to tear him apart.

He turned to flee, but before he could move, tendrils of dark, clawed hands shot from the earth, seizing his legs, pinning him in place. The demon's jaws opened wide, and he felt the horrific rush of its teeth sinking into his flesh, ripping him apart.

Pain exploded through him, an unrelenting agony as his body was torn to shreds. His mind screamed, but no sound escaped—only the torment as his remains were swallowed whole. The creature's digestive acids burned away the remnants of his life, erasing him from existence, leaving nothing behind but the empty echo of his pain.

***

Gideon jolted upright in bed, his body trembling violently, drenched in sweat from the nightmare that clung to him like a suffocating fog. His heart raced, his breath shallow, but it was the figure before him that froze him in place. Abaddon sat at the foot of the bed, her presence like a heavy weight pressing down on his chest.

Before he could even summon the words to speak, she opened her mouth, her grotesque form shifting as a tentacle shot out from her throat, striking him hard on the forehead.

In an instant, the world around him shifted violently.

The air thickened, and he found himself standing in a barren, desolate landscape at the foot of a towering mountain, its jagged peaks looming over him like the fangs of some ancient, slumbering beast. Massive boulders lay scattered across the ground, and one, in particular, caught his eye—a stone etched with a strange, foreboding symbol, as though carved by an unseen hand. The air seemed to hum with an eerie energy, and then, a voice shattered the silence.

Azazel's voice echoed through the mountainside, deep and cold, sending a chill down Gideon's spine. "When the time comes, Gideon, I trust you will not fail me again."

Gideon's knees buckled, and he collapsed to the ground, desperation flooding his every thought. "No, my Lord! I swear it—I will do everything in my power to free you!"

"I certainly hope so, for your sake. I will not be so forgiving next time."

The words cut through him like a blade. He clenched his fists, feeling the weight of the promise crushing him, the knowledge that failure meant more than death—it meant endless suffering.

The vision suddenly vanished, and Gideon found himself back in his bed, gasping for air, heart pounding in his chest. Abaddon was gone, her sinister presence fading as quickly as it had arrived. He lay there, alone in the darkness, his mind reeling.

Failure was not an option. If he faltered, if he gave in, the future awaiting him would be one of unending agony, a fate sealed in eternal torment and despair. And deep down, he knew there would be no second chance.

CHAPTER 22

Heaven itself seemed to mourn, a silent anguish hanging in the air on the anniversary of the day the world lost one of its greatest warriors in the battle against darkness. As Matthew and Grace made their way toward the Grotto, the sky darkened, clouds swirling overhead to obscure the sun, as though even nature felt the weight of the loss. Moments later, a light drizzle began to fall, cold and unrelenting, washing over the land.

Grace tugged at her jacket, trying to wrap it tighter around herself, but the chill still seeped through. Matthew watched her struggle, an amused chuckle escaping his lips. Grace glanced up at him, narrowing her eyes. "Are you laughing at me?"

His grin widened, "Of course not."

"I'd like to see you try carrying this child around for nine months, then come out in this freezing cold, and not be able to button your own damn coat!" she snapped.

Matthew placed a hand gently on her belly, his smile softening. "Do you have any idea how beautiful you are right now?"

"I feel like a whale," she muttered.

He chuckled, "But you're my whale."

"Hey!"

Her tone shifted as she pressed closer to him, her voice softening, "Do you think they'll show?"

Matthew's expression grew serious. "I'm not sure. I hope so. But we don't really know much about them."

"I know it's a crazy request," she said softly, "but I just thought we could give him one final goodbye."

Her voice broke as she buried her face against his chest, holding him tight, needing the comfort.

"It's not crazy at all," Matthew said quietly, his arms around her. "Solomon meant a lot to all of us."

"That he did," a voice suddenly interrupted from behind them.

Turning, they saw Pascal approaching, carrying Rumple on his shoulder. Behind them, Morgan and Victoria followed, the latter shrinking slightly behind Morgan when her eyes landed on Grace.

Grace scowled at the sight of Victoria, but quickly softened. "Look, I'll never forget what you did. But I also don't want to live the rest of my life in hatred. My parents would want me to forgive you and move on."

Victoria's head lowered in shame. "It's more than I deserve."

Morgan pulled her closer, offering her a silent gesture of comfort.

Grace watched the exchange, a tight feeling in her chest. "Saving my ass was a good start, though."

Pascal added, "Not to mention stopping the apocalypse."

Matthew nodded, a dry laugh escaping him. "Yeah, would've been nice to finish Gideon off once and for all, though."

Grace's voice sharpened. "Isn't that really why we're all

here?"

The group looked at her, confusion flickering in their eyes.

She pressed on, "I know I asked you all here to pay our final respects to Solomon. Since we couldn't do it after... the incident. But I was also hoping we could make a sort of pact. Between all of us."

Morgan raised an eyebrow, "What exactly are you hinting at?"

Grace met her gaze, unwavering. "We all know Gideon's not done yet. He'll come back with something else, something worse. I just want us to have each other's backs if it goes down again. We stand a better chance of ending him once and for all if we work together."

Morgan crossed her arms. "I don't really work well in groups. I prefer to be alone."

Victoria spoke up, "What about me?"

Morgan leaned in, pressing a quick kiss to her cheek. "You're the exception, sweetie."

Rumple spoke then, his gravelly voice surprisingly firm. "I'm in."

Pascal raised an eyebrow. "But I thought you were retired?"

Rumple shrugged. "Well, consider me unretired. If Solomon's death taught me anything, it's that evil never sleeps. And neither should we."

Pascal let out a breath, shaking his head. "Well, shit. Guess that means I'll have to stick around to keep you out of trouble."

The others turned to Morgan, waiting. She sighed, finally giving in. "Okay, whatever. If you need me, just call me."

Morgan walked over to Grace, her expression serious. "May I?"

Grace nodded. "Of course."

Morgan placed her hands gently on Grace's stomach, closing her eyes. After a moment, the baby kicked, and Morgan pulled her hands away, her eyes growing distant. A moment passed before she returned to herself, a soft exhale leaving her lips. "Wow... haven't had one of those in a while."

Grace's eyes widened. "What's wrong?"

Morgan didn't answer right away, her gaze distant. Grace's nerves began to fray as silence stretched between them.

"Don't worry," Morgan finally said, her voice steady. "It was just a little premonition. Nothing bad."

"What did you see?" Grace asked nervously.

Morgan hesitated. "It was hard to piece together. Too many images... flying at me all at once. But I can tell you one thing. You're going to have your hands full with this one. She's going to be a firecracker."

Matthew's grin returned, "That's not surprising, given who her mother is."

Grace punched him playfully in the arm. "Hey!"

Morgan cleared her throat, breaking the moment. "Can we get back to the reason I thought we were brought here?"

Both Matthew and Grace nodded somberly in unison.

Morgan reached into her pocket, pulling out a small seed. "Everyone, form a circle around me. Hold hands."

They complied, gathering around her. She touched each of their foreheads with the seed, murmuring an incantation with an ancient cadence:

"Take me now, take me now to face the Summerlands. By the earth and wind and the fire and rain, I'm on my way, remember me."

She turned to the North. "Take me now back to the air from which we spring and then return. I shall cross over, now it is my turn. I am not afraid, remember me."

To the East: "Take me now back to the fire from which we spring and then return. I shall cross over, now it is my turn. I am not afraid, remember me."

To the South: "Take me now back to the water from which we spring and then return. I shall cross over, now it is my turn. I am not afraid, remember me."

And to the West: "Take me now back to the earth from which we spring and then return. I shall cross over, now it is my turn. I am not afraid, remember me."

She blew softly onto the seed, and then, her voice stronger, she chanted:

"Blood of my blood; Bone of my bone; Flesh of my flesh; Keep my soul alive. I will live on within your hearts. I am not afraid. Remember me."

She flung her hands skyward, releasing the seed into the air. For a heart-stopping moment, it hovered, suspended in the wind. A bolt of lightning tore through the sky, striking the seed with a brilliant flash. The impact sent shards of light scattering in every direction, a storm of shimmering particles spinning wildly through the air.

A gust of wind whipped up, carrying the ashes away, creating a dazzling light show as the clouds parted above them. The sun broke free from the darkness, its golden rays flooding down, as though Heaven itself had decided to celebrate Solomon's life rather than mourn his death.

"Wow!" Grace exclaimed, breathless, as a butterfly landed on her hand. For a fleeting moment, she felt as if Solomon himself was there, saying his final goodbye. "That was incredible."

Morgan, without a word, simply turned and began walking away, her task complete.

"Wait!" Grace called out. "How do we contact each other?"

Morgan's voice floated back over her shoulder, calm and knowing, "We're all part of a coven now, connected by a psychic bond. Just close your eyes and concentrate. If we're alive, we'll hear it."

She continued walking, then paused, glancing over at them. "By the way... I hope you're okay with tattoos?"

Grace blinked in confusion as Morgan and the others began to fade into the distance. After a moment, only she and Matthew remained.

"What was that about?" Grace asked, still trying to process.

Matthew simply shrugged. "I have no idea."

***

They walked in silence for a few moments before Pascal broke the quiet, his voice low and sharp. "You saw something, didn't you?"

Morgan's gaze remained distant, her expression clouded with something darker than the overcast sky above them. "Yeah," she replied softly, her words carrying a weight that seemed to hang in the air. "I saw something."

Rumple grunted from behind them. "What was it?"

Morgan's jaw tightened, and for a brief moment, she hesitated, her thoughts clearly far away. Then her eyes met theirs, and her voice dropped to a whisper. "Let's just say that somewhere down the line, the world is going to go to shit. And Grace's little girl? She's going to need our help... badly."

The air seemed to grow colder, as an unspoken fear lingered between them.

The End.

BOOK SIX PREVIEW

Hellish Book Six:
Hope Destroyed

By Scott Dokey

CHAPTER 1

It was happening again, and Matthew felt the sick churn in his stomach, like a storm rising inside him. No matter how many times he'd tried to escape it, disaster found him, lurking like a shadow he couldn't shake. He pushed the gas pedal down, weaving through the clogged streets, his eyes darting from one panicked person to another, all racing the same hopeless race. Every face he saw through his car windows wore the same look: the hunted desperation of those who knew they were running out of time.

The reports had come like a wave, crashing and deadly, before communications went dark. A missile attack, of all things, like something ripped from a nightmare, had hammered the West Coast. Some said it was Russia, others China, but the truth lay buried under static now. And while Palm Springs sat a bit inland, far enough from the coast to escape the initial devastation, Matthew knew better than to believe they were safe. This was the end, he could feel it, pulling them all toward something dark and hungry.

He whipped his car into the driveway, tires screaming as he slammed on the brakes. Grace burst out of the house with their daughter, Hope, following right on her heels. Both were crying desperately. Matthew jumped out of the car toward Grace with his hand held out, intending to pull them into the car and speed away, but then the ground buckled beneath them, a tremor so fierce it threw all three to the ground like discarded dolls.

The earth itself seemed to roar in fury, cracking open right before Matthew's eyes. His car teetered, then plunged, swallowed whole by a black chasm that cut through their street, extending down the block. The rumbling grew louder, the earth convulsing in violent fits until the chasm gaped wide enough to consume more than a dozen cars in its jagged maw. Matthew could only stare as his last hope for escape disappeared into the depths.

He yanked Grace and Hope to their feet, ushering them back to the house as the ground continued to tremble. They clung together on the front porch steps, hearts pounding, breaths coming in harsh, frightened gasps, waiting for the violent quakes to subside. When the final tremor rolled away, a horrifying silence settled over the area. Trees that once stood tall and unshakable lay uprooted, their roots like long, twisted fingers clawing at the air. Houses sagged, roofs collapsed under their own weight, and all around them lay the shattered remains of life as they knew it.

Matthew's cell phone was dead. He cursed, wondering if he'd ever hear from anyone outside this wasteland again. Faint sirens wailed in the distance, but soon even that thin lifeline was choked out by the heavy silence. And then, next door, he saw movement: Nathan, their neighbor, staggered out, his forehead split open, blood streaming down his face, while his wife Mary clutched a broken arm to her chest.

"Stay here," Matthew murmured to Grace, squeezing her shoulder. She nodded, her face pale, her eyes wide with fear. He pushed through the rubble, his heart pounding as another aftershock shook the ground beneath his feet. "Are you guys okay?" he asked as he met Nathan and Mary.

"Yeah," Nathan said, the words sounding hollow. "Banged up but alive. You?"

Matthew nodded, glancing back at his shattered car swallowed by the earth. "We're outside, so we're... lucky. Car didn't make it, though."

Nathan's face twisted, his eyes haunted. "Is this... the end?"

Matthew held his friend's gaze, a grim determination hardening his jaw. He'd been here before, close to the edge, and knew the war wasn't over until it was lost. "Not if I can help it."

Together, they agreed on a plan—such as it was. Check the damage. Gather whatever supplies they could find. Then see if there was any hope of restoring communication. When Nathan mentioned the blackout—TV, internet, everything— Matthew forced a chuckle. "Yep, technology's great. Until it isn't."

Both men managed a faint laugh, but it was brittle, like dry twigs snapping underfoot. As they turned back to their homes, Matthew looked over his neighbors, the people he'd seen walk with pride, now shuffling broken and weary. This was just the beginning; he could feel it in his bones.

Back inside, Grace wrapped her arms around him, her face streaked with tears. "Matthew, I heard the news... and then everything went dead. I think—I think this might be the one we don't make it out of." She buried her head in his chest, sobbing softly.

Matthew glanced at Hope, who looked as if she'd crumbled inward, her once-bright spirit caved in by the horrors around her. He held her, too, the three of them clutching each other, unwilling to let go, even if it felt like the world around them was crumbling.

When they finally separated, Matthew headed toward the garage to grab a few flashlights. He was met by the sight of their living room, littered with broken glass and twisted furniture. The chandelier had come down with the force of a sledgehammer, smashing the dining room table in two. Shattered crystals lay like scattered jewels, mingling with shards from the blown-out picture window. And there, face down, was his TV, his one outlet to the world—a notice that the normal life he'd clung to was as broken as the glass on the floor.

A soft whimper from the corner snapped him out of his thoughts. He turned and saw Buddy's black tail sticking out from under a fallen bookshelf. His heart clenched as he and Grace raced over, lifting the bookshelf to free the dog, while Hope pulled him free. Buddy staggered up, licking Hope's face with reckless fervor, making her laugh for the first time since the attack began. It was a momentary relief, but the tremor returned, shaking them all to their core.

"It's just an aftershock," Matthew muttered in a strained voice.

Grace looked at him fearfully. "How bad is it?"

Matthew held her close, his voice barely above a whisper. "I don't know."

She pressed her face into his chest as he gazed out the shattered window, catching sight of a shadow slipping into the tree line—a large, fast shape, too big to be anything normal. Buddy's growl rumbled deep in his chest, his eyes tracking the thing until it disappeared into the darkness.

They needed to prepare, to make some kind of plan, however hopeless it seemed. And as Matthew patched the windows with trash bags and duct tape, he couldn't shake the feeling that this was it, the last fragile hold they had on their world before it spiraled into the void. He watched his family as they moved around the dim house, and with every look, every gesture, he knew they were all he had left.

***

After Hope shut her bedroom door, she snatched her cell phone from her pocket and held it tight, as if sheer willpower could make it work. She knew it was pointless, knew the signal was gone, despite that, her fingers slid instinctively to Jason's number. The screen blinked, stubbornly empty, the call refusing to connect. She let out a low, frustrated groan and threw herself face-first onto her bed, pressing her face deep into her pillow, where the tears finally came, hot and thick.

Jason wasn't just a boyfriend. They'd only been together a few months, but he was the first person who'd seen her—the real her—this shy, small-town girl with a love for all things fantastical, from the battles of Middle Earth to the spells of Hogwarts. He was the first boy to really understand the hours spent bent over her comic books, or her excitement at a new anime release. And he didn't just tolerate it; he dove into her world with her, even helping her pick out the right fabric for cosplay costumes, getting into the thrill of each new game. She'd never felt this way about anyone. The thought of him being out there, maybe hurt, or worse—she shut her eyes tighter, trying to block the dark thoughts clawing up her mind.

A soft knock at her door snapped her back from the darkness. "Honey, are you all right in there?" Grace asked from the other side.

Hope bit her lip, letting a few seconds pass, hoping maybe her mom would take the silence as an answer. But Grace was already coming in, taking a seat on the edge of Hope's bed, and resting her hand on Hope's shoulder.

"Are you okay, sweetie?" Grace asked softly.

Hope forced herself upright, hurriedly brushing her eyes dry. "Yeah. I'm fine," she said, forcing a brave, brittle smile. "Just trying to make sense of everything."

Grace gave her a knowing look, one that softened around the edges. "Have you heard anything from Jason?"

Hope blinked, stunned that she'd guessed. "How did you know?"

"Because I'm your mom. I know everything." Grace's gentle smile only lasted a moment, though, before it faded into worry. "It's a rough night. Just don't let yourself spiral into the worst-case scenario."

Hope looked away, her voice barely above a whisper. "I know. I just keep hoping he's okay, that maybe he's..."

"Maybe he's at his place, helping them pick up the pieces," Grace interrupted softly. "Or maybe he's been trying to get to you just as much as you are to him."

Hope sank into her mom's shoulder, her voice small and raw. "Yeah. You're probably right."

Grace gave her a squeeze and then gently pulled her up from the bed. "Come on, honey. Let's get some rest. Tomorrow's gonna be a busy day."

Reluctantly, Hope followed her out to the living room, where Matthew had stoked the fireplace. The flames flickered in the darkness, casting long, dancing shadows that somehow made the room feel cozier. They each grabbed a blanket, bundling close together near the warm crackle of the fire. And despite the looming uncertainty, the unspoken fears thick in the air, they found themselves slowly drifting into a restless sleep. The fire crackled low, and soon enough, each of them was breathing heavily, lost in fitful dreams as the world outside lurked, dark and restless.

***

At first, Matthew thought it was part of a dream—the shrill, garbled hiss cutting through the silence. He jolted awake, his heart pounding in his chest, his eyes locking on the shifting shadows around the dying embers. The sound rose again, and this time Grace and Hope shot upright from their sleeping bags, panic flashing in their eyes.

"What was that?" Hope whispered, her voice tight with fear.

Matthew's gaze was fixed on the darkened windows. "I don't know, but it sounds close."

Before they could react, a scream tore through the night, shrill and desperate, followed by a gunshot. Grace gasped, clutching his arm. "That sounded like Mary!"

Matthew scrambled to his feet. "You two stay here."

"Where are you going?" Grace's grip tightened, her voice trembling. "You don't know what's out there. I saw something earlier—I couldn't be sure, but it terrified me, Matthew."

He hesitated, a shadow of his own memory rising—a fleeting, dark figure slipping into the trees at the edge of their property. "I have to check on them. Mary and Nathan... they're our friends. They'd do the same for us."

He kissed her forehead softly. "I'll be careful. I promise."

He quickly made his way to his study, unlocking the gun cabinet and pulling out his shotgun. He loaded a handful of shells into his pockets and grabbed a flashlight, casting one last look at Grace and Hope before he slipped out the door into the cold, watchful night.

The distance between his house and Nathan's stretched about forty yards, a gap now divided by the massive trunk of a tree toppled in the chaos. As he neared their house, another scream pierced the air, and he saw Mary and Nathan running toward him, their faces twisted in terror. Nathan's gun went off, firing blindly over his shoulder at the creature chasing them, a dark silhouette bounding forward on powerful, muscled legs, its long claws reaching out hungrily.

As she stumbled, the creature's momentum carried it past her, snarling in fury as it skidded to a halt, lowering its goat-like head and narrowing its eyes on her prone form, the jagged edges of its horns glinting in the moonlight. Matthew raised his shotgun and fired, his breath catching as the shot hit its back, but barely slowed it. It turned, eyes blazing with fury, and refocused on him.

For a brief, desperate moment, Matthew's life flashed before him—Grace, Hope, the warmth of home, everything he'd built and loved. He leveled the gun again, steeling himself, and fired directly into the creature's face. This time, it dropped in a heap, its burning gaze extinguished.

Before he could even catch his breath, Grace and Hope were racing toward him, pursued by a second monstrous figure, its eyes glowing as it closed in on them. Out of nowhere, Buddy charged from the side, intercepting the creature just long enough to throw it off balance. It swatted him aside, but the moment was all Matthew needed. He reloaded, aimed, and fired, sending the beast crumpling lifelessly into the dirt.

Grace threw herself into his arms, shaking uncontrollably, tears streaming down her face, while Hope kneeled beside Buddy, who lay whimpering, a dark streak of blood trailing from a gash on his neck. She tore off her sweatshirt, pressing it against the wound, her hands shaking as she tried to stop the bleeding.

Matthew held Grace close, whispering soft reassurances,

though his heart was pounding, fear clawing at him. After a minute, her trembling began to ease, her breathing slowing. But as her weight grew heavier in his arms, he noticed the blood staining her shirt, spreading from a wound in her stomach. His breath caught as her eyes fluttered open, her hand finding his cheek, her voice a faint whisper.

"Take care of our baby," she breathed, her voice weak but steady. "Tell her everything—about us, about who she is."

Matthew's throat tightened, tears threatening to spill as he struggled to keep his voice steady. "It's going to be okay, Sweetie. I promise, everything will be okay."

Grace's hand moved weakly, brushing his cheek, her touch already growing cold. "Promise me," she said, her gaze locking onto his. "She has to know."

A tear escaped as he nodded, unable to speak. A faint, peaceful smile crossed her face, and with a final, shallow breath, she slipped away, her hand falling gently from his face.

CHAPTER 2

Matthew clutched Grace's body, struggling to steady his breath, his heart breaking more with each passing second. For a fleeting moment, he pictured life without her, an unbearable emptiness stretching before him. But as he looked over at Hope, who was tending to Buddy and blissfully unaware of what had just happened, he knew he'd have to find strength—somehow.

"Hope, I need you," he called, his voice frayed.

Hope looked up, instantly recognizing the grief etched into his face. She hesitated, torn between her father and the wounded dog, but then rushed over to him. Her heart sank as she saw her mother in his arms, her eyes wide and fixed on the heavens, blood pooling beneath them.

"No!" she sobbed, dropping to her knees beside them.

Tears streamed down their faces as Matthew reached for her, holding her close. They didn't have time to process the pain before a chorus of unsettling howls filled the air. Matthew staggered to his feet, Grace's body held close, his eyes flicking toward the house. A split-second later, another demon barreled across the field, its eyes trained on them.

"Shit!" Nathan joined them, glancing around in horror.

"How many of these damn things are there?"

"Too many," Matthew said, starting toward the house. Nathan and Mary fell in behind him, but he stopped abruptly when he realized Hope wasn't with him. Terror shot through him as he turned around and saw her running toward Buddy, with the demon closing in fast.

"Hope, no!" Matthew yelled, but it was too late. Just as she reached Buddy, the creature lunged with a guttural snarl, launching itself into the air. Hope looked up at the last second, rolling forward as the demon flew overhead and crashed to the ground. She grabbed a sharp stone in her fist and hurled it, striking the creature squarely in the left eye. The demon shrieked, convulsing violently before falling still at her feet.

Shaken, Hope looked down at her trembling hands, her eyes widening as they glowed an eerie, pulsing red. She turned to her father, terror written across her face, wordlessly pleading for help. Before either of them could react, another demon lurched toward her, only to stop abruptly, staring at her glowing hands. With a deep, feral growl, it backed away, retreating into the shadows.

Hope looked down, blinking as her hands returned to normal. For a split second, she thought it might have been a trick of the mind—until she spotted a faint mark on her left hand, a dark symbol etched into her skin. She tried to brush it off, convincing herself it was just dirt, but a chilling instinct told her otherwise.

Matthew's voice jarred her back to the present. "Hope! We need to get inside!"

Scooping Buddy into her arms, she stumbled toward the house, relieved to see Nathan's outstretched arms ready to help. She handed the injured dog to him, and together they bolted for the door. Once inside, Nathan set Buddy on the couch as Hope rushed to her father's side, where he kneeled beside Grace's lifeless body, desperately attempting to revive her. Finally, he looked up at Hope, his eyes pained with sorry, and she let out a broken cry, sinking down beside her mother.

A tremor rumbled beneath them, a deep quake rattling through the house, sending books and knick-knacks crashing to the floor. The ground's trembling seemed to echo their grief, as if the earth itself mourned with them. When it finally stilled, Matthew rose slowly, placing a gentle hand on Hope's shoulder. "Come on, help me bring her to the bedroom."

Hope nodded, wiping the tears from her eyes as she stepped back to allow him enough room to carry Grace's body down the hall. She followed, her heart heavy, regret gnawing at her for every word left unspoken, every moment she'd never get back. She feared the weight of it might crush her.

As they reached the bedroom door, she brushed against Grace's hand, and suddenly an image flooded her mind: she was standing in a shadowed chasm, a massive wall looming before her, twisted bodies contorted in agony, reaching for her, their wails filling the air. She stumbled, the vision dissipating as abruptly as it came, and she collapsed against the wall.

Matthew hurried to her side as she collapsed. "Hope, are you alright?

Her voice shook as she replied, "I don't know, Dad. It feels like everything's falling apart, and I can't stop it."

He pulled her close, whispering words of comfort, though his own heart felt on the verge of breaking as well. "I'm here for you. We're going to get through this. Somehow."

"But what's happening?" She looked up at him, her eyes filled with confusion and terror.

"I wish I knew." Grace's words echoed in his mind: *Promise me you'll tell her everything.*

Hope slumped back, her thoughts tumbling into one another. "First the quake, then the demons, and Mom…" She hesitated, glancing down at her hands. "And then this."

Matthew's brow furrowed. "What are you talking about?"

"When I touched her just now, I saw… something horrible. Like a wall of tortured souls reaching out for me. And earlier, with Buddy—when the demon attacked, my hands… they started glowing."

"I thought I saw something, but everything was happening so fast…"

"I did too, at first. But then… then this happened, and I don't know what's real anymore."

Matthew knew he couldn't leave her in the dark, but he also knew it wasn't the right moment. As she slumped against the wall, he struggled to find the right words to break through the whirlwind of terror surrounding them. Then he glanced at her hands, and his breath caught. Marked into the skin on each one were strange symbols—runes or glyphs that pulsed faintly under the dim light.

"Please tell me those are tattoos I didn't know about," he murmured, though he feared the answer.

Hope's face fell, her voice barely above a whisper. "I think they scared the demon away… I don't know."

A sob escaped her, and she wrapped her arms around him, clinging tightly. "I'm so scared, Dad. I don't know what's happening to me."

Matthew held her close, his heart breaking as he whispered, "Shh, it's okay, sweetie. I'm here for you."

CHAPTER 3

The first tremor rolled through the valley like the shudder of an ancient beast waking from a long and bitter slumber. Jason felt it in his bones before he heard the rattle of dishes in the cabinet or the deep groan of the earth beneath his feet. His first thought was of Hope. Her wide eyes, the soft way she said his name—the image pierced him as the second tremor surged, fierce and sudden, making the walls shudder and the light fixture swing like a decapitated pendulum.

When his cell service sputtered out, a spike of dread crawled up his spine. His father muttered something slurred and incoherent from the worn recliner, and his mother shifted on the couch, her legs lazily draped over the edge as if the world weren't shaking itself apart. Jason ignored their oblivious murmurs and bolted for the door.

The world outside was a cacophony of honking horns, distant screams, and the sharp wails of car alarms. He jumped onto his bike, his breath coming in ragged bursts as he pedaled hard. Each rotation of the wheels seemed slower than the last, as if he were fighting the tide of an invisible current. Fred Waring and Portola loomed ahead, choked with a chaotic river of vehicles. Drivers shouted at each other as their cars jostled for inches of space. It was as if the entire town had been overtaken by a primal urge to flee.

Jason ducked and weaved between cars and flailing pedestrians. His legs pumped hard, his muscles straining as he neared the bridge spanning the dry wash. Just as he reached its midpoint, a deeper and stronger tremor surged through the ground. The pavement cracked with a deafening shriek, splitting open to reveal a large chasm yawning before him.

He barely managed to throw himself from the bike as it tumbled into the abyss, metal and rubber swallowed by the darkness. A screeching sedan pitched forward, front wheels hanging over the void before gravity claimed it. The plunge seemed endless until a fireball erupted below, lighting up the night in shades of orange and sickly red. Jason's heart slammed against his ribs as he clawed for a twisted length of rebar, its sharp edge biting into his palm.

The screams of those trapped in their metal coffins pierced the air, sharp and abrupt as they were cut off by another explosion. The ground beneath Jason quivered, sending ripples through his aching limbs. The silence that followed felt more sinister than the quake that had preceded it.

"Hope," he whispered, her name trembling from his lips like a prayer.

A raw, jagged breath rattled through him as he hauled himself up, the taste of blood and smoke coating his tongue. Around him, the streets had become an inferno—fires crackled hungrily, devouring buildings with tongues of flame. Smoke billowed across the horizon, a fiery orange against the darkening sky, the cacophony of sirens and panicked shouts of desperate people echoing through the air. His knee screamed with pain where he had twisted it, sending sharp jolts up his leg with every step.

He stumbled toward a nearby playground and grabbed a tattered shirt left abandoned on the ground, twisting it tight around his knee, grimacing as he tied it off. The makeshift brace would have to do. He glanced up and saw dusk creeping in, shadows lengthening like claws over the carnage.

At Deep Canyon Drive, a flicker of movement drew his eye. He paused, heart hammering, as the hair on his neck stood on end. But whatever it was, disappeared into the shifting dark. Jason shook his head, pushing away the creeping dread as he slipped through a gap in the chain-link fence and limped down the steep embankment, each step a needle of pain. He reached the wash's dry, cracked bottom and looked up the other side, already streaked with blood and grime. Halfway up, a low, guttural growl slithered through the air, freezing him in place.

Before he could react, a woman's scream split the silence—a shriek so raw and agonized that it sliced through him like a blade. Then, it stopped, severed mid-cry. A wet thud followed, and Jason's blood turned to ice as a severed head tumbled down the slope, coming to rest inches from his face. The eyes stared sightlessly, mouth opened in a final, silent scream. His breath caught in his throat as something heavy moved above him, the sound of claws scraping dirt and stone. A stench rolled down, fetid and wet, and he clamped his lips shut to keep from retching.

A shadow loomed menacingly above him, sniffing the air, sharp snorts of frustration and rage punctuating the silence. Jason pressed himself flat against the slope, his heart hammering in his chest, until at last the thing slunk away, leaving only the echo of its ragged breathing.

When he dared to move again, the world seemed even darker. Fires painted grotesque shadows that danced over the broken landscape. He reached the top, taking in the devastation: homes crumbled like sandcastles beneath the weight of the inferno, and bodies littered the ground everywhere he looked, frozen in the last moments of their horror.

Suddenly, a massive shadow passed overhead, blotting out the fiery sky. The thick smoke shifted just enough to reveal a passenger plane descending wildly, lurching side to side as if an unseen hand had grabbed hold of it. Jason's jaw dropped as it disappeared beyond the rooftops, followed by a muted thud and the billowing of an inky column of smoke in the distance.

"Holy shit," he breathed, the words barely a whisper. The screams of those in the doomed aircraft seemed to echo in his mind.

A snarl jerked him back to reality, and he spun to find himself face-to-face with something pulled straight out of Hell. Its eyes, red and burning with an insatiable hunger, locked onto him. Jason dodged to the side as it lunged, but its claws sliced through his arm, leaving a trail of white-hot pain that made him stagger back, vision blurring.

As the demon loomed over him, its mouth oozing black bile that dripped and sizzled on the scorched earth, Jason closed his eyes. A tear traced down his cheek as he thought of Hope —her laughter, her warmth, the words he never spoke. The only light in this infernal night. We wished he could tell her he loved her, just once. His eyes shut tight, and he waited for the darkness to take him, his undeclared love cursed to remain silent on his dying tongue.

"I'm sorry," he thought, as the darkness began to claim him, a silent confession lost to the roar of hell's embrace.

Scott Dokey is a creative force whose storytelling spans across writing, filmmaking, and visual art, delivering haunting, immersive experiences. Growing up in the shadow of Notre Dame's Golden Dome, Scott discovered early on the magic of turning a blank page into a captivating work of art. This love for creation only grew, leading him to explore writing and filmmaking, with a special focus on horror and the supernatural. His novels, including the Savage Apocalypse series, and the acclaimed *Hellish* series (*Tortured Souls, The Chosen, Unholy Religion,* and *Vizibir*), have cemented his place as a master of dark, psychological terror, where human fears are confronted with unrelenting force.

Scott's career isn't just about writing; he's an award-winning screenwriter who has produced and directed several short films, along with a no-budget feature that showcases his resourcefulness and vision. His dedication to the indie film scene is highlighted by his previous role as president of Mid-America Filmmakers, where he helped foster new talent and bold ideas. As with his novels, his films create unsettling atmospheres where the supernatural meets real-world anxieties.

Now living in Southern California with his wife, Jennifer, and their daughter, Kaylee, Scott enjoys the extreme contrasts of desert life—the blistering 120° summers balanced by the bliss of an 85° winter. His life and work continue to push the boundaries of what horror can achieve across multiple mediums. For more about Scott's creative journey, you can visit his website at www.scottdokey.com.

Be sure to check out all of the titles in the Hellish series:
    Book One: Tortured Souls
    Book Two: The Chosen
    Book Three: Unholy Religion
    Book Four: Vizibir

Also available, The Savage Apocalypse saga:
    Book One: The Cry Of The Dead
    Book Two: The Howl Of The Dead